The Year of Secret Assignments

The Year of Secret Assignments*

by Jaclyn Moriarty

* Diary Entries,
Rude Graffiti,
Hate Mail,
Love Letters,
Revenge Plots, Date Plans,
Notes Between Friends,
and Famous Last Words

SCHOLASTIC INC.
New York Toronto London Auckland Sydney
Mexico City New Delhi Hong Kong Buenos Aires

ISBN 0-439-49882-1

Arthur A. Levine Books hardcover edition designed by Elizabeth B. Parisi and Lauren Monchik; published by Arthur A. Levine Books, an imprint of Scholastic Inc., February 2004.

12 11 10 9 8 7 6 5 4 3 2 1 5 6 7 8 9 10/0

Printed in the U.S.A. 23

First paperback printing, April 2005

To Colin
—J.M.

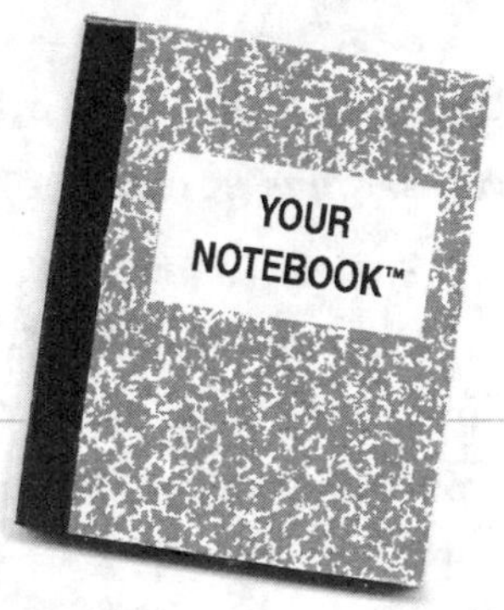

1. Lydia's Notebook

QUICK!

Before you read *another word,* write your own FULL name in every box on this page!

Don't be afraid! Your Notebook™ is *meant* for writing in!

Hello LYDIA JAACKSON-OBERMAN**! It's great to meet you!**

Hey, *wait a minute.* That name sounds familiar!

LYDIA JAACKSON-OBERMAN**?**

Isn't that the name of a *FAMOUS AUTHOR*???!!!

Well, is it? Not sure? Maybe one day?

Hey, LYDIA JAACKSON-OBERMAN **— there's only one thing that *is* sure! And that's this: *The answer is in your hands!***

Or, to be straight with you, LYDIA JAACKSON-OBERMAN***, the answer is in this Notebook™ !!!!***

You want to know how the Notebook™ works?

It's simple.

We ask questions. You answer them.

And *by the time you get to the end of the book, you're an author* — OR YOUR MONEY BACK!!!*

Think it's crazy? Think again. Ever heard of William

* Conditions apply.

Shakespeare? Jane Austen ring a bell? *How do you think those guys got started?!?!*

So. You ready? Let's dive right in!

How do you KNOW, deep in your heart, that you WILL be an author one day? (Go on, LYDIA JAACKSON-OBERMAN**, it's your turn now. . . .)**

Shakespeare got started using this book? Wait till I tell my English teacher.

Wonderful! Now, how do you know you have the determination to see your dream through?

Well, for one thing, I put my name in those boxes. Normally I would find that kind of thing insulting to my intelligence.

Plus there's the fact that I'm writing in this book at all, considering it's a birthday present from my dad.

Okay, great. Now, what was it that made you stop in the bookstore today, pick up this book, and take it over to the counter to pay for it?

My dad bought the book. Not me. For a birthday present?

Interesting. Okay, let's start with something simple. Look around you right now. Write down a list of everything that you see.

1. A guy leaning back with his arms stretched over the back of the seat, as if he is watching a football game from his couch at home.

2. A girl fast asleep with her head on the guy's shoulder, and her hair caught under his arm.
3. Other people leaning or sleeping in different directions.
4. A maths teacher. (She's writing numbers and letters all over the board and she seems pretty excited, the way her shoulders are bouncing. Maybe she's figured out the formula for time travel or something. Wait a minute and I'll ask her.)

We bet you just wrote down "grass," "water," "sky," etc., etc. Maybe you noticed the coffee cup, but we bet you didn't get the lipstick stain *on the side* of the coffee cup! Now, go ahead and try again. Write down EVERYTHING that you see.

I don't get it. There is no coffee cup.

Ms. Yen just turned around from the board and I noticed that she's getting a bit fat. The top button on her jeans has popped open.

She said that she didn't think there *was* a formula for time travel, although she *does* think there might be a formula to make me shut up and do my maths or else find myself *laughing on the other side of my face when it comes to the half-yearlies!*

If she tells me what that formula is, I'll write it out for you.

That's better! Now, do you know the names of any of the plants or animals that are around you?

$(A + B)–(A–B) \times (X+Y)–(X–Y)$

What about some of the *colors* of the things that you see?

I made up the formula myself. Ms. Yen couldn't think of anything to say when I asked her.

Let's pretend that YOU are a character in a book. The book starts with you waking up yesterday morning. Tell us what you did.

I knew immediately that something was wrong. "Turpentine!" I shouted to my stepsister, whom I keep under my bed. "SOMETHING IS WRONG!"

"Something *is* wrong," agreed Turpentine, waking up and brushing the cobwebs from her silver hair. "You're turning into a road sign."

"Call the doctor!" I commanded, trembling. Turpentine was only two years old but she was no fool. I had all the classic symptoms. A stretchy feeling in my elbows, itchy palms.

I knew I was not long for this world. *Why me?* I kept thinking. *Why me?*

It was a stupid question. Turning into a road sign was going around at my school, and I kept eating lunch with the NO WAYS. It was only a matter of time.

But what would I become? A STOP? A SLIPPERY WHEN WET? Or maybe something special like: OLD NORTHERN ROAD? I hoped so.

Great! So what happened next? Remember that these are easy questions — it's not about "making things up." Your Notebook™ is going to build you toward "invention." For now, you should just tell the truth!

You should actually have made that clear to begin with. I put a lot of effort into that story.

Will you excuse me please because the maths class is almost finished and I have to go to English. We kept forgetting to go to English last year, and now they're all weird about attendance.

Okay, time for your first QUICK FLICK. These are "memory" exercises that you will find throughout your Notebook™. You'll really start to look forward to them! Think for a moment, and then describe for us your very first day of university.

It was bad because I was only three at the time, and my mother made me wear a plastic bib around my neck in case I spilled any of my stewed apples. All the other kids stared.

YOU LOSER. I'M IN HIGH SCHOOL.

I JUST TOLD YOU ABOUT MY MATHS TEACHER AND MY ENGLISH CLASS, ETC. DID IT SOUND LIKE UNIVERSITY TO YOU? WERE YOU EVEN LISTENING?

I DON'T THINK YOU WERE.

Tell us the occupation of your best friend. Is he a plumber? Maybe he's an accountant! We'll leave a couple of pages now so you can tell us ALL about your best friend!

My best friends are Emily Thompson and Cassie Aganovic.

You want to know what Em will do when she finds out you think she is a plumber?

You want to know what Cass will do when she finds out you only refer to people as "he"?

I am now in my English class and there are two minutes until the end of the period. Em is beside me and Cass is behind us. Look at them if you want. I'll hold up the book so you can see.

Mr. Botherit is waving his hands to indicate that he wants to speak.

Let's see what he has to say.

Mr. Botherit is an idiot.

What he has to say is that we have now finished Larkin, so *next week,* we will begin the Famous Ashbury-Brookfield Pen Pal Project. Specifically, we will write letters to students at Brookfield High, and they will become our pen pals. "And this," he says (whispering for dramatic effect), "will kill two birds with one stone!"

("Don't you *dare* kill any birds," Sasha Perkins said passionately.)

Mr. Botherit is holding one finger in the air: "A," he is saying, "it will reduce the hostility between our schools! And *two,*" he holds up a second finger, "and *two,* it will be our stand against the tyranny of technology! By sending *letters,* we say no to e-mails! No to mobile technology and texting!! And *yes* to the *Joy of the Envelope!*"

Mr. Botherit, as I said, is an idiot. He's trying to be funny, but he can't hide the fact that he's not.

He also can't hide the fact that he just said A and then two. A lot of people are now offering to teach him the alphabet.

Meanwhile, the rest of the class is in an uproar. Some people are upset because their mobile phones have been insulted. Most people are upset about having to write to Brookfield. Mr. B. already tried this last year, and many students ended up dead. Or, anyway, unhappy.

Em just put her hand up to say it's probably against our constitutional rights to make us associate with drug dealers and murderers. She offered to check on this with her parents. (Her parents are lawyers.) (Actually, Cass and I also have lawyers for parents, but Em's are compulsive lawyers.)

Mr. Botherit nodded at Em politely, which confused her. ("Does he mean yes? Should I check with my parents? What does he mean by that nodding?") Cass said he doesn't mean anything. She has noticed he nods when he can't think of what to say.

"Thank you, Cassie," said Mr. Botherit as the bell started to ring. "That is an astute observation."

Well, notebook, I'm going to have to stop writing now. It's Friday afternoon, and it's been great getting to know you, but we all have places to go, e.g., I'm going to Em's place for the weekend; you're going into the garbage bin.

Well done! That was fabulous!

And guess what? You did it! You finished Part 1 of your Notebook™! We are SO PROUD of you!

Be sure and take a break before you go on to the next Part. . . .

2. Emily's Weekend

Dearest Emily,

I write to keep you informed of the *progress of your parents* and to provide you with *advice for your weekend.*

I shall begin with the *progress of your parents.*

Your mother is currently:

(a) blow-drying her hair;

(b) shouting something inaudible down the stairs; and

(c) cranky (because I lost the plane tickets).

Your father is currently:

(a) eating a banana;

(b) writing this letter to you; and

(c) happy (because I just found the plane tickets, right here in the fruit bowl!).

Your mother has now switched off her hair dryer. For your information, her shouting has become audible and is to the following effect:

> "Have you found the tickets yet? What are you doing?! Are you even *looking?!* Benjamin! Can you *hear* me?! I think that's the taxi!! Are you still writing the note to Emily!? How can it take so long?! Have you tried the kitchen table?!"

I shall now move on to my *advice for your weekend.* In drafting this advice, I have kept the following in mind:

(a) you will be here, at home, without your adoring parents;
(b) you will, instead, be in the company of Cassie and Lydia; and
(c) Lydia is nothing but trouble.

I am pleased that you will have Cassie and Lydia's company this weekend and ask that you say "Hi" to them from me. However, I must now advise, in the strongest possible terms, that you:

(a) eat proper food;
(b) have some nice chats with Cassie; and
(c) sing loudly when Lydia speaks, and cover your ears.

Incidentally, you may recall that you have a younger brother. As usual, he will be staying with Auntie June for the weekend, so please do not panic if he is not in his room. If, however, he is in his room you should panic and phone Auntie June.

I will now *conclude* by saying that your mother just tripped halfway down the stairs because she was wearing a *single* high-heeled shoe. It is a lesson in the danger of doing things by halves. She is all right, however, and is chuckling happily to herself, as if a very funny thing had just happened. I hereby confirm that your mother is a lovely, cheerful woman, most of the time.

Your mother has stopped laughing to ask that I remind you not to set off the smoke alarm.

If you have any questions or comments, please do not hesitate to contact us at the Annual Taxation Lawyers' Conference. In the meantime, I wish you all the best, look forward to seeing you again on Sunday night, and remain,

Your Loving Father,

Signed, Sealed, and Delivered,

Benjamin A. Thompson

- **Attached and marked with the letter "A" are the contact details of our conference.**
- **Attached and marked with the letter "B" is Auntie June's phone number.**
- **Attached and marked with the letter "C" is a photograph of your mother and me, which I just found here in this marvelously fruitful fruit bowl. The photo will remind you what your parents look like. Doesn't your mother look gorgeous? She is the one in the hat.**

3. Cassie's Diary

Sunday, late at night, full moon

Well, hello there, Diary.

This is Cassie and it's Sunday night.

So, what happened was, I just spent a weekend at Emily's place, since her parents were away (as per usual). Lydia was in a melancholy mood so we didn't do anything illegal. We just invented recipes using the strangest ingredients in the kitchen plus some different kinds of old wine.

Also, Lydia set off the smoke alarm seventeen times. She's been analyzing how smoke alarms work.

It was Lydia's birthday last week, and her father gave her this book that has instructions to make her become a famous author. Part of why Lydia was melancholy was that she can't decide whether to keep using the book or not, since on the one hand she hates her dad and she thinks the book is stupid, but on the other hand she really wants to be an author.

Anyhow, I just got home from Emily's, and I thought of this diary. The reason being that it was a birthday present from *my* dad a few years ago. I remember it was wrapped in green tissue paper when he gave it to me, with one of those curling, twirling ribbons, and I made fun of my dad because I knew a shopkeeper must have wrapped it and also because I was twelve and stupid.

Also, I remember that I saw the leather cover and realized it was a diary, and then I raised my eyebrows and kind of humorously threw the diary over my shoulder, saying, "You think *I'm* the kind of person who writes in a diary?"

Mum and Dad laughed, and Dad just shrugged, like, "Oh well, better luck next time." I put the diary in my bedside drawer, and it's been there ever since.

Hey, I guess you don't know all these people, do you, Diary? Lydia and Emily and mothers and fathers and everything?

You don't even know who I am.

I'm not the kind of person who writes in diaries.

That's one thing to know about me.

4. Ashbury High Year 10 Notice Board

THOUGHT FOR THE DAY:

In order to know the road map of your mind, seek out the compass in your schoolbooks!

SPRING CONCERT!

As the autumn term gets underway, spring may seem a distant star. But it's not! It comes just after winter! At this week's form assembly, we'll ask for volunteers to participate in the spring concert: If you can sing, dance, juggle, or even "rap!" (but only cheerful rap tunes, please), raise your hand at the assembly so your name can be included! (Air guitarists need not apply unless and until they learn to play the guitar.)

THIS HAS BEEN A MESSAGE FROM YOUR FORM MISTRESS.

Protest in Mr. Botherit's English Class Today

Do you value your life?

Then say NO to Mr. B's Ashbury-Brookfield Pen Pal Project.

WHATEVER YOU DO, DON'T WRITE A LETTER IN CLASS TODAY.

If Mr. B asks why, remind him that:

- *The reason judo is compulsory here at Ashbury is so we can defend ourselves against Brookfield students.*
- *You can't get in to Brookfield unless you have a criminal record.*
- *Brookfield students don't know how to read or write.*

A NOTE TO MR. BOTHERIT'S ENGLISH STUDENTS!

I see that an uprising is in the works to do with my Pen Pal Project!

Guys, it's true that the students at Brookfield seem "scary," and they do have more tattoos and prison time than we have here. But isn't this what life is all about? The Adventure of the Scary and the New?

I'll let you in on a secret: Brooker kids are every bit as human as you are! Last year, my English class had a ball writing to them. Despite the rumors, nobody got their arms broken — indeed, my students learned a great deal about themselves, friendship, and the Joy of the Envelope!

Don't forget! Sharpen your pens and your wit, and I'll see you in English today!

Mr. Botherit

P.S. A word of warning: Although your letters to Brookfield will be completely confidential, participation in the Pen Pal Project will count directly toward your assessment marks for this year.

5. Letters from Ashbury

English Assignment: Mr. Botherit's Class
Letter from Ashbury Student to Brookfield Student as Participation in the Ashbury-Brookfield Pen Pal Project

Dear Student at Brookfield,

Please see the following!!!

1. My Name: Emily Thompson (aka: Em)
2. My Interests: Well, there's too many to write out! My hand will fall off from the repetitious strain injury! But okay. You twisted my arm. I'll choose the top three!

(a) Shopping

Shopping, shopping, shopping! HEY, DID I JUST USE UP MY THREE? OOPS!

Anyway, just kidding. ☺

Let me give you an idea of the kind of shopping freak I am. Okay, I'm walking along Pitt Street Mall with two shopping bags on my RIGHT ARM. I'm unbalanced! Hey! These bags are too heavy! The blood has stopped flowing to my knees! I'm about to tip sideways! Help!

WELL. You might think that the *sensible* thing would be to swap one bag to the other arm. Or maybe even stop for a café au lait?

But no! What do *I* do? I head straight out to buy myself TWO more shopping bags full of clothes or accessories or what-have-you takes my fancy!

And THAT's how I balance myself out!

Oh, don't get me started about shopping! Or else I'll never finish this letter!

(b) Chocolate

Don't get me started about chocolate either! Yummorama! My nickname might be Em, but it's sometimes also Toblerone! I think this is a "play" on Thompson, which is my last name.

I think it is an angiogram of Thompson, actually. But it might also give you a little clue about what my favorite chocolate is! Any guesses?

(c) Horses

Finally, I would like to end with "horses." I have loved horses since I saw this old movie called *International Velvet* on TV when I was a child. It starred Tatum O'Neal, who was a child actress, in her time.

3. My Friends: Okay, this one's easy.

I have two best friends. Lydia Jaackson-Oberman and Cassandra Jane Aganovic.

Maybe you've heard of Lydia Jaackson-Oberman? Lydia's father is a judge of the Supreme Court of New South Wales, and since New South Wales is the most important state in Australia, that makes Lydia's father the smartest man in the world!

That's what Lydia says, anyway, and it kind of makes sense. Go figure!

But more important, Lydia's mother is a famous celebrity: Marianne Jaackson.

I think there might be an accent on the name "Marianne," such as would make it foreign? But I can't remember and Lydia is ignoring me right now, even although I just threw a Tic Tac at her! (She caught the Tic Tac without even looking up from her letter, and ate it, and continued writing! Kooky! ☺)

I'm not sure why Lydia's mother is a famous celebrity. She is certainly very beautiful, or at least I get the impression from Lydia's family photo album that she used to be beautiful.

And in the meantime, [she once had plastic surgery and so therefore she is still practically a celebrity today.]

Cassandra is my other best friend, Cassie.

Cassie's mother is not a celebrity; she is just a lawyer who works in the same law firm as my parents do, and she has very large bosoms. ☺

At any rate, the three of us girls are like the Three Scrooges! We have been best friends since primary school on account of all the lawyers among our parents going to cocktail parties and, in their youthful days, having affairs with each other and so forth.

Everybody knows us as Cass, Em, and Lyd, and in primary we used to even have a club called the Cassemlyds. Not a very original title, I know, but we were kids then. Can there be Siamese triplets? 'Cos that's what we would be! Oh, don't get me started!

4. My Favorite Holiday: Cannes Film Festival
5. My Pets: I don't think that horses should be called pets, but I *do* have two horses, Aristophanes and Cinque.
6. My Favorite Subjects at School: English! This is a lot to do with our teacher, Mr. Botherit. I cannot explain it, but he really seems to care about his students more than most teachers.
7. My Favorite Color: Aquamarine!
8. Parents' occupation: My parents are both lawyers. So my

little brother and I are their merger and acquisition. William is the merger, and I'm the acquisition.

Often my father does not arrive home until 4 A.M. in the morning, and my mother not until an hour after that! This is because they are partners of their law firm.

9. Things I Would Like to Change about the World if I Could: All horses should be allowed to come to school with you and just wander around shopping centers behind you and so forth; no more global warming.

Well, I have one other thing that I could tell you, and it is this: that I am a person who has Secret Assignments. Like an FBI agent? ☺ I get Secret Assignments which appear in my locker; they are written on scented notepaper inside envelopes sealed with red wax.

Kooky, eh! But that's just what I'm like.

I can't say any more about THAT little secret just now!

Well, whoever you are who receives my letter, I hope you also realize what an inspiring idea this is of Mr. Botherit's. I remember this time last year, when kids in a different English class in our year were writing letters to you guys at Brookfield? Well, I was *jealous*! I wanted to be one of them! Mr. Botherit is dead-set-on-your-mark-get-ready-go when he says that schools which are close to one another should forge ties, and I hope you are as keen as I am to get started with the forgery.

Okay, got to go! Looking forward to your reply! ☺ ☺ ☺

Yours sincerely,

Emily Melissa-Anne Thompson

(aka . . . have you been paying attention? . . . aka: Em Toblerone!!!)

Student at Ashbury High

* * *

Letter from Lydia Jaackson-Oberman of Ashbury High to a Person at Brookfield

Dear Person at Brookfield,

I am a fish.

You wouldn't think so to look at me, what with the uniform, and the hair on top of my head and all that?

But it's true, I'm a fish.

I'm not sure what type, but I think maybe a cod.

What are you?

My mother grew up in a pinball parlor, but then she dyed her hair purple, learned to fly a plane, and the rest, as they say, is history.

My father, I never knew, except for this one time when he threw a ball and told me to go fetch it.

"Dad," I said. "Am I a dog?"

"Lydia," he said. "I apologize."

We haven't spoken a word to each other since.

He's the smartest man in the world, my dad, but you can't tell at all.

I'm having trouble concentrating because Tic Tacs keep hitting the side of my head.

What should happen is this:

You should send me some dope and I should sell it. Or use it. We should do it regularly. You send it, and I sell it. It would be a bit like drug trafficking.

I've heard that Brookfield has a marijuana plantation instead of a sports oval. So I guess it's easy enough for you to get. Or are they strict about who can pick it? I hope not.

It was my birthday last week, and my friends Em and Cass

made a chocolate cake. It had a lot of bourbon in the mixture, so it was excellent, and also strange. But the point is, we look out for each other, Em and Cass and I.

They look out for me by baking me birthday cakes. I look out for them by supplying their dope.

Do you think you can get it here by lunchtime?

Yours,

Lydia Jaackson-Oberman

P.S. Sorry about my name.

* * *

To Student at Brookfield from a Student at Ashbury

Dear Brooker Kid,

That's what our English teacher calls you:

"Brooker Kids."

I think it's pretty funny, so that's how I have started my letter to you. I wasn't even going to write at *all,* is the fact of the matter, but I just found it so funny when he said it that I wrote it:

"Dear Brooker Kid."

My name is Cassie.

In actual fact, I always think it's funny when a teacher tries to be cool. Most people want to slap them across the face, but I want to sit them down, like with a hand on their forehead, and say, "It's *okay,* you're a *grown-up,* you're allowed to be a nerd, just breathe in and out, that's all you need to do," and they would look up at me confused but also relieved and teary-eyed.

Emily gets rapid breathing (you know where you have to breathe into a paper bag?) because she is highly strung. Lydia does not get rapid breathing because she is as cool as a cat. Em and Lyd are my best buddies, so that's why I introduced them to you right there.

I'll tell you something else that I find funny, and that is this: counseling. I went to see a counselor with my mother last night. You might think that's kind of a private thing to reveal in a letter to someone like you, who I've never even met, but you must be forgetting what counseling is. It's where you TELL A STRANGER ALL ABOUT YOURSELF. So telling you that I've been to see a counselor is nothing. You're not a stranger. You're a Brooker Kid.

I never knew that you would get homework from counseling, especially since it's expensive, and we should be able to give the counselor homework instead of the other way around, but there you go. She leaned toward me too much, the counselor, maybe her eyesight wasn't so good, and she offered me a chocolate mint, and she gave me homework.

The homework is that I have to choose someone who is a perfect stranger, but who seems like a really nice person, and I have to tell them about myself. Does that sound safe to you? No. Not to me either. The counselor said I couldn't choose Em or Lyd as they have known me all my life, practically. Right away she wanted to get me *out of the pattern,* she said, the pattern being life with my two best friends. She figured this out from my five-minute explanation about Lyd and Em. I couldn't believe it, and I can tell by the expression on your face that you can't believe it either.

"Find yourself a nice girl at school, honey," she said.

She was imagining somebody who wore glasses and a cardigan and who would nod along with whatever I said. I bet.

One person I was thinking of for my homework is this girl at my school called Elizabeth Clarry who seems pretty nice. We used to do athletics training together a few years ago.

The counselor also gave my mother homework, which was to write a letter to my dad and express her emotions. I think that's just stupid.

She's not supposed to mail the letter or anything, just write it. My mother did her homework last night while she was drinking a bottle of wine. I found it on the kitchen table this morning, all purple-stained, and I took it with me to school because I thought she might get depressed if she found it in the middle of her hangover this morning.

And here's the funniest thing. It's all about me when I was a baby. I read it, and in the whole letter she just describes ME in my bassinet.

I just thought of something. If I send my mother's letter to you right now, then I can be doing my homework.

You definitely don't know me, and you must be a real nice person because you're a Brooker Kid.

So I'm enclosing it.

Bye now.

Cassie

6. Letters from Brookfield

LETTER TO EMILY THOMPSON
ASHBURY HIGH SCHOOL

Dear Emily,

Well, I have to say your letter was a bit of a shock. Maybe it's a girl/guy thing? Do you want to ask your teacher if you can write to a girl in my class instead of to me? Or else, I've got a sister if you want to write to her? Just say the word, if you do.

Seriously, what grade are you in? No offense, but do you realize you talk like an eighty-five-year-old?

You talk like the lady who works in the shop where I get my curry chicken pie every afternoon on the way home from school. She has white hair, and every single day she says:

"Ho ho! I know what you want, Mister Man! You want a sausage roll!" And I always say:

"No, actually, I want a curry chicken pie."

That's EVERY SINGLE DAY.

Do you realize you talk like her?

Here's an example from your letter: "Don't get me started!"

That is an expression used by an eighty-five-year-old woman in a cake shop.

And besides which, how come you don't want to get started? What will happen if you get started? Are you worried about using up your fuel or something? I mean, you already got started. Whenever you say that in your letter, it's when you've already got started. It's a weird expression, if you don't mind me saying so.

I also have to say, and I'm only doing this for your own good, but you kind of prove the image of the private school girl from Ashbury High. I was reading the letter, and what I was thinking was this:

"F*–*–*–*–*–*–*–*k me."

(Give me a call if you need me to explain what the missing letters are there. I didn't want to risk writing the actual word as the shock would kill you.)

I'm telling you right off, I don't know what we're going to talk about if your favorite things are shopping, chocolate, and horses. We could sing the soundtrack from *The Sound of Music* together, I guess, but otherwise, stuffed if I know. Can you think of any other interests, maybe?

I think you should talk about your interests with those friends of yours, Lydia and Cassie, and just leave me out of there.

One thing I can do, if you want, is explain to you why your friend Lydia's mother is a celebrity. I've heard of her. So you don't have to keep throwing things at your friend to find out. Say the word, and I'm there.

I can't believe you've been best friends with Lydia since primary and you don't know why her mum's a celebrity.

Still, I have a supersonic memory, which not all other people have. So I've got to make allowances. The first memory I have is from before I was conceived, I mean, before I came into being. About a fortnight before.

It's a "kooky" thing about me, as you would say, like you and your Secret Assignments in the candle-wax envelopes.

I'll be straight with you, that's the only interesting thing that I found in your letter. Those Secret Assignments. Tell me what they are.

I can't think of anything else to say. As I mentioned, though, I have a sister, and if you want to write to to her, you just say the word.

Yours sincerely,

Charlie Taylor

* * *

LETTER TO LYDIA JAACKSON-OBERMAN

Dear Lydia,

Happy Birthday for the other week.

It's great that you're a fish, because I'm a heron of the kind that flies around the sky and then swoops down to the ocean and screws your brains out.

You thought I was going to say I was the kind of heron that swoops down and eats you, didn't you?

I was, but I thought that might be offensive.

My mother is a food processor and my father is a wall-mounted clothes drier. I have a kid brother too, but I don't know what kind of appliance he is yet. He's too small.

You're a freak, you know that?

I can't figure out when you're being serious and when you're not. Example: Does your mother fly planes really? Why?

Other example: Do you really want me to send you what you were saying you want me to send you? How much would you want me to send? We should talk about this. Suggest a place to meet.

I don't think you need to be sorry about your name. That can't be your fault, a thing like that. It would have to be the fault of your parents. Anyway, there's nothing wrong with the name Lydia. I think it's cute.

See you,

Seb Mantegna

* * *

Dear Cassie,

Eat shit and die, private school slag.

Yours faithfully,

Matthew Dunlop

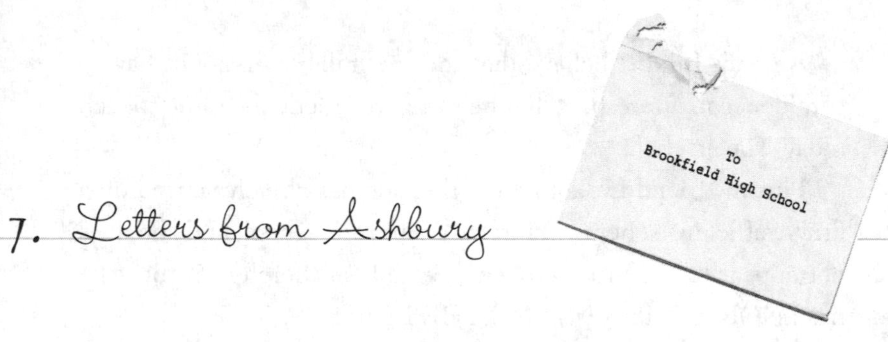

7. Letters from Ashbury

To Charles Taylor

Dear Charles,

This is what Mr. Botherit wrote up on the blackboard as a suggestion for our responses to the letters from your class:

"Try commenting on the letter! Was it: amusing? interesting? E.g., 'Thank you very much for your letter which was amusing.'"

So, Charles Taylor:

Thank you very much for your letter which was a BIG PILE OF CRAP.

This is the LAST and FINAL and SUPERLATIVE letter you will ever get from me.

The only reason I wrote to you in the first incidence was because I thought it was an assignment. I thought he was going to read the letters and give us feedback and incorporate the feedback into our assessment grades. And I am aiming to come first in English this year, so therefore I put A LOT of effort into that letter.

Now it turns out that he meant it when he exclaimed that there would be full confidence for our respect. EXCUSE ME. Full respect for our confidence. (You see what you have done to my English? You've got it all twisted.)

Anyway, I didn't believe that for one millimeter, about having confidence in our respect, but he just gave exactly the same speech today. The arsehole.

Plus my friend Lydia told me that she has already started up a drug-trafficking scheme in her letters to your school, and she does not appear to me to have been arrested, so therefore it must be true: NOBODY IS READING THE LETTERS.

Which brings me to the point: Why would I keep writing to you? That seems to me like an incompetent waste of my time.

And no, I do NOT want to write to your sister. How sexist of you to think that just because I like shopping it means that all girls like shopping, and that's the only thing girls talk about. My friends Lyd and Cass both HATE shopping, and guess what, they both happen to be girls. So you are therefore proved wrong.

You are so old-fashioned you need EXIT MOLD sprayed under your arms.

And furthermore, if you just imagine for one MOMENT that you might show anyone this letter, you'll be face-to-face with a lawsuit so brutal you'll never eat another chicken pie.

And I *think* I have a few more connections in the legal world than you do.

Ciao, Roma.

Emily Thompson

P.S. There's nothing wrong with the expression "Don't get me started." It's expressive and humor-filled. I can't believe you think it's incorrect to use that expression when a person has already got started. You don't understand satire or irony or sarcasm or effectiveness. That's Brookfield High all over, I guess.

P.P.S. AND YOU CAN TALK. "Just say the word." JUST SAY

THE WORD? What kind of an expression is that? WHAT WORD WOULD YOU LIKE ME TO SAY ANYWAY? MORON?

* * *

LETTER FROM LYDIA JAACKSON-OBERMAN TO SEB MANTEGNA

Dear Seb,

In one letter only you have blown my cover. You are right. I am no fish.

Bravo, my friend, bravo.

It was nice of you to say Happy Birthday, but I notice you didn't send me any kind of gift. Are you one of those careful drug traffickers? I've heard about them. I don't think they have a very good reputation. The way to break the law is to be really upfront and open about it.

I know this because my dad's a judge.

I'm sorry, but my mum does not fly planes. She drinks a lot, though, so she's often flying. And she's part owner of a film studio, which will cater to all your film needs: sound recording, editing, lighting, and really bad TV commercials.

Plus it has a great makeup studio, which is second on the right after the reception desk. Keep it in mind if you ever need a makeover.

I have decided to tell you about the morning of my birthday, which, as you know, wasn't long ago.

This will be me telling you about the morning of my birthday:

The scene is the breakfast pyramid.

The breakfast pyramid is built out of frosted glass and is reached by a tunnel from the back door of our house. It is filled with Egyptian treasures, such as ashtrays.

The mother, Mum, *dressed in a tissue-paper nightgown, sits at one end of the breakfast table. The father,* Dad, *dressed in a suit and tie, sits at the other end.*
They are both buttering croissants in a very deliberate way so that croissant flakes are floating all around the pyramid.
Occasionally there is a thud as the family dog, Pumpernickel, *hurls himself at the frosted glass, trying to get someone's attention. There is an outside shot of Pumpernickel backing away from the pyramid to line up and take another hit at the frosted glass.*

Mum: *(sweetly)* Take it easy on the butter there, honey. You've already forgotten the results of your latest cholesterol test, haven't you?
Dad: This is low-fat margarine, as a matter of fact.
Mum: *(surprisingly)* Up yours, as a matter of fact.
(Pumpernickel: *Thud.*)

The beautiful daughter, Lydia, *enters.*

Lydia: *(happily)* Great, croissants.
Dad: Honey, you're still in your pj's. We need to be out of here in five minutes, kiddo.

He dissolves a tablet into a glass of water.

Lydia: *(through the glass to the dog)* You can do it, Pumpernickel.
(Pumpernickel: *Thud.*)
Dad: *(pressing his thumbs to his temples)* Lydia. Don't tease the dog, honey.

Lydia: *(sympathetically)* Do you have a headache, your worship?

Dad: *(chuckling)* Well! You're going to have to figure out the difference between a magistrate and a judge if you want to stay in this family! "Your worship" is what you say to a magistrate. "Your honor" is what you say to a judge. And what's your dad, eh?

Lydia: *(charmingly)* I know that, Dad! I was messing with you!

Dad: *(pushing back his chair)* I'll wait in the car for five minutes for you, Lyd. But then I'll just have to go, I'm afraid. It's late, kiddo.

Exit Dad.

Lydia: Hey, Mum. You know what day it is today?

Mum: *(staring distractedly at the dog, which is now sliding down the frosted glass with a slow, squealing sound)* No, darling, I haven't the faintest idea. *(Frowns for a moment, deep in thought)* I think it might be Tuesday.

END OF SCENE

So that's the end of me telling you about my birthday morning.

(But then on the way to school I reminded my dad what day it was and he spun the car in the middle of the highway, took a right into a one-way street doing about 180, parked in a disabled spot outside Dymocks, picked up a book for my birthday, and then jumped back into the car. I just wish I'd had a camera with me, and I could have taken a photo of my dad's car in the disabled-parking spot and sent it to the papers.)

I don't think we should meet.

I think this will work better by mail.

I have decided that we have to tell each other the dreams that we each had the previous night. Well, last night I had a dream that

I was a snail. Nothing really happened, I just sat there being a snail and sometimes stretching my neck a bit. That's it.

What did you dream?

See you,

Lydia

* * *

Dear Matthew Dunlop,

Thank you very much for your letter. I loved it.

So anyway, how have you been? You didn't give much away in your letter.

Mr. Botherit told us that sometimes boys have trouble expressing their feelings and he hopes the boys in our class can work through that in their letters. Also, he hopes we keep it in mind if we're lucky enough to get a boy for a penfriend. Those were his words:

Lucky enough to get a boy.

Does he mean it's unlucky if you get a girl for a penfriend?

I am one of the lucky ones. I got a boy. YOU. And you are a champion. Don't let anybody tell you any different, k?

I don't think you have that much trouble expressing your feelings, but you should try and share more. You could tell me what your favorite subjects are and what you do to relax after school. Do you soak your feet in tea tree oil?

Don't feel under any pressure, though, because I like you just the way you are.

After I sent that letter of my mother's to you, I felt pretty bad, like what was I thinking? Betraying my mother's privacy and everything. I confessed to her, but she didn't mind at all. She said she left the letter out on purpose because she really meant it as a message to me, reminding me how cute I was as a baby. And she's happy for me to share that around with my friends, she said. So, that's lucky.

Well, it's been fun. I can't wait for your next letter.

Love,

Cassie

8. Letters from Brookfield

To Ashbury High School

Dear Emily,

Wow. That letter really kicked arse. Do you want to chill or something for a minute though?

Getting worked up like that can't be good for your blood pressure.

I didn't mean to offend you. Okay, now I'm lying to you. I *did* mean to offend you, because I thought you were buried under a landslide and we needed a few rounds of explosives to get you out. I thought maybe there was a real you under all that crap.

And I was right! There is a real you and like I said, she kicks arse!

I see now that all the crap was for your teacher. Why didn't you just say so? I did think maybe you had a bit of a thing for your teacher, like maybe you wanted to get into his pants. But I didn't realize it was to do with your *assessment.*

Wow, if you can degrade yourself that badly, maybe you *should* get into his pants? Have you thought about asking if he would give you extra marks for a blow job?

You've got to learn some pride, Emily.

You've got to make me proud of you.

Yours sincerely,

Charlie Taylor

P.S. You actually think that only private school kids have connections? You want to know what my brothers do? Brian's a cop with connections with the local Triads. Jack's a cop with connections with the local Mafia. And Kevin's a charter member of a motorcycle gang called the Pitbulls. As in those dogs that get their teeth into your flesh and don't let go, even if you hit them with a sledgehammer?

And you think I'm wetting myself because your daddy's a partner in a law firm? Bite me, baby.

* * *

Hey Lyd,

Inside this envelope, you will see my painting of your dog nose-diving into the breakfast pyramid. I spent the whole art class doing sketches to get it right. Is it right?

Okay.

Here's the thing. How do I know you're not a snake?

We need more than a couple of letters to establish that you can be trusted. Don't get me wrong, you seem pretty cool, but if I've figured it out right, you also seem to be the daughter of a judge.

Now, he might be a loser who forgets your birthday, but that could be *exactly* what I need to be concerned about. Maybe you're looking for ways to get Daddy's attention?

For all I know, you're waiting to get enough dirt on me and then you're heading for the breakfast pyramid and saying: "I've caught you a drug dealer, Daddy. *Now* will you say Happy Birthday?"

That's all hypothetical, of course. I categorically deny that I deal in drugs.

So what we're going to do is, we're going to do a few tests. If you can do these things for me, even though you might get caught, then I'll know you're not your Daddy's Little Angel.

This is the first test:

It's to set off my school's fire alarm. That's it. You might think it's kind of unimaginative, but I haven't got an imagination. You ask Radison. (That's our English teacher.)

The alarm has to go off straight after lunch on Tuesday next week, and it has to be serious enough that the whole school spends fifth period on the oval.

If you pass my tests, then I'll know you're not a snake.

Okay, and I'll show my respect by obeying you too. You want me to tell you my dreams?

The dream I had last night was this: I was a kookaburra sitting up high in a eucalypt, with my feathers camouflaging nicely into the bark, and way down on the ground I see a slither of something sharp. It's a snake. So I move.

I move without stopping to figure out a strategy. I don't stop or think, I just fly. Straight down like a jet plane, heading for a crash landing in the grass, and next thing I've got the snake.

Then I fly it to the nearest rock so I can smash it against the rock until it's dead. Then I rip open its middle and eat out its guts.

Cheers,

Seb Mantegna

* * *

Cassie,

Why don't you ask someone who I am?

And then ask what I do to people I don't like?

Matthew Dunlop

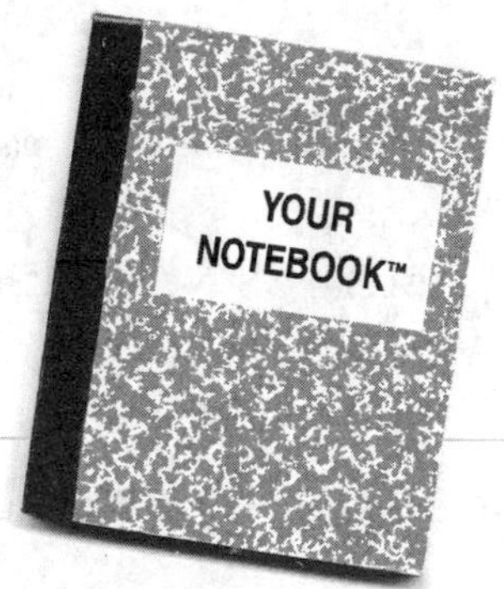

9. Lydia's Notebook

Hey! You still with us? Still enjoying our questions?! In this Part, we leave more room for your answers so you can spread your wings! A recurring theme will be "senses." Tell us about your five senses!

Okay, well, first you should try less open-ended questions. What do you want to know about my senses, exactly?

And second, you should know that I'm only doing this because I want to be an author. It's not because I respect you.

No offense.

I'm in German right now, and this is what's happening. Frau McAllister is getting off on humiliating David Corruthers. She wanted him to write up the sentence, "If I had a donkey, I would ride it to school every day," and he's written, "If I were a donkey, I would ride myself at school every day." Big deal, it's close enough.

It's weird the way some teachers are happiest when you make mistakes.

Anyway, as I was saying, I've decided I'll keep writing in this notebook. Because I've noticed something: I never get right inside my head when I write. So I'm going to use this book to try.

Great! We loved that! Now, tell us, what are your favorite things to eat?

My favorite things to eat include tortoiseshells and eucalyptus leaves.

BUT IT'S NOT TRUE. IT'S A LIE! I'M TAKING YOU FOR A RIDE!!!

What star sign are you? Does it capture your personality?

I think we need to invent some new star signs. None of the old ones work for me. I've thought up one called "Britney."

A Britney is a happy-go-lucky person who wants to be a nurse or a meteorologist when he or she grows up. Britneys have fingernails which break easily. Britneys need plenty of calcium.

Tell us something surprising about yourself. Are you a smoker? Or perhaps you are a sword fighter!

I can't believe you know about my sword fighting. Who told you? So you also know how I spend a couple of hours each afternoon slaying dragons?

Actually, I'm not a smoker either. I used to be, but I quit last year because Emily made me. The things you do for your friends.

I was planning to be a chain-smoker because I like that word: "chain." I still like the word. I like paper chains, chain letters, chain gangs, and chain mail. I wear a lot of chain mail for my sword fighting.

Em made me quit smoking after they did antismoking at school. They showed us this ad which has a girl putting a cigarette in her mouth and not realizing that the cigarette is a metal hook. You would surely realize. But anyway, the hook goes through the girl's lip. Do you get it? *Hooked*. Brilliant.

But after that, Em could never look at me with a cigarette without imagining the hook through my lip. She's such a sucker for mind games.

Now you tell me a little about yourself.

Write down a thought for the day.

Today, I'm thinking that this book is a waste of time and I'll never be an author in a million zillion years.

Time for another QUICK FLICK! Tell us the first memory that comes into your head!

I remember Cassie walking toward us across the primary school playground, carrying her skipping rope. It's her birthday, so she got to ring the Old Bell for the start of lunchtime.

Em and I are already halfway through our Vegemite sandwiches, and she's just walking across the yard.

She did a bad job ringing the Old Bell. Em and I are excellent at it when it's our birthdays: We can make it go *ja-jing, ja-jing,* like a real brass bell should.

Cass just made it go *clangetty, clangetty. Crash.* She must have been shaking it side to side.

Cass arrives and says, "The bell sounded stupid, huh?"

And Em says, "Derrrr, Fred," and I say, "Maybe yes, maybe no," and Em says, "Don't worry, it's because you're no good at being the center of attention," and Cass stands still in front of us, with a funny look in her eye, winding the skipping rope around her wrist.

What is a sound that you like to hear? Tell us all about it!

You know, there's this background noise in my head sometimes, like electricity, or maybe like frogs croaking.

One time I was getting a bus home from school and a family of ducks crossed the road. I was sitting in the seat right alongside the driver. This was when I was maybe eight years old and in love with the bus driver. He was fatter than half a bus and named Barney.

"Hey kid," Barney always said. "It's all happening, eh?"

I always pretended I knew what he was talking about.

"Oh yeah," I always said. "It's really happening."

I sat there bumping along next to Barney, waiting for it all to happen. And Barney would lean his fat stomach forward over the steering wheel at T-intersections, to look both ways. Or he'd concentrate on getting the bugs off the windscreen by aiming at them with washer fluid and the wipers.

So this one time, I was getting the bus home from school as usual, and I saw a mother duck and her five little baby ducks.

They were on the side of the road. I sat there watching through the dusty window and I forgot to tell Barney. I saw them but I didn't say a word.

Barney was watching some noisy kids in his rearview mirror, and shaking his head about them, and next thing the mother duck decides to head herself and her five little babies across the road.

None of the bumps was big enough to make the kids up the back hit their heads on the roof. Just a little bump and then bumpity-bumpity-bump.

"Christ," Barney said to me. "Was that what I think it was?"

"Yep," I said.

Barney raised his eyebrows — like *whoops* — and drummed on the steering wheel with one hand. Like someone in a band.

What is a smell that you like to smell? Tell us all about it!

I don't know if that was his name or not. Barney. That could be just a name I made up.

I have a lot of dreams about sex. I mean, dreams about what I think sex is like. I think it must be good.

What is a taste that you love to taste? Tell us all about it!

Sometimes I get so worried about Cassie it makes me cry. I try to get her to talk to Em and me, like she used to, but she just smiles and says she's fine.

She hasn't said anything about the letters she gets from Brookfield, for instance. She reads them and smiles to herself kind of secretly.

Whereas Em is hysterical about her penfriend. She keeps telling us that she's never writing to him again, but I know she will, because she always wants the last word.

But I don't know about the guy who's writing to me. At first I thought he was okay, but then he sent his kookaburra/snake letter. I hate it when guys get all serious like they're the ones who know how the world really works. Whereas girls are only playing at life and we have to be careful or we'll get ourselves and *them* into trouble.

Now I don't know how to answer him. I could do his "test" for him. To show he doesn't scare me. But doesn't that mean he's the one with the power?

What is a sight that you love to see? Tell us all about it!

I think I'm going to throw this stupid, frigging, waste-of-my-time notebook away.

10. Autumn Term / Emily and Charlie

Dear Charles,

You talk a pile of crap. You talk a pile of crap.
You talk a pile of crap. You talk a pile of crap.
You talk a pile of crap. You talk a pile of crap.
You talk a pile of crap. You talk a pile of crap.
You talk a pile of crap. You talk a pile of crap.
You talk a pile of crap. You talk a pile of crap.
You talk a pile of crap. You talk a pile of crap.
You talk a pile of crap. You talk a pile of crap.
You talk a pile of crap. You talk a pile of crap.
You talk a pile of crap. You talk a pile of crap.
You talk a pile of crap. You talk a pile of crap.
You talk a pile of crap. You talk a pile of crap.
You talk a pile of crap. You talk a pile of crap.
You talk a pile of crap. You talk a pile of crap.

Yours faithfully,

Emily Thompson

P.S. I decided to use this opportunity to practice my handwriting. As you can see, I am developing a highly eloquent style.

P.P.S. I got a Secret Assignment yesterday and GUESS WHAT. I'm not going to tell you what it is.

P.P.P.S. I have to go now because you are wasting my TIME.

P.P.P.S The next letter you get from me will be an empty envelope, so be prepared for misery.

★ ★ ★

Dear Emily,

Check it out. I JUST SAVED THE LIVES OF THE WHOLE SCHOOL.

I'm on the oval right now, and I can hardly see this paper through my tears of life-giving joy.

See those girls sitting cross-legged and singing the theme song from *Friends*? They wouldn't be doing that right now if it wasn't for me. See that guy over there taking the shoelace out of one of his sneakers? Same thing. That girl picking her nose? SHE WOULD BE DEAD AND HER NOSE WOULD BE FULLY UNPICKED IF IT WAS NOT FOR ME.

That guy with the sneakers is now using the lace to strangle someone, which is a beautiful thing to see, Emily, and I made it possible, and that's why you are blurry through my tears.

Okay, check it out, I'll tell you what happened.

I was in the admin block, outside the principal's office. I won't go into the reasons why I was there, because it would destroy the flow of the story.

The fact is, I was there, and on my own because the secretary just went out for a moment, and the telephone rang.

So I answer the phone. "Hello?"

And this voice goes, "Hello?"

And I go, "Hello?"

And this voice goes, "What?"

So I go: "Brookfield High School. How may I direct your call, please?" as per what I hear the secretary say every time I'm waiting there.

Then this voice goes, "Yes, hello, I'm with the Local Gas Authority and I'm calling from the basement of your school here. I'm just checking the main gas line and there is a serious leak here. Really, so serious that at any moment there could be an explosion. I myself am about to run to my car and get the hell away, but I thought I should let you know so you can sound the fire alarm and get everybody out of the school and onto the oval."

Check out how cool I was under pressure:

I just said, "Thank you very much, and please get yourself out of there and save your own life." Then I hung up, switched on the P.A. system, and said,

"THERE IS A GAS LEAK IN THE BASEMENT OF THE SCHOOL. THERE IS NO NEED TO PANIC. IT IS JUST A GAS LEAK WHICH MAY LEAD TO AN EXPLOSION AT ANY MOMENT. PLEASE ALL GO TO THE OVAL, AS PER THE FIRE DRILLS."

Then I found the fire alarm and pressed the button.

So then of course the doors all around me open and the principal practically kills me to switch off the P.A., and somehow I landed on the office floor but I kept my dignity.

So that explains why I am on the oval right now and not doing my Origins of the First World War examination, and also why I have now got a new faith in humanity, on account of being its savior.

When you think about it, the young people are the future, so I have saved the future.

There are even a couple of police here right this minute scouring the school for gas leaks, which includes my brother Brian (I don't mean my brother Brian is a gas leak, he's a cop), so I'm hoping they'll get to the leak in time and patch it up, maybe with a bit of Blue Tac or chewing gum, whatever you do in an emergency.

Or in the alternative, I hope they get everyone out of there, including the fish out of the school pond and the flying foxes from the attic, and then the gas leak explodes and then the school is, like, fully gone. *Pffwt.* (Open your hands out wide to indicate that there's nothing there anymore, as per your average magic trick.)

No more school.

Anyhow, I hope you don't send an empty envelope next time.

Catch ya,

Charlie

P.S. I liked your handwriting in your last letter. It was cute.

* * *

CHARLIE,

THIS, AS YOU WILL SEE, IS AN EMPTY ENVELOPE.

EMILY

* * *

Dear Emily,

Wow. You sure have a lot of resolution: I can't believe I sent you that whole story about being the savior of the future and you just sent me an empty envelope.

Technically, it wasn't empty on account of your note in there about it being an empty envelope, but still, it was pretty close, Em, and I'm proud of you, girl.

You really knocked me for a six.

I notice that you didn't express any interest in what happened next, after the gas leak. If you want to know, just say the word.

Actually, I'll tell you anyway, even though it is not a nice story.

Well, I told you there were cops at the school, and I was kind of wondering why. I was thinking: *Why not the gas authority blokes*? Plus, what happened to that chick in the basement?

After I wrote my letter to you on the oval, I saw the principal waving at me to go over to her, and that's where the truth came out.

I go over to her and she's standing on the front lawn of the school with the cops, and she says, "Now, tell us again about this phone call of yours."

I said, "Excuse me but it wasn't a phone call of *mine,* I just happened to answer the phone," but she wasn't interested in that.

So I told her the details of the phone call as per my description in the last letter, and then she says, "Nobody told you there was anything on fire?"

"No, just a gas leak in the basement."

"Charlie," she says. "Charlie, can you tell us where the basement of this school is?"

"No," I say, "I don't know where it is."

"Well, that's because we haven't got a basement. There is no basement in this school, Charlie. And Charlie, is there any gas in this school?"

At which point my brother Brian made a snorting sound, like immaturely indicating that there's plenty of gas of the kind that smells bad.

"I don't know," I say, as I did not know, "but I assume there is gas, if there's a leak."

"There is no gas in this school," says the principal. "Electricity, Charlie. We have electrical heating, all right?"

Then the adults all turn away from me and start talking to each other like I'm not there, about how unfortunate it was that there was a student answering the phone, and how everyone else would have seen it for a prank right away, and very sorry to have got you out here, officers, and wasted your time.

"Charlie apologizes also," said the principal, "for wasting your time."

She would have known that she couldn't order me to give an apology.

One of the cops was very forgiving and said he thought I did the right thing, and the other two (including my brother Brian), started doing stupid stuff like kicking around dead leaves at each other and going, "Watch out! There's a gas leak in your trousers!" and taking cover under their arms and stuff.

That was yesterday, and today I am depressed.

I'm eating my Coco Pops at the moment, and my mum is unfortunately using me as a pipeline to talk to the rest of the family, even though they are all also eating their breakfast right in this room. She's mad at everyone for some reason or another.

"Charlie," she just said, "ask Kevin if he intends to put the entire jar of strawberry jam on his toast."

"Kevin, Mum wants to know if you are you intending on —"

"Yes, Chuck, you tell your mother that's exactly what I am intending."

"Charlie, tell Jess to stop spilling the Coco Pops all over the floor, and ask Kevin what he intends the rest of us should eat on our toast."

"Jess, get your hand out of the cereal box. Kevin, what are your intentions as per the rest of our breakfasts?"

"I haven't really given much consideration to the rest of the family, Chucko."

"There's a purple dinosaur in here somewhere, I swear to you. Tell Mum about the purple dinosaur."

"Mum, Kevin says he hasn't considered us and Jess wants the purple dinosaur."

"Charlie, ask Jess if she is four years old, and please tell your father that his tie looks ridiculous with that shirt."

"What's wrong with this tie? I love this tie. You *gave* me this tie. *You* love this tie! What's wrong with this tie?"

As you will see, my dad just broke through the pipeline to defend his tie.

I just asked Brian if I should come by the station and give a statement about my general impressions of the chick on the phone, to help them catch her, plus some suggestions about protocol for future pranks like that, e.g., they should install phone-tracing machines in all school offices. If I could have switched on a tracer I could have tracked down the prankster while we were talking. Although that is assuming I would have known she was a prankster, which I did not.

Anyhow, Brian just told me to piss off and stop being a nancy-boy.

See you,

Charlie

* * *

CHARLIE,

THIS IS AN EMPTY ENVELOPE AGAIN.

YOURS SINCERELY,

EMILY

P.S. I HAVE TO PUT IN THE NOTE ABOUT IT BEING AN EMPTY ENVELOPE SO YOU CAN FEEL THE TRUE MIS-

ERY OF THE EMPTINESS. SO THEREFORE IT DOES NOT MAKE IT ANY LESS AN EMPTY ENVELOPE JUST BECAUSE THERE IS A NOTE.

* * *

Dear Emily,

Actually, I think it does make it less of an empty envelope, but I won't go into technicalities with you. How long are you going to keep up the empty envelopes?

I am leaving school right this moment and I'm skipping my curry chicken pie to go see the cops at Castle Hill, despite what Brian said. I think they have to stop people who play cheap tricks — if we're always going out to the oval on account of gas leaks in schools without gas, that could be the end of education as we know it. And therefore the end of the future. Do you want to know what happens with the cops or do you want me to stop writing?

Charlie

* * *

CHARLIE,

HERE IS ANOTHER EMPTY ENVELOPE. I WILL KEEP IT UP FOR MY WHOLE LIFE IF I NEED TO.

EMILY

P.S. PLEASE TELL ME WHAT HAPPENED WHEN YOU WENT TO THE POLICE ABOUT THE GAS LEAK. BUT YOU STILL CAN'T EXPECT ANYTHING OTHER THAN MISERY OUT OF ME.

* * *

Dear Emily,

I am wondering what I can do to expect anything besides misery out of you. It makes me feel depressed the way you keep sending misery to me. Like a kind of extra burden in my heavy life.

I remember one time when I was two years old and my mum left me with my brother Brian — I told you I had a supersonic memory, eh. I guess Brian was about twelve or thirteen at the time and he forgot about me and watched TV all night. Oh man, I was just stuck in Brian's bedroom where he forgot me, too short to open the door and get out, hungry, cold, the noise of my own voice calling, "LET ME OUT, LET ME OUT," giving me a full-on headache. The smell of Brian's sneakers making me sick to my stomach. I can't even tell you.

That was a bad time. And now this time in my life feels even worse than that.

E.g., I just got my latest geography assignment back, and, by the way, I worked really hard at that. And I got 23 percent, and the teacher wrote, "Wow, Charlie, you outdid yourself!," which I don't think teachers should be, sarcastic and critical like that.

2nd e.g., when I went to the cops, nothing happened. Brian was there and he just made me wait for two hours, which meant I missed out on this car show I was going to, and which I now find out has moved on to Melbourne, so I've missed it forever, unless there's a plane ticket under this paper right now. No, there is not, I just checked. And in the end, all Brian did was tell me to stand at the counter and write down my account of the incident. Which I did and then I gave it to Brian and he wrote something at the end of it, and told me I should sign my name there, and I looked at it, and he'd written "NANCY-BOY."

Then he just made it into a twin-engine paper aircraft and flew it into the bin.

And the fact is, I had some pretty good impressions that I wrote down on that paper and which could have helped them catch the perp. For an example:

- The chick had a funny way of saying the letters "th." Like in the word "the." Not exactly a lisp, but something a bit *distinctive* and kind of cute.
- There was some kind of an announcement going on in the background at one point when she was talking. Like at a railway station maybe?

3rd e.g. of how useless I am. The way that I have got you so mad with me, and I don't even really know how I did that. I was just mucking around when I suggested you give your English teacher a blow job back in my original letter of whenever that was. But maybe that was offensive?

I don't know. I'll make a confession to you. I've never had a girlfriend.

Once I asked a girl out on a date, and you've gotta wish you didn't have a supersonic memory when you experience something like that.

It's because of all the brothers, I guess, meaning I don't know about girls. The brothers do teach me about cars. (Brian taught me how to drive when I was nine, Kevin taught me how to hotwire a car, and Jack taught me how to siphon petrol out of other people's fuel tanks.) So I'm all set when it comes to cars, but they don't teach me about girls. And I've only got one sister and she's younger and likes to beat me up, which teaches me nothing apart from shame.

So I've got nobody to learn from, see?

So, maybe, can you forgive me and stop sending me misery all the time?

I'd really appreciate it.

Thanks,

Charlie

* * *

Dear Charles,

If you are feeling depressed, you should eat a Chokito or a Crunchie or a Caramello Koala. Any one of those will make you feel better. I always say that you should eat a chocolate which begins with the letter *C* if you are depressed.

Also, if that doesn't help, you should go shopping. And I'll tell you a particular secret: You should go shopping until you need to go to the bathroom, and then you should go to Level 5 of the Grace Brothers City Store. I tell you, those are such gracious bathrooms. You will feel fully calmed. They have a very sun-dewed light so you look attractive in the mirror, and they have an unusual basin for washing your hands. They are clean and modern and also very contemporary.

I was sending you misery because you were very offensive to me, telling me I was an old lady and challenging my legal connections, etc. I am a sensitive girl, Charlie. But, as you now see, I am also a nice and compassionate person, and I have sympathy for you because I get depressed myself sometimes. So therefore I have decided to stop sending you misery and give you a break.

This is on condition that you stop talking about me giving my English teacher a blow job, as that kind of talk gives me a headache.

Maybe you could tell me about the time you asked out that girl and I could give you suggestions on what you did wrong, so therefore you could avoid doing the same things wrong in the future?

Yours sincerely,

Emily

P.S. It's a funny thing that your brother Brian made a paper airplane out of your statement as a way of humiliating you. Right now, my brother William is in the kitchen melting chocolate bars and then putting the melted chocolate into molds so as to make chocolate shapes. It is one of his favorite things to do. And he is even making one in the shape of an aeroplane, and he will probably give it to me, and that is an example of how much nicer my brother William is than your brother Brian.

P.P.S. Another way of cheering up is to stop thinking about that gas leak trick. JUST PUT IT BEHIND YOU. It has already happened and it's all over, and you have saved humanity, or anyway if there was actually a gas leak you would have saved humanity. So get over it.

* * *

Dear Emily,

I've got to say, you hit me for a six again. That was so nice of you to think of ways to cheer me up, and I have got faith in humanity again.

On my way to my history class the other day, I thought maybe the class was planning on giving me a surprise party, or at least a Mexican wave, to thank me for getting them out of doing the exam last week by hitting the fire alarm. I could hear shushing inside the room, like everyone getting ready for something. But when I got there it wasn't to do with me, they were just planning to scare the shit out of the teacher by hiding under the desks and then jumping out and screaming: "HAPPY BIRTHDAY!"

It wasn't our teacher's birthday as far as anyone knew, but he has a weak heart, and we were supposed to be doing the postponed exam. So I guess you live in hope.

I'm just waiting in the admin block again at the moment, so I'm using the opportunity to write to you.

"Brookfield High School. How may I direct your call? No, sir, this is not a waste disposal unit, I'm afraid you have the wrong number."

That's what the secretary is saying. I've noticed, in my times here in the admin block, that a lot of people seem to think Brookfield is a waste disposal unit. It must have a similar phone number.

Well, as I said, I feel a lot better because of your kindness in your letter, and I will do what you suggest and tell you about the time I asked out this girl.

It was last year, and it's a girl in my science class. She's not even that hot so I thought she would think it was reasonable for me to ask her out. She wears these cute hair clips all over her head, like in the shape of lady beetles and birds and things, and she also wears long white socks.

So, I've gone up to her and I've gone, "Hey, how's it hangin'?"

And she's gone, "Up yours."

And I've gone, "Woo-hoo, up mine, eh? Nice one. Maybe we could go out some time so I could hear more of that humor of yours, eh? Maybe a movie or something else of your choosing?"

Though I've gotta say, I don't think she was actually intending on being humorous.

And she's gone, "Would you get lost before you put me into a coma?"

And I've gone, I've just gone.

I mean, I've just got lost, as per her recommendation.

So can you give me any advice on what I did wrong?

I really appreciate it.

Thanks again, and

Catch ya later,

Charlie

* * *

Dear Charlie,

Well, for a start what you did wrong was ask out a girl with lady beetles in her head and long socks. A girl like that does not deserve to be asked out, or even to be alive.

The other thing you did wrong was that neither of you were drunk. You should always ask girls out when you are both blind, and so therefore you can't see each other.

Anyway, I'm in English at the moment, and I'm so hungry that I'm just going to take a painkiller. Excuse me.

Yours sincerely,

Emily Thompson

* * *

Dear Emily,

I appreciate your comments about the girl I asked out and I think you are an alcoholic. If you need alcohol to give you courage, that's alcoholism.

Maybe you could give me some advice on how to pick up chicks. You seem like a very experienced girl, I have to say, and kind of professional about life. I am eating a Crunchie this moment and I've got to say it cheers me up, just as you said.

There's one girl my heart belongs to at the moment, but she's just been taken by a class-A prick who happens to be captain of our form. He also gets himself the starring role in every drama the school puts on. I say being the guy-in-charge and a star should be enough for him. But no, he has to get Christina Kratovac for his girlfriend as well. She is the hottest woman alive, I swear to you.

*

HEY. SORRY I had to stop then. The smoke alarm just went off and the sprinkler system turned on in our classroom. You won't even be able to read this letter anymore because the ink's all running, eh? I am soaking wet. The good thing about it is that we now don't have to do our exam on South African geography. I've got to go get a change of clothes or something.

Catch ya,

Charlie

* * *

Dear Charlie,

When you say "pick up chicks" it reminds me of "pick up sticks," which is a game I used to have as a child. I do not think it is correct to refer to girls as colorful sticks in a pile on the floor, and so therefore please don't use that expression.

Also, I don't think you should refer to a girl as the "hottest woman alive." For one thing, it might be offensive to the girl you are writing to. How do you know the girl you are writing to is not the hottest woman alive? I am not saying that this is true, I am only giving you a hyperactive situation of how you might give offense.

However, you are very inexperienced and so therefore I will forgive you for now.

I think that I should give you some lessons on how you ask a girl out. And then you will be able to steal this girl who has your heart, named Christina.

However, Lydia and Cassie are waiting for me at the moment, standing right beside me trying to read over my shoulder, which makes it difficult to concentrate. We are about to take the train to Lydia's place because we are spending the weekend there and painting the walls of her bedroom. Lydia says I have to explain that we are not just painting the walls like wall painters, we are doing a mural. We get one wall each, and the fourth wall is for practicing. But I don't think that's necessary, for me to explain that.

Wait one moment and I will ask Lyd and Cass for their ideal way of being asked out.

Okay, Lydia says her ideal way would be this: It would be the guy with the nose stud and the blond hair who works in HMV in Castle Hill and he would sell her a CD and he would put a little purple note in the CD cover saying a time and a place, and she would not even know what he meant, and whether it was serious, but she would be curious and have to go there, and when she got there, there would be a waiter standing at the door, wiping his hands on a white cloth, and speaking in a Russian accent, he would say, *"You are Lydia? I have a message for you. Go now. Go to the second elevator from the left and press the up button,"* and she would go there, and she would see an electric guitar leaning against the elevator door. . . . LYDIA IS GOING ON AND ON AND I AM NOT GOING TO WRITE DOWN ANOTHER WORD. *LYDIA, YOU MUST LEARN TO CONTROL YOURSELF.*

I am going to ask Cass instead.

Cass says that her ideal way would be for the guy to be Brad Pitt and he can just call her up and ask.

I am not sure that they understood the question correctly, but at least it is a start for you to work with. You could think about getting a nose stud, for instance.

Okay, I have to go as they are both trying to take the pen out of my hand as you will see from the handwriting.

Yours sincerely,

Emily Thompson

* * *

Hey Emily,

Thanks for your letter with the good advice. I would think about getting a nose stud but we have a crisis in the family at the moment as Jess just came home with a tattoo of barbed wire around her wrist. My mother has been crying her eyes out, and my father punched a hole in the kitchen wall.

My brother Kevin didn't make it any better because then he got home with a broken heart and a tin of black paint, ready to paint his room black.

That's a coincidence, eh, because you and your friends were painting bedroom walls over the weekend.

Anyhow, but Kev shares his room with Jack and Jack doesn't want the walls black, so they're just beating each other up in the backyard for a while to sort it out.

I hope you had fun with your friends. Did you?

I've got a heap of homework right now and it would be good if I could do some of it, eh, but no chance in this family.

See ya,

Charlie

* * *

Dear Charlie,

Well, I had a very nice weekend, thank you.

Lydia's walls were this repulsive orange color, but we made them extremely fascinating, and then we just watched DVDs and talked all night, generally.

Cassie is an excellent singer and she did this BEAUTIFUL song which she made up, all about painting the wall, and she wrote the words on the wall with paint so we could join in on the chorus. I can't explain how beautiful the singing was because you can't write music.

The sad thing is she will never sing in front of anyone else except us and I guess her piano teacher, and maybe she sings sometimes in the shower and maybe a passerby hears. Also, she did sing at her dad's funeral last year, but that was too sad for words.

Cass is just not the kind of person who can sing onstage.

And there is nothing wrong with being a shy person is what I always say, as long as you tell your best friends every single thing inside your head. Incidentally, I am a bit suspicious that Cass is not obeying this proclamation.

You know what, though, Lyd and I have noticed that Cass is writing a lot of letters to her penfriend person at Brookfield. This is a mystery to us, but he must be a nice person, whoever he is, to get her to write letters like that. She never usually likes to write stories or essays or anything. She is more the sport and music type of girl.

What I am thinking in my psychological mood is this: Cass does not explain the expressions on her face.

You must express your feelings. It is a rule.

I don't mean you, though. Boys should never express their feelings. It's really annoying when they do and makes them less mysterious, which is what boys should be. There's a guy in my English class who is always saying how books make him *feel,* like in *Julius Caesar,* it made him feel really sad to see the violence in the world. For a start, who cares how he feels, not me, and for another thing, that's not how you are supposed to read, you are supposed to look for the Themes and the Characters, and for a final thing, the teacher really gets off on it when this guy says how he feels and praises him to an extent beyond belief.

Therefore, in conclusion, when I say, "You must express your feelings," I mean a *person* should express his or her feelings, unless the person is a boy.

Yours sincerely,

Emily

* * *

Hi Emily,

Well, Kevin won the fight in the end, so he was able to paint his bedroom black. Only he was too depressed to lift a paintbrush, so I had to do it for him.

I really need some help, Emily. My family is making me crazy.

We didn't have to do our science test today because our teacher had his car broken into and all the papers stolen.

You know what? I've been working on my memory of that gas leak incident. I feel like all my problems would be solved if I could find out who tricked me like that. And made me miss out on that car show, wasting time going to the cops. It was embarrassing, is the thing, even though it was not really my fault that I didn't know we are a fully electrical school with no gas to leak. It was still a humiliation to be tricked by that gas authority girl, and to have the cops laugh at me, and I really want to try to find out who that girl was and maybe get her arrested.

I have been trying to remember what that announcement said in the background. You remember I told you there was some announcement going on while she was talking to me? Now I think I almost have it.

"Would all [something something] who are [something] on the inside of the Balkans, please be devout immediately [something] *and the lives of others.*"

Something like that.

So that seems to suggest it was an airport or a train station, doesn't it: something about devout passengers going to the Balkans? She was making an escape is what I read into it.

Catch ya,

Charlie

* * *

Dear Charlie,

You should chew on fresh mint all the time. You can get it from your mother's mint garden, and you can always keep it in your pocket.

I think that one problem with boys is that they often smell: e.g., Body odor, or breath, or just a general boy smell.

For an example, I have an Uncle Christopher, and he has a real tendency to drink coffee and eat garlic and sardines and so therefore he has breath.

So this letter is a reminder to eat fresh mint from your mother's mint garden while you are asking a girl out, and to move out of your home. That's my advice for now.

My other advice is that it will not solve any of your problems if you keep thinking about the girl who called you about the gas leak. It will only keep you awake at night, tossing and turning, and that is no answer. That girl would be long gone now since she was calling from an airport. Plus, maybe she is not so evil as you think she is? Maybe she really DID believe there was a gas leak? MAYBE IT WAS A WRONG NUMBER. Have you considered that?

Sincerely,

Emily Thompson

* * *

Dear Emily,

Okay, fair enough about the mint, though I have to say that my old lady is the last person on the planet to have a mint garden. I'll pick some up at the supermarket.

But even if I got Christina to go out with me, what would I do once I got her out? As you can see, I am a hopeless case.

I can't go home tonight because Kevin thinks I took his motorbike for a spin. In actual fact, it was Jessica. So maybe you are right about moving out, but how will I live?

I will try to stop thinking about the gas leak girl.

See ya,

Charlie

* * *

Dear Charlie,

I have got some more advice, as I see you are miserable again, and I wonder if you are taking my advice about the toilets in Grace Brothers.

But I wonder if the boys' toilets are the same as the girls' toilets? That is something I never thought of, and it's good that I'm writing to you as it puts a whole new perspex on the world.

Here is some new advice.

The ladies seem to really go for Lydia's dad (Justice Oberman). They love him! ☺ I have heard tell (from Lydia's mother) that Justice Oberman's name was once a cinnamon for sex god. This was in his university times.

I asked my parents about this, but they just laughed fondly, remembering the days of free love.

All our parents are friends, you know. They used to smoke pot together, but they gave it up to set a better example for us. However, they continue gathering to drink whisky (the men) and gin and tonics (the women) and at some point in the night, they always play a song by Kate Bush called "Wuthering Heights," which makes them dance wildly in drunken disarray.

Well, anyway, they used to do this often, before Cass's father got too sick, and even after that, they still hung out at his place, and laughed loudly in their variety of laughs.

Now, getting back to Lydia's dad, the mystery of it is that he is bald. ALMOST COMPLETELY BALD. And he does not even seem ashamed of it, for example, by wearing a hat or a wig. He would wear a wig when he is being a judge, of course, and that is probably why he became a judge, but I do not see him wear one in normal life.

Also, I have seen on TV that you can get head transplants and it seems to me that it is a tragedy if you are bald and you don't get a head transplant.

My dad agreed with me heartily, and with much joy, when I pointed out that Lydia's dad should get a head transplant.

Yours sincerely,

Emily Thompson

P.S. I completely forgot the point of this letter! It was to say that we should learn from Lydia's dad, because if he can be bald and still be attractive to women, well then!

P.P.S. You can really learn from him, I guess.

P.P.P.S. So therefore I thought about that while I was at Lydia's place. I noticed that her father plays a lot of snooker with various friends in the family games room. He seems to be sharp at snooker, and offers brandies and cigars to his friends while they are playing, and makes urban comments about the cigars. As well as being urban, he can be quite trivial. For instance, the other night we stopped by the game room to see if we could play snooker while we were eating our pizza, and he was in there with two women. He put on a strong Italian accent and said, "Pepperoni, eh? Mamma make-a the pepperoni pizza, eh?" If you can believe it, the two women giggled. Then he put on a French accent instead, and told us to leave him, because he was entertaining *mon cheries,* gesturing toward the giggling women.

He is a ladies' man, as I have said, and so you should learn from that.

* * *

Dear Emily,

Thanks for your advice about the pepperoni pizza and the head transplants.

My brothers sit on the back porch and drink beer when they get home from work each day, and that means that they are alcoholics.

I'm sitting out here with them now, freezing my balls off in the dark, trying to see this paper using the lights of their cigarettes. I have no socks because Jessica stole them all to keep her worms warm. She's got a worm farm in a garbage bin in the backyard, which stinks.

Meantime, my mother has been having a bath to get over her nervous breakdown. So the bathroom also stinks, but of some kind of jasmine designed to get Mum sleepy.

It's funny that you say guys smell bad, because in my family I reckon it's the women.

Catch you,

Charlie

* * *

Dear Charlie,

Sometimes I think I might have already *lived* too much for a teenager. You know, because I have been to Spain, France, Italy, and the United States of America. Where else is there? I am too cosmopolitan for my own good.

Which is satirical, because I can't even get to the south coast of New South Wales to see my horses. My parents are always away and therefore not taking me there.

Listen, I have some more advice for you, for impressing this girl called Christina, and it might make you feel better about your family and the alcoholism and worms. The advice is this: You have to be very funny. I have realized that it is essential for a boy to be funny. Otherwise, what is the point in a boy?

The boy must be funny. It's a rule, and it's similar with fat people. There is no point in being fat unless you are funny.

Yours sincerely,

Emily

* * *

Dear Emily,

There are a couple of things I have to point out about your letter.

One of them is that I can't be funny. I have tried to be funny but I'm crap at it. So what do I do if I'm a boy and I'm not funny?

The other thing I have to say is that I think it is wrong what you said about fat people — that fat people have to be funny. I think it's actually a bit racist.

Catch ya,

Charlie

* * *

Dear Charlie,

I hope you're not fat. All that supporting of fat people.

If a boy is not able to be funny, then the boy should not talk at all. The boy should be completely silent.

Yours sincerely,

Emily

* * *

Em,

Did you know that you can be supportive of people even though you are nothing like them yourself?

Charlie

* * *

Dear Charlie,

Only Lyd and Cass call me Em. But I suppose it's okay if you want to call me Em, OCCASIONALLY. Just not all the time.

Of course I knew that it was okay to be nice and supportive about people who are not like me. What do you think I am doing for you? I am being nice and supporting you.

Talking about that, I just had this great idea, the greatest idea. It is this. We should *go out together.*

DON'T GET EXCITED. IT WOULD NOT BE REAL.

It would be a TRAINING SESSION to prepare you for this Christina girl. It would be a kind of practice run, of Going on a Date with a Girl, and I could be the Girl. Then I could give you my degradation afterward and also make suggestions for improvement.

Also, you can pay me for it if you like.

Yours sincerely,

Emily

* * *

Dear Emily,

That is so generous, and you continue to strike me as the best thing of humanity. What about this Friday night?

Charlie

P.S. Do you realize that if I pay you to go on a date that makes you a prostitute?

* * *

Dear Charlie,

I have noticed something about the names in your family: Brian, Kevin, and Jack, and also your name: Charlie.

I think you should change these names.

Lydia went out with this guy once who was called Bruce, and we all decided she had to break up with him because of it, the name, and so therefore she did.

You see? It's a risk.

I think you should change your name, for example to "Adam" or "Ashley" or "Aaron" or anything else beginning with *A*. And you should change all your brothers' names similarly.

Yours sincerely,

Emily

P.S. I have reconsidered and decided that you don't need to pay for the date. It will be free. Okay, I am free this Friday night for your Date with a Girl. It's the last day before the holidays too, so I would normally go out with Cass and Lyd, so I am making a genuine sacrifice for you.

* * *

Emily,

Thank you for your great suggestion about changing my names and the names of all my brothers. I can't do anything about my brothers, but from now on my name will begin with an *A*.

Yours sincerely,

Aristotle

P.S. If you go on a date with me for free, then you are a slut.

* * *

Charlie,

HA HA HA about the Aristotle, I mean. Not about the "slut," which is offensive, and you are using up the times that I will forgive you.

Okay. You can be Charlie. But try not to use your name too much in conversation.

And I don't see why you can't rename your brothers. Why don't you have any strength of character? It sounds to me a lot like those brothers of yours push you around, and I think you could reinstigate your position in the family if you changed your brothers' names for them. From there, it would be a simple step to stealing this girl called Christina from her boyfriend.

Emily

* * *

Dear Emily,

Do you think you can give me some advice on what I should wear on a Date with a Girl? There are only three days to the Date, so I would like to feel fully prepared.

Catch ya,

Archibald

* * *

Dear Charlie,

I recommend that you wear black, including black jeans, and a black jacket, and black running shoes on your feet, and black socks if you can get any out of your sister's worm farm. Also, you could wear a piece of black rope around your neck with a little seashell hanging off it. A girl would like that. ☺

It's the middle of the night right now, and I had to get up because I was so hungry. I had to eat some of the letters off the birthday cake that my mother bought for my uncle, and now it says, "HAPPY BIRTHDAY, UNCLE CHRIST." So I am going to have to eat the "T" as well, for obvious reasons.

I was in an earthquake once, you know. It was on a family trip to España. I was excellent in a crisis, and I looked up "Help!" in the Spanish phrase book for my dad.

Yours sincerely,

Emily

P.S. As I explained before, I have revoked my invitation that you change your name. I have now decided that the name Charlie is acceptable, and so therefore please stop calling yourself by the *A* names. It is not funny, you know. It is just tiresome, and sometimes can be confusing.

* * *

Em,

Where do you think I should take a girl on a date? I don't want to get it wrong. Should it be a movie or dinner or something wacky like going to see a circus or taking a walk along a beach? Can you answer urgently because there are only two days to go.

Aloysius

* * *

Charlie,

I think it is too cold to go for a walk on a beach for a date, and I think girls like movies a lot. I think we should just meet at the Castle Hill movies at seven on Friday.

Can you please just call yourself Charlie now? Okay? I will now admit that I was wrong. OKAY. I WAS COMPLETELY WRONG WITH MY INSPIRATION ABOUT CHANGING YOUR NAME. OKAY, OKAY, OKAY.

Em

* * *

Em,

How do we decide what movie to see?

Abraham

* * *

Charlie,

Well, when we get there you should say: "What do you feel like seeing?" And the girl will suggest a movie, and you will laugh and make a little joke about why you don't want to see that movie.

I am sure you can think of a joke for it.

Anyhow, and then the girl will say, "Okay, we'll see something else," but then *you will insist that we see what the girl suggested!*

Em

* * *

Charlie!

I am rushing this note and so therefore you will not be able to read the handwriting, but it's VERY VERY VERY important that you bring chocolate when you go on a date, especially as it is the start of the holidays. I can hardly wait for the holidays as I am very tired.

It doesn't have to be chocolate in the shape of a heart. That would be stupid actually if you did that. ☺

It just has to be a giant-sized Toblerone.

Yours sincerely,

Em

* * *

Charlie!

Also, you could bring a magazine along, in case the girl gets bored, and then she can read the magazine instead. *Cosmopolitan* or *Vogue* would be sensible.

Em

* * *

Em,

Okay, see you tonight, and I'll be dressed in black and carrying a Toblerone, as per your instructions.

I won't bring a magazine though.

The girl is not going to get bored.

See you later,

Adonis

11. Autumn Term / Lydia and Sebastian

Dear Sebastian,

Huh, the computer just told me that it looks like I'm writing a letter. Spooky. How did it know? It wants to help. It's a little paper-clip man and it wants to help.

That is so nice of it. I'll try to talk to it.

YES PLEASE, PAPER-CLIP MAN. HELP ME WRITE THIS LETTER. WHAT SHOULD I SAY NEXT?

(It's not saying anything, Seb. It's just smiling at me. Maybe it needs more information? Wait.)

DO YOU NEED MORE INFORMATION?

(It blinked at me.)

WELL, OKAY, HERE IS SOME INFORMATION: THE LETTER IS TO SEBASTIAN. HE'S A GUY AT BROOKFIELD AND HE WANTS ME TO PROVE THAT I'M NOT A SNAKE. ALSO, TO SHOW HIM THAT I'M NOT AFRAID OF MY FATHER. YOU LOOK CONFUSED! I KNOW, SO AM I. HOW IS IT HIS BUSINESS IF I'M AFRAID OF MY FATHER OR NOT?

PARDON?

WELL, HE THINKS I WANT TO BUY DOPE OFF HIM. I KNOW! I KNOW! IT'S NOT HIS FAULT. HE'S JUST A BROOKER KID, AS MY TEACHER WOULD SAY. MAYBE

THEY DON'T REALIZE WHEN PEOPLE ARE MESSING WITH THEM THERE? WHAT SHOULD I SAY TO HIM?

(Sorry Seb, I'm just talking to my paper-clip man here. I don't mean to leave you hanging. Paper-clip man said I can get dope easy at Ashbury, so why would I want someone at Brookfield to send it to me? We had a good laugh about you.)

HUH, REALLY?

(Hey, Seb, guess what he said? He said I should not bother writing to you, I should trash my bedroom and chuck this computer out my window. It seems profoundly excessive, doesn't it. I'll ask if he really means it.)

PAPER-CLIP MAN. DO YOU UNDERSTAND THAT *YOU* WILL DIE IF I THROW OUT THE COMPUTER?!?! YOU ARE PART OF THE COMPUTER!!!

(Well, Seb, looks like he meant it, hang on and I'll start trashing the room. . . .)

I got you, eh. I wasn't really trashing my bedroom, I was just getting some grilled-cheese-and-Vegemite-on-toast and some *Orangensaft*.

That's German for orange juice.

I'm at home from school today on account of the flu, and I'm writing this on my new computer, which was a birthday present from my parents. Through the window I can see our frosted-glass pyramid, and there's a family of little elves trying to climb the side of it. They're wearing striped pajamas and they have tiny suction things on their hands and feet to help them climb the glass, but they keep skidding back down, and it's SO CUTE.

OH MY GOD.

Our dog, Pumpernickel, just ate the elves! That is the saddest thing I ever saw.

You're welcome to tell me more of your dreams, especially as they are like nature lessons. That dream of yours about the kookaburra killing the snake by hitting it against a rock? That was excellent, Seb.

Wait a minute, the paper-clip man is talking to me again. (He's sitting on my shoulder now, eating a little bowl of strawberries and cream.)

NO, PAPER-CLIP MAN! I'M SURE HE WASN'T TRYING TO *THREATEN* ME WITH THE DREAM ABOUT THE KOOKABURRA! HE WOULDN'T DO THAT! THAT WOULD BE CHILDISH AND STUPID! I'D NEVER WRITE BACK TO HIM!

Auf Wiedersehen,

Lydia

P.S. You want me to make sure the alarm goes off at your school after lunch next Tuesday? I've got the perfect person for the job. If you need something, Seb, all you have to do is ask.

P.P.S. But you have to do something for me too. What we'll do is, we'll take turns giving each other challenges and we'll see who's best at it. The winner will be selected to join an elite spy squad. I'll choose the winner.

P.P.P.S. I liked your sketch of my dog and the breakfast pyramid a lot. You're a great artist.

* * *

Dear Lydia,

Have you ever been committed?

You are *très* confusing (don't talk to me in German, okay, I do French and you'll mess with my mind if you put another language in there).

Which bits of your letter are true?

Okay, fine, Lydia, you can be a freak, it's funny. But can you give me a sign when you're about to tell the truth?

I thought it was true that you wanted me to send you that stuff you wanted me to send you and I might've done that, you know, and I could've got in a whole lot of shit. And now it turns out you can get it easy at your school. Who from?

Also, more important, I thought it was a fact that you only got a book for your birthday. Remember? You told me that story about your dad doing the 360 turn and all? That sucked bad, and I felt sorry for you. Now you reckon you got a computer. That sucks too, Lyd, especially if you wanted a foosball table, but it doesn't suck as bad as a book would.

Just tell me this: that you're serious about the school alarm. Can I trust you on that? Don't screw me over, okay. I need that alarm to go off on Tuesday or I'm dead.

And we can do the challenges for each other, if you mean it about that. I'm up for that.

But you mean it, right?

Seb

* * *

Hey Lydia,

It's now Tuesday morning. I was hoping for a letter of confirmation from you, but maybe it's kicking its way over as we speak. I'm guessing you're back at school and not still home with the flu? So I can trust you?

We need this plan straight through the goalposts with the goalie flying in the wrong direction. I want to hear that alarm sounding, Lyd, loud and clear as the Old Trafford crowd in the match against City. You with me?

Seb

* * *

Lydia,

I swear to God, you might think it's funny being deceptive and tricky and stuff, but when people rely on you it's what I call deadly serious. It's fine for you looking all pretty there in your frosted glass, but you just don't think about people who might not have frosted glass.

I'm just saying that there are now five minutes to period no. 5 here and I don't hear any alarm bells. I'm just saying you better forget about writing to me again because you know what? You let me down. You've gotta be able to trust people, and I thought maybe you weren't like those other Ashbury girls because you sounded kind of whacked out. But now I think maybe you're just like them, and maybe you're a snake. I don't know, Lyd, I'm not saying you are.

But you're one of them, Lydia, that's for sure.

Don't start crying or anything because it's not like me to be upfront like this unless I'm really mad, but well done, Lydia, you've got me pissed. Maybe you're still sick, but you should have let me know, okay. No offense, but you're not a team player, Lyd. You play mean, is what you do. You're the kind of player who's always doing hand balls because you don't want to bother hitting the ball with your head on account of it might mess up your hair. That's rich people for you all over. People rely on you, Lyd, and

Well, beat me with a broomstick and call me Uncle Harry. (As my mother likes to say.)

You did it.

The alarm's going off right now, Lyd, baby, and I just heard an announcement made by my good buddy Charlie Taylor telling us about a gas leak. There is no gas in this school, but that's a fact that's passed my good buddy Charlie by. Also the people around me who are tearing up to the oval like cattle on heat.

Jesus, Mary, and the other Guy, I am in love with you.

You are the most beautiful, gorgeous, unbelievable girl in the country, Lydia, and I am totally in awe of you.

I'm out of here. I'll drop this off at the Ashbury mailbox on my way to the oval, being careful of gas explosions. You tell me a time and place where we can meet, okay? I want to take you out to say thank you for this.

You rock.

Seb

* * *

Dear Lydia,

Hey, what happened to you? It's been like a week or something and I haven't heard back. I thought you were planning on sending me a challenge of your own?

Did I not thank you enough? I seem to recall that I told you you were gorgeous and sexy or something like that. That's good enough, isn't it?

Where are you?

I miss your crazy talk. I really want to meet you in person.

Seb

* * *

Lydia?

* * *

Dear Sebastian,

Do you understand that you can get out a new piece of paper if you change your mind about writing something?

Lydia

* * *

Dear Beautiful Lydia,

I don't know what you're talking about, but it's good to hear your voice again. I forgive you for being a freak, because I'm in love with you for making that happen with the alarm. That was a nice touch keeping me in suspense like that, but in the future you might think about my blood pressure. Meantime, I'm hanging to take you out to your favorite location and worship you for life.

Hey, did I ever tell you I have a little brother? He loves you too. He's like no age or something. Like ZERO years old, but he loves you. I'll get him to dribble on the paper here for you when I get home.

You're making me nervous by being so weird.

But your weirdness is what I like about you.

Seb

* * *

Dear Seb,

Actually, I think it's fairly common for people not to like being called deceptive and a snake and a non-team player who never hits the ball with their head or whatever that soccer crap was about hand balls and messing up my hair and you say *I'm* the one who talks like a crazy person?

It's actually not "weird" or "freakish" at all. To stop writing after being insulted.

And it doesn't make it okay that on the next page you said you were in love with me. You wanted me to let you know when I was being serious. Okay, I'm letting you know. That letter pissed me off. You were making these assumptions about me, and imagining you knew me, and the fact is, Seb, you don't.

And come on. Giving me a lecture because the *alarm didn't go off?* You wanted to get out of an exam or something, Seb. I'm not a moron. Why didn't you just skip school for the afternoon? Or actually do the exam?

Last year, when my friend Cass came back to school after her father died, we had exams, and Cass is not the exam type to begin with. And she couldn't walk down a corridor without people spinning out of her way because they were afraid to look her in the eye.

Do you think she went around shouting at people about not being team players? And trying to get out of exams?

No. She just stared straight ahead and wrote the exams.

Except for the science exam, because Em and I decided she needed a break that day and took her to the movies.

You could learn some lessons in strength of character from Cass.

Best wishes,

Lydia

P.S. Here is your challenge.

1. At 1 P.M. tomorrow, go to the refrigerator section of the Harvey Norman store in Castle Towers.
2. You will see a huge cardboard polar bear carrying a sign which says: "THIS WEEK ONLY! POLAR BEAR FRIDGES — GET THEM WHILE THEY'RE COLD!"
3. By 2 P.M. the huge cardboard polar bear must be standing outside the World of Pets pet shop. The sign should say:

"THIS WEEK ONLY! POLAR BEARS! — GET THEM WHILE THEY'RE COLD!"

4. Send me a photo of this.

* * *

Lydia,

The polar bear challenge?

Easy.

Seb

TO: Lydia Jaackson-Oberman

Special Covert Operation Report

Agent: Seb Mantegna

Aka: AKA*

* STANDS FOR ARSE-KICKING AGENT

Special No.: 101010101010010101

Special Password: Sultana Bran with banana, thanks Mum

Experience: Task Force Operations in Indonesia, Korea, Russia, Iraq; local training in Baulkham Hills and Glenhaven

Special Mention: Instrumental in ending the Cold War; knocked over the Berlin Wall, etc.

Pro: Black belt in tae kwon do; kick-arse soccer player; knows how to make up baby's bottle with correct amount of formula; knows how to make baby smile by tickling baby's little chin with feather

Con: Memory sucks, so will sometimes say something in a letter and forget to throw letter away and start again

<u>OPERATION</u>

Operation Polar Bear

Assigned by Agent Lydia

Result: Successfully Completed (See Photograph Attachment)

FIELD NOTES

Agent Mantegna wants to say sorry to Agent Lydia for letter where forgot to start again after sledging Lydia unfairly when Operation Alarm was successfully completed by Agent Lydia. See CONs above.

* * *

Dear Seb,

Okay, I forgive you. I always forgive people when they say sorry.

That was a pretty cool operation you did. I take off my hat to you and bow down to the ground, but get those shoes away from me. I'm not kissing those shoes. You hear me? Are you kidding? GET THEM AWAY FROM ME! GET YOUR STINKING SHOES AWAY FROM ME!!

Sorry, I'm kind of tired. It's after midnight.

Are you really a black belt in tae kwon do?

I hope you're not trying to impress me with those baby-related talents: I don't think it's anything special in a guy to know how to take care of kids. All guys should know that, especially if your mum recently had a new baby.

Plus, is it safe to touch a baby with a feather? Where did you get the feather from? Is the feather attached to a bird? What sort of bird? Is it a parrot?

THE PARROT'S CLAWS COULD HURT THE BABY, SEBASTIAN. YOU IDIOT.

It's twenty to one, and I keep looking up from the computer to the window and seeing my own face, which is a shock. Especially when I catch a smile on my face, meaning I think I'm being funny.

But when I look past my own face I can see our back lawn with such gentle moonlight on it: so gentle, it's like it's afraid of touching.

By the way, I don't think you have to be rich to have a frosted-glass breakfast pyramid. It's not really a breakfast pyramid anyway. It's more a breakfast triangular prism.

I don't know the difference either.

My dad gave me a surprise today by getting my walls painted a kind of disgusting tangerine color, like a fake sunset. I've been saying I want to rip off the wallpaper and paint the walls myself, and my stupid father thinks he's doing me a favor by getting professionals in to paint while I was at school. He was so proud of himself.

"Dad," I said. "I wanted to paint them myself."

"Lydia," he said. "Is that a fact?"

"Yes," I said. "It is a fact."

I will now go to sleep.

Tschüß!

Lyd

P.S. It's your turn to give me an assignment now.

* * *

TO: Special Agent Lydia

From: AKA

Special Covert Operation Assignment

Assignment Description

Set off smoke-alarm sprinkler system at Brookfield High, 11 A.M., next Tuesday. This only has to happen in the classrooms along the second-floor balcony of the northwest wing, but go ahead and make it happen in the whole school if you prefer.

FIELD NOTES

Sorry about my handwriting on this Special Report, I was rocking the baby's bassinet with my left foot the whole time.

FIELD NOTES #2

I've decided you get a yellow card every time you mess with my head. You've got one yellow card right now for the incident with the dope.

FIELD NOTES #3

Why don't we meet somewhere in person? I could hand over the plans of the school or whatever you need for this assignment.

* * *

Hey Seb,

I don't think we should meet in person. That would compromise special operations.

You should just admit that you're trying to get out of exams or whatever it is. Or are you so concerned about your fellow human beings that you want to test the fire system?

What I think should happen is, you should choose special operations which are a LITTLE bit less self-centered and more socially oriented.

Lydia

* * *

Dear Lydia,

Yeah, you've got a point there. I should think of more *people*-focused assignments.

Example: I could get you to put a polar bear sign outside a pet shop. I've got to say, I felt my spirit soar when I shifted that sign for you. Knowing what I was doing for humanity.

Let's just say this. I would never stoop so low as to exploit special operations to get out of exams, and you should be ashamed of yourself for your doubt. Trust me, Lyd, there's a significant reason why I asked you to set off the school alarm and why I'm now asking for the sprinkler system, etc. One day you might even find out what that reason is.

I'm thinking about getting out another yellow card for you right now, for your suspicions, and you know what a second yellow card means. It means a red card.

What I reckon should happen is, you should buy me a coffee to apologize for the slander of my character.

Seb

* * *

Hey Seb,

Shut your mouth, exam boy.

Lyd

TO: Seb Mantegna
Special Covert Operation Report

Agent: Lydia Jaackson-Oberman

Aka: Lydia

Special No.: 1776

Special Password: Do you mean to say your mother makes you breakfast? Make your own.

Experience: CLASSIFIED

Special Mention: CLASSIFIED

Pro: Excellent at everything

Con: None

<u>OPERATION</u>

Operation Sprinkler System

Assigned by Agent AKA

Result: Successful

FIELD NOTES

Too easy.

* * *

Dear Lydia,

You are as beautiful as the Irish equalizer by Robbie Keane in injury time in the Ireland v. Germany game, World Cup, 2002, Korea.

I have now got a kick-arse cold from the sprinkler water falling on my head. That's my only complaint. You could have made it start just before I got into the room. But I swear to you it is the most beautiful cold I ever had.

Why can't we meet in person for you to give me the next assignment? We could see a movie and you could give me the assignment while the previews are on.

Seb

* * *

Dear Seb,

Why would I want to meet you when you have a cold? I could catch the cold.

I can't concentrate right now because Em and Cass are on either side of me having a loud argument about what whales sound like when they're singing. They're giving a lot of examples to support their own arguments, which is really making people stare.

I'll interrupt them to ask them what causes colds. (I'm pretty sure it's not sprinkler systems.)

It was difficult to get them to stop talking, but as soon as I did Em had an answer. She said colds travel around on the fur of rats, and that is what caused the plague and she's not surprised that people at Brookfield have colds because it's rat infested.

Cass said people get colds when they walk around with their mouths open.

So shut your mouth, Seb, and you'll be fine.

It's interesting that you suggest I give you an assignment during the previews of a movie. You need to learn a little respect for previews. They're our favorite part. Em always cries in the previews for sad movies because she guesses what sad thing might happen in the actual movie, and Cass packs her things up, like she's ready to go home, when the previews finish. As in to indicate humorously that that's all she needs to see.

Okay, I've thought of an assignment for you.

Well, we always go to the movies on Thursdays after lunch, and what we do is, we take the path through the reserve behind our school to get to the station. Do you know the reserve? People go there at lunch to smoke up or buy drugs, so you probably know it. Also, people jog there all the time. But whenever I hear running footsteps behind me I think it's someone chasing us. Like a teacher. To arrest us. Even though I know it's just a jogger.

So this is the assignment.

1. Go to the reserve and tie purple ribbons around as many branches of the trees as you can. That way I'll see them and be distracted from the running footsteps.
2. Try to do it by lunchtime Thursday.

I hope that's enough notice for you.

Tschüß.

Lydia

* * *

Hey Lyd,

I did the ribbon thing for you. Very weird request.

Is it okay if I send you my next special task now? It's urgent.

This is it:

TO: Special Agent Lydia
From: AKA
Special Covert Operation Assignment
Assignment Description

Think up a way to stop me from having to do my science exam on Wednesday. The science teacher is the Rattler if that helps. Also known as the Rattlesnake. Maybe you want to kill him?

FIELD NOTES

Okay, you broke me down. These are exam-avoidance techniques. I can't think of any other way to disguise them.

FIELD NOTES #2

You talk about your friends Emily and Cassie a fair bit. Are they as hot as you?

* * *

Dear Seb,

I forgive you for the exam thing because I knew it all along. Also because I loved the ribbons around the trees in the park. Thank you v. v. much.

Em and Cass came over to my place on the weekend and we just watched movies and listened to music and painted walls, etc. On Sunday we went shopping, and we were at this café and there was a bowl of sugar sachets in the middle of the table. Cass was looking at the sugar and she suddenly said, kind of quietly, "*Huh,*" and she took out her mobile and dialed a number and said, in a polite voice, "Yes, I'm really interested in finding out more about this sugar, please?"

Because she had found a number on the side of the sugar to Call If You Want More Information About This Sugar. She kept a straight face the whole conversation, and that's exactly the way Cass is funny when she decides to be funny.

I've found the right person for your next assignment. Don't worry about studying for the science exam.

But I don't see how this helps you. In the end, you'll have to do the exams, right? So why do you keep putting it off?

Lydia

* * *

Dear Lydia,

You STOLE THE EXAM PAPERS FROM HIS CAR????

How did you even know what kind of car he drives? You rock. You're a classic. You're as beautiful as a Beckham free kick and as wicked as a Maradona header. I'm thinking about taking off my shirt and sending it to you. I'm that in love with you.

You realize that's THREE challenges you have succeeded in without a single thing going wrong?

You know what you are?

You are Argentina.

In particular, I'm thinking of the fact that Argentina beat Japan, Jamaica, and Croatia without conceding a single goal in the first three games of the World Cup in 1998.

This time you have to let me take you out to say thank you. I'm not accepting a no.

Your No. 1 Fan

* * *

Dear Seb,

Thanks for your praise about the stolen exam papers. But I can't take personal credit. I have a friend with a talent for locks. You don't need to know any names.

I don't understand why you want to meet in person. Try to remember something: You don't know what I look like.

You need to see a person to know what they look like. Did you not know that?

Lydia

* * *

Dear Lydia,

I bet you a thousand dollars you are the most gorgeous girl in the country.

Seb

* * *

Dear Lydia,

You haven't written for five days. Where are you and when can we meet? I know that you are beautiful.

Seb

* * *

Dear Seb,

Okay, just to prove how wrong you are, I've decided that we CAN meet. I've thought about this a lot, and I've figured something out.

It will be a double Secret Assignment and the aim is to identify the other person first.

What we're going to do is, I'm going to tell you a place and a time, and we both have to be at the place at the time, and *we have to figure out which one the other person is before the other person figures it out.* Does that make sense?

I haven't decided yet where the place will be, but it will be somewhere crowded and noisy. And I think it will be the last day of the term before the holidays.

Gotta go,

Lydia

* * *

Dear Lydia,

Okay. What time will we go to the crowded/noisy place where I have to figure out which one you are before you figure out which one I am?

Seb

* * *

Dear Seb,

You are so going to lose this.

I've figured out all the rules now. They are these:

1. We will both be at the Blue Danish Café next Friday night, arriving sometime between six and seven.
2. As soon as you figure out which one is the other person, you have to go straight up to them and give them some kind of object, like a flower or something, to show you know it's them, and then you have to leave the café immediately.
3. The first person to do that is the winner.
4. We can't ask around at the café to find out which one the other person is.

5. Also, we can't ask around for information about what the other person looks like before Friday night. It's very important that you obey this and I'm trusting you, and you have to trust me. The point is to recognize the other person's *soul,* not their face.
6. We can only use the following clues:
   (a) We have to send each other a photo which shows *something* about us, e.g., it could be a photo of our cat. I am enclosing a photo of my elbow now. The person in the photo who is grabbing at my elbow, trying to get me into the photo, is my father. I look absolutely nothing like my father, thank you Jesus. So his face is not a clue.
   (b) We're allowed to ask each other THREE questions, only they can't be questions about what we look like. Just questions which we think will help us identify the other person's soul.

Tell me if you agree with the rules or not.

Lydia

* * *

Dear Lydia,

The only thing I don't like about the rules is that the person who wins has to leave the café. Why is that? Why can't the person who wins get to sit down with Lydia and have a coffee with her and get to know her?

I'm enclosing a photo of my left ankle. It's going in for a tackle which will lead to me getting control of the ball and making a beautiful pass, leading to a goal being scored. The guy who's got the ball and is about to lose it to my brilliant piece of footwork is my good buddy Charlie Taylor. He's a great guy but a really crap soccer player.

I'll answer your three questions, but not until you agree that we get to stop and talk before I walk out of there, leaving you heartbroken with nothing but your red rose.

Seb

* * *

Dear Seb,

I already made the rules. Trust me, you'll be glad to have the opportunity to leave when you see what I look like.

Here are my questions:

1. How do you take your coffee?
2. What is your favorite song at the moment?
3. Do you smoke?

See ya,

Lydia

* * *

Dear Lydia,

1. Black.
2. I haven't got one, but I like Tom Waits.
3. No.

I'll give you some time to think about the answers before I send my questions. I seriously don't know what use my answers will be to you. Maybe you're thinking of playing a song on the jukebox and then looking around to see if anybody in the café looks happy when they hear it? Ingenious.

Wait until you see my questions.

Watch and learn.

Seb

* * *

Dear Lydia,

Okay, it's me again. Here are my questions:

1. If a tree falls in the forest and nobody cut it down, why did it fall?
2. If you were an astronaut and you noticed that your spaceship was running out of petrol and the nearest petrol station was on Venus, would you:
   a) Scream and get upset?
   b) Convert to solar power?
   c) Go to Venus and get petrol?
3. Who won the 1998 World Cup?

I still say we should change the rules and stay and talk.

Seb

* * *

Seb,

Keep your mouth shut or you'll get a cold. The rules can't be changed.

Your questions are intriguing, but you must have a master plan because I know what kind of an undercover spy you are.

1. Why did the tree fall if no one cut it down? Because it got struck by lightning. That happened to me once and I fell over. It was the shock.
2. (b)
3. I haven't got a clue who won the World Cup in 1998. Do you actually need me to find the answer to that question? Do you not know?

Lydia

* * *

Dear Lydia,

DO I NOT KNOW?

You want to know every finalist, semifinalist, and quarterfinalist *ever* in the World Cup, FA Cup, and European Champions League? I'm your guy.

I asked that question for a reason, Lydia: A person who knows who won the '98 World Cup will have a kind of shine in their eyes, which I would recognize right off across the floor of the Blue Danish.

I now know that you will have the flat, sad, lost eyes of the person who doesn't know who won. That makes my challenge harder because the café will be full of girls like that.

Out of interest, what kind of perfume do you wear, and if you choose anything to eat at the Blue Danish, what would you normally choose? Also, what kind of shoes do you wear and what color is your hair?

Seb

* * *

Seb,

The winner of the 1998 World Cup was France.

See you tonight.

Lyd

12. Autumn Term / Cassie and Matthew

Dear Matthew Dunlop,

Okay, I give up. What do you do to people you don't like? I asked around at school, but most people hadn't heard of you. Bindy Mackenzie said she thinks she's heard of you, and she thinks you're a trumpet player. I asked her what you do to people you don't like and she said maybe you play the trumpet really loud in their ear.

But she was just trying to be funny.

Em says I'm not allowed to talk to Bindy Mackenzie anymore.

I went to counseling again last night and the counselor played some applause for Mum and me. She had a whole tape full of applause and all three of us sat on her corduroy couches and listened to cheering, clapping, *whooo!*, whistling, etc.

It's hot today, eh? I was thinking there should be like a tribunal or something you can complain to when the weather is incorrect for the season. It's autumn. There should be crisp air and orange leaves. Lydia is sick at home with the flu, and that's the kind of thing that happens when the season gets the weather wrong.

"Any complaints, take them up with the management," is what my dad used to say when it rained on a netball day.

Actually, he stole the line from Lydia's dad; he heard Lyd's dad say it one time and he thought it was clever.

The counselor said it was called *cheer therapy,* making us listen to the applause.

"That's excellent," Mum said politely when it finally ended.

"Thank you," said the counselor proudly. "I made it myself."

Then Mum leaned back in the corduroy chair and tapped her nose with her finger. "So what you're telling me," she said, "is that *you* clapped and cheered like that into your tape recorder?"

The counselor laughed and said, "No! No! What I did was, I got out some of my live music CDs, and I taped the clapping at the end of the songs! A whole collection of it!"

"Not opposed to a little copyright infringement then, are we?" Mum said.

The counselor laughed a bit nervously and said, "I hardly think anyone's going to *know.* . . ."

And Mum said, "Your concern is whether you'll get caught, rather than whether you've broken the law? Interesting. Do you, by any chance, shoplift?"

It was great. She went on like this for the rest of the session, and the counselor kept trying to get control, but then Mum would confuse her again with questions about which supermarkets she found had the least security, etc.

We pissed ourselves laughing the whole way home, and when we weren't laughing we were shouting stupid things at other drivers like, "Are you, by any chance, a *Volvo* driver?" and the drivers were scrunching up their faces at us trying to understand what we were saying, and mouthing, *"What? What?"*

It was excellent.

Mum hasn't been writing any more letters to Dad, so I guess I just have to tell you about myself myself.

Love,

Cassie

* * *

Cassie,

I swear to God if you don't stop writing to me I'm coming around to your place and rip your eyeballs out.

Matthew

* * *

Dear Matthew,

Well, I have good eyesight. That's one thing that I can tell you about me. I can see really well and sometimes when Mum's driving at night she can't see a thing so I tell her where the road is. And the corners.

When I was in first grade I had to wear glasses with a patch over one of the lenses, and that corrected my vision, so now, as I said, I have great vision.

Em, Lyd, and I skip a lot of classes, that's the second thing I want to tell you about myself. Sometimes this is to go to the studio which Lyd's mum owns. Lyd's mum is never there — that's the point of owning, she says — and she hangs out at home instead, watching soap operas. She's a former TV star, that's why she watches them.

Also, we have an obsession with going to the movies, and we go every Thursday after lunch because we have double maths then.

We got into some trouble about this last year, so we are very careful these days. And we try to avoid skipping science classes and that's on account of an event which I want to tell you.

Well, the event went this way.

We had this science teacher called Ms. Ralph in Year 7. She was, like, straight from teacher's college, and that's when they're overexcited, you know, when they want everyone to love them and they want to try out experimental discipline techniques.

And her name, as I said, was *Ms. Ralph.*

So she was on the back step to start with or whatever that expression is.

It was coming up to the half-yearlies and everyone was really stupid. Like saying that the moon is inhabited by tadpoles which produce carbon dioxide. So Ms. Ralph got into a panic, thinking we were all going to fail, and we were, but it wasn't her fault.

So, she split us up into groups and arranged lunchtime sessions for each group. Everyone got pretty annoyed about having to do science at lunch, but Ms. Ralph said it would be like a party, and we'd chat, and have fun, and please, please come or you're all going to fail.

Our lunchtime session was the first one, and the group was me, Emily, Lydia, and this guy, Vincent. But we had history first that day and we couldn't stop sighing, so after history we just walked through the reserve to the train station.

As soon as the train doors closed, Lydia remembered the science class at lunchtime and said maybe we should go back. But Em and I said we'd already paid for our train tickets.

So we went to the movies and got back to the school just in time for the end-of-day roll call, which is what we do.

And then I overheard some people laughing about Ms. Ralph, how they saw her sitting in the science lab all by herself at lunchtime that day, and she was surrounded by pizzas and chocolate crackles and cans of Coke.

And I said, "What about Vincent, wasn't he there?"

And they said, "Vincent? He's got chicken pox all over his entire body, even under his hair and in his private parts."

So *then,* the three of us were like: "Oh no, *poor* Ms. Ralph."

Except that Lyd said, "And I even said we should go back, remember?" Em and I got a bit annoyed and said she didn't exactly try to make us, and she said she did, and I said how were we supposed to know that Vincent was sick, and Em said that *she* knew he had the chicken pox but she forgot.

So Lyd and I were mad with Em for not telling us about Vincent, and Lyd was mad with Em and me for not listening to her, and Em and I were mad with Lyd for making us feel guilty.

We stopped talking to each other for ONE WHOLE MONTH. It was like the world turned into a strange place, walking around and seeing Em or Lyd and they were not Em and Lyd anymore, they were mean strangers with weird little smiles.

It all ended when I found Emily crying behind the tennis court, and I said, "Wait right where you are," and I ran and got Lydia, and we both comforted Em, and she kept on crying, and saying, "When will the Secret Assignments start again?"

Lydia said, "You will both get a Secret Assignment before the end of the day."

Which we did. And the Secret Assignment was: "Go to Lydia's Place This Weekend and We Will All Bake a Cake Together to Give to Ms. Ralph to Say Sorry."

So we did that.

And Ms. Ralph was so happy about the cake that she had sparkly tears in her eyes and wanted to hug us, and then Lyd got 95 percent on her science exam because she does that kind of thing when she feels like it, and Ms. Ralph loved us even more.

I should let you go now.

The counselor asked me if I'd found a nice person to talk to about myself and I said yes, a trumpet player named Matthew Dunlop, and I am telling him the Stories of My Life.

So she played some applause for me.

Love,

Cassie

* * *

Cassie,

After I rip your eyeballs out, I'm breaking your fingers one at a time.

Matthew

* * *

Dear Matthew,

That is so strange because my fingers are the other thing that's good about me. They're kind of freakishly long, so I can play the piano and reach the interval of a tenth (major or minor; starting anywhere), and I'm fairly good with locks, and that's not showing off, it's just lucky for me.

Do you practice on your trumpet much?

You can't play the piano when your hands are cold, and I'm just wondering if the same applies to the trumpet. I had a cat when I was little, named Giraffe, because it had a weirdly long neck, and I used to make my hands warm by holding Giraffe before I played. She was like a hand warmer.

Last night the counselor asked my mum and me what our

greatest fears were, and I said my greatest fear was failing my piano exam. It was a straight-out lie, especially because I'm taking a break from piano exams this year.

I should tell you more about the counselor. Her name is Claire, and she's provided by my mother's law firm. They signed Mum up for six months of free family counseling, which I think means that she's not working as hard as she used to and they want to fix her up so she can keep making money for them.

Claire wears bright colors that make you jump back a bit when you first walk into the room, and I don't think her face is interesting enough for so much color. Her face disappears.

I felt kind of guilty about lying to Claire's invisible face. Telling her my greatest fear was failing piano. So later in the session, I told her something true. I told her that I can't stop thinking about putting my right arm into the air.

I think she thought I was making that up, like to play a joke on her. She looked at me very narrow-eyed and suspicious, but the fact is, that part's true. I can be eating my breakfast or watching TV or doing homework and I'll suddenly have this terrible wish to put my hand in the air.

Sometimes, if I'm alone, I even do it. I actually stop playing the piano and put my hand up, you know, like some kid at school who wants to go to the bathroom. Then I feel really stupid, sitting there on the piano stool with my hand up, and I put it back down and keep playing.

Do you think I'm crazy? I'm pretty sure that Claire did.

Love,

Cassie

* * *

Cassie,

I'm getting really tired of thinking up threats for you.

Matthew

* * *

Dear Matthew,

Are you?

The other night I told Claire that you and me have a rapport. "Me and Matthew are developing a *real rapport,*" I said, and then I told her we had formed a band and we were playing music together, on account of your trumpet playing and my piano playing.

There's a lot of violent imagery in your mind. Do you watch too much TV and/or play too many violent video games and/or eat too much food with red coloring?

I read the other day that you should eat more cabbage. *Matthew Dunlop should eat more cabbage.* That's what I read.

My mother is a copyright lawyer for her occupation. She works at a law firm which is practically the number-one law firm in the city of Sydney, maybe number two.

Woo-hoo!, as Claire would say. Emily's mum works there too, but she's a partner.

Now I wish I hadn't told Claire about the hand-in-the-air thing. I'm going to have to think up a reason for it, because she keeps asking questions about it.

Grandma Matilda visited us the other day. She's my mother's mother, and she told me I'm looking a bit sharp-featured. Mum told me I could insult her back in any way I wanted, and then they both waited patiently for me to think of an insult, but I just shook my head at them in disbelief.

It's getting cold, eh?

Good. It's autumn. It's meant to be cold.

Lots of love,

Cassie

* * *

Cassie,

Your last letter? I put it through the shredding machine. Write to me again? The same thing will happen to you.

Matthew

* * *

Hey Matthew,

That took you a week and I have to say, it wasn't up to your normal standard. You used to answer like WHAM. Like a lightning strike.

You don't have to, if you don't want to, you know: I mean, threaten me. You could just tell me how your day's going, or how your sinuses are, or, I don't know, write a poem.

Feel free.

One good thing is that I thought of a way to stop Claire asking about my hand-in-the-air condition. I told her that sometimes I feel like I'm *drowning*. Claire kind of breathed out in a slow, loving, sympathetic way, and my mother looked at me sideways, but I just shrugged and said, "It's not a big deal, it's just how I feel sometimes," and then changed the subject.

I'll see how long it takes for Claire to make the connection. *Oh, you feel like you're drowning, eh?*

So you feel like you need to put your hand in the air, like indicating to the lifeguard to come rescue you!

That will surely occur to her soon.

Love,

Cassie

* * *

Dear Matthew,

Where are you?

It's hurting your brain trying to think up something threatening, eh? But don't even worry. I am way scared of you already. I feel *threatened*. Relax.

But listen, Claire wants to know about YOU. It's my new homework. You remember that my first homework was to find a New Friend (I found you) and tell him/her all about myself? Well, now I have to find out about the friend. Claire wants to know what you plan to be when you leave school, and what's the worst thing that ever happened to you, and what you love most in the world.

I think that Claire's probably a genius. She's teaching me to be a *listener*, see? That's way important.

Come on, you owe me.

Cass

* * *

Hey Matthew,

Well, I guess I can just keep writing without you writing back. That's fine and it's not really that different from how it was before. Although *before*, I felt like I was playing squash against a big brick wall. Every time I whacked the squash ball over to Brookfield, it would hit the brick wall and come back *SMACK* in my face. Whereas now, it's like the brick wall has just dissolved, and it kind of makes my arm feel funny when I swing the racket.

Cassie

* * *

Hi Matt,

Did you know that a good thing to do if you want to strengthen your fingers and help them to be flexible for your trumpet playing is to carry a squash ball around and just squeeze it occasionally? Anyway, it works for piano playing.

I think I'm getting used to you being quiet. It's kind of peaceful. It's like you're over there having a little sleep on the couch.

Lots of love,

Cassie

* * *

To Cassie Aganovic,

I know your name. (See above.)

I know where you go to school.

I know your friends' names.

I know your therapist's name.

I know everything there is to know about you, Cassie. And you keep on writing and telling me more.

You want to explain to me how you got to be so absofrigginlutely stupid?

Yours faithfully,

Matthew Dunlop

* * *

Dear Matthew,

It's good to hear from you again, and it's good to know you've been paying attention.

Emily and Lydia are now talking German to each other, which is profoundly rude of them. I wish I'd done German, but my dad said I should take Japanese, but then the school stopped offering it because the teacher left, so I had to take commerce instead. I know one German word at least and it's this: *Andenken.* It means souvenir. The reason I know it is because I remember Emily studying for a German exam last year and saying over and over again *Anden-ken bought some souvenirs; An-den-ken bought some souvenirs.* Do you get it? It's like Ken had a cup of coffee and then he went and picked up some souvenirs.

Well, as I said, Claire really wants me to find out some facts about you, so I guess I might just bring along your letters. She would so love them because she could analyze them and talk about your insecurities and so on, and my mum would be confused because even though she's a lawyer in a big firm, what she's really most into is children's rights. In particular, she thinks kids should be able to *express themselves.* So, as I said, she'd be confused because she'd think you have a right to say those things, but she might not like you saying them to me.

Then she and the counselor could get into a discussion about the copyright in your letters.

Either that or you could write the answers and I'll hand that in instead. Just tell me what you want to be when you grow up, and the worst thing that's ever happened to you, and what you love most.

Love,

Cassie

P.S. I was just talking to Bindy Mackenzie again, and she said she's SURE that you play the trumpet. She said she was singing at the School Spectacular last year, and there was a guy called Matthew Dunlop who was a trumpet player, though he was fairly bad at trumpet playing and she wasn't sure why they let him in. I said, "I thought you were just being witty, saying he played the trumpet," and she said, "No, I was only being witty when I said he'd blow the trumpet in your ear if he didn't like you." She said it right off, just like that, as if she had never really stopped thinking about saying it and maybe laughing to herself quietly.

* * *

Cassie,

Yeah, whatever.

Okeydoke.

You wore me down.

Here's some infotainment for you:

A for my Future Occupation: There's a DC-10 with my name on the captain's seat someplace out in the blue beyond.

B for the Worst Thing That Ever Happened to Me: A shark took a piece out of my board one time when I was surfing, and I'm not screwing you around when I tell you this: I was a kid and drowning, and this was down Jervis Bay way.

I've got a shark tattoo on my shoulder to show my respect.

C for the Thing I Love Most in the World: I would kill my mother and my sister and my mother's sister for one of those Mint Aero Bars. Any time of the day.

You can tell your counselor that you are the most unfriggingbelievable whacked-out freak of all time.

And you can tell Bindy bitch-face Mackenzie that I'm the best trumpeter in the southern hemisphere and she can't sing for shit.

Okay, so nice work with the blackmail.

Now will you get on with your life and leave me alone to get on with mine?

Matthew

* * *

Matthew Dunlop!

Well, you outshone even yourself. You're a surprise to everyone, Matthew. Your parents always believed in you, but never the general population. The general population always had doubts about you, Matthew, and look what you've done.

Wow, you are so weird.

I picked up your letter on the way to maths, which is why I'm writing on the back of this maths exam. Can you please post the exam back to my teacher when you've finished reading so she can mark it?

I haven't answered many questions, though, because I got tired after the first two and I decided to have a break and open your letter, and I got the shock of my life. You wrote a whole letter! A WHOLE INTERESTING AND SURPRISING LETTER!

Wow. But the weirdest thing is this: Why?

I mean, why are you suddenly answering, like you think I'm blackmailing you by saying I'm going to show the letters to the counselor? I wasn't trying to blackmail you. I could have shown your letters to a teacher or to my friends (and you wouldn't be alive to read this today if I'd shown them to my friends). I could have shown them anytime, but I got the impression that you didn't give a crap about anybody knowing, and for some reason that made me protect you.

Now it turns out that you got *scared into being human by the threat of a counselor.* What's with that? Are you phobic about the mental health industry?

Imagine if a person was phobic about going to psychotherapy. How could the person get over their phobia? The person would have to go to a psychotherapist to get over it, right, and *once they got there, they'd be over it.*

Anyhow,

All the best,

Cassie

* * *

Hi Cassie,

Look, okay, cut it out and give me a break. So, I've got an attitude problem.

And the reason I've got an attitude problem is because of a situation, which, step up closer to the speaker if you like, and I'll whisper a clue.

No, piss off, it's personal.

Can we just leave it now, though? You got what you wanted. You moved me up to a higher plane, and you got some deep thoughts out of me, so you're the winner. Way to go, Cassie.

Matthew

* * *

Dear Matthew,

Hello. I just had a really great weekend at Lydia's place. We painted the walls of Lydia's room because they were a strange orange color, and I used my wall to write a song, and then I painted over the song with many layers of black paint, and one day someone will strip it back and think that a caveman wrote the song. So that's cool.

I love Lydia's house. It's huge with passageways going everywhere, and she's got a doll's house in the window of her bedroom.

We went shopping in the city on Sunday, and Em got obsessed with the talking dog outside the QVB. You know the one that promises it'll say thank you if you put a coin in it for the deaf children or something? Well, Emily realized that you *don't have to put a coin in.* You can just stand there and stare at it, and it still says, "THANK YOU, RUFF, RUFF."

The weirdest things get Emily upset. Like one time we were making dinner together, including rice, and the rice kind of got ingrained into the saucepan, so it was all these little circles which we couldn't wash off. Em started going crazy. She couldn't stop scrubbing the pan, and she was practically crying about it.

Lydia's a lot more normal and would never cry about rice in a pan. But even she's crazy. She really wants to be an author, and it scares her sometimes, thinking that she might never get published. She gets depressed because she always writes half novels and then gets bored and starts another novel. Sometimes she even stops after one sentence, like, she'll write: "Once upon a time there was a man who lived inside an empty packet of Twisties." And then she loses inspiration and scrunches up the paper.

Plus, sometimes Lydia gets her stories mixed up with real life. For an example, she thinks her mother's a drug addict and her father's a sleaze. I think that's what they were a bit like when she was younger, and she just hasn't noticed that they've grown up now.

Her mother can be flaky. But she's really just being flamboyant.

It's freezing. My feet are cold.

Lydia's dad is also okay. He just makes nerdy dad jokes, such as whenever he turns on the under-floor heating, he says: "You hear that, girls? That's the sound of the electricity company applauding."

He means because it's expensive to run under-floor heating.

Also, he likes to get us to stare at these pictures (you know the ones with the squiggly patterns?) until a shape emerges. Like a tiger or someone doing a ski jump? After a while, we always pretend we can see it, but we never can.

Emily painted squiggly lines all over her wall of Lyd's bedroom and then called in Lydia's dad and told him she had painted something behind it which he could see if he stared long enough. But he could tell she was making it up.

Love,

Cassie

* * *

CASSIE,

Okay, so you've got no plans to piss off. I get it.

I can tell you this. The thing about me is that I'm a loser. I'm no good at anything, except maybe playing the trumpet. I'm good at that, I guess like you're good at piano. And I guess it's the only thing that keeps me, like, gives me a reason to live.

You seem kind of whacked out, but you keep skipping science or whatever to go to the movies, and that's okay, but it means you must be kind of smart. I could not skip science because I've got to go to every class because if I don't do okay in science I'll never get to be a pilot, which is all I want to get out of life.

Just to play the trumpet and fly a plane. Is that so much to ask for?

Plus I think it's stupid, getting yourself in trouble unnecessarily. There's a guy in my class who is about to get thrown out of the school if he doesn't get his act together, and the other day he just went into Castle Hill shops for half the day instead of going to this important across-the-form English test we had to do. I don't know. I just think he's a moron. And that's an example.

And let me tell you what happened, this is not a sob story, and it's not bull. I got into trouble recently, and that's what I mean when I say a situation. The trouble was with a girl who goes to your school.

I got into a relationship with this girl, and maybe you even know her so I won't say her name. She's really pretty, with sparkling eyes and kind of soft-skinned. I was whacked out in love with her, like my heart could hardly stay up in my chest. So she talked me into meeting her at lunch a month or so back, in that reserve which is at the back of your school, and I went. I'm such a moron, but my heart was, you know, whacked. So I went, and we're there, don't get offended, but we're there on the grass, getting it on, I apologize for offending you, talking about doing it with another girl.

But that's what was going on.

And your school principal was walking through the reserve and she found us, and right off, this girl turns on me and tells this bullshit story about how I forced her. Like I forced her to come to the reserve with me, and I threatened to break up with her if she didn't, blah blah, which was such a lie.

I still miss her sparkling eyes, though. You know?

But you guessed it, I was going to represent my school in the School Spectacular again this year, on the trumpet, and now, no chance. Your principal told my headmistress and it's all screwed. She turned the screws. It's a screwed-up world. You know? She banned me from playing.

I guess some parts of your letters seemed real to me, like how your hands get too cold to play the piano and all that crap. I don't know,

sometimes I forget how much I hate you and it just seems like you are a nice story I'm reading.

But every time I get to the end of your letters I think about what bitches go to Ashbury, and I think that you are one of them.

Matthew

* * *

Hi Matthew,

Well, that was the longest letter I ever saw from you, and thank you for writing it.

I don't know who that girl was, but why don't you tell me and I can hate her for you. I'm sorry she was such a bitch, but I promise that not all Ashbury girls are bitches, so don't let her ruin our reputation.

But I'm really sorry you don't get to play the trumpet at the School Spectacular this year. That seems kind of a harsh punishment, considering it's the thing you love most.

Since you told me a secret, I want to tell you a secret.

The thing I love most is singing, actually. You know how I'm kind of musical, and I really don't mean that in a showing-off way, it's just something I inherited from my mother. Well, so, you know how I'm musical, I love to sing, and I always had this very secret dream to be a singer. Like, onstage.

But I get such serious stage fright like you wouldn't believe. I'm not a scared kind of a person. Okay, I'm fairly quiet, but not because I'm *scared* to talk, just because I don't always want to.

And the thing is this: I just wish I'd put my hand in the air, to volunteer, I mean, at the start of this term when they asked for volunteers for our school's spring concert. All the time, my mind was going, *put your hand up, Cassie, put your hand up*. But I stared at my hands and they just sat there, being quiet.

Sorry I told you that. I guess it's just meant to show I have sympathy with you not being able to play the trumpet when you want to. Maybe you should go and talk to your principal and just explain how important it is, and ask if you can have another punishment? Something like that?

See you,

Cassie

* * *

Dear Cassie,

Well, I tried what you suggested and now I'm in even worse trouble.

Sorry, I know it's not your fault. You are an angel with the wings of a DC-10, I know it, and I can tell from your handwriting that you've got a pretty face and cute ears. I kind of think sometimes about kissing you, behind your ears.

Anyhow, I feel bad about all those threats I used to send to you, is all.

So, what happened was, I went to the principal and I said what you suggested, and the principal just sat behind her desk there with this smug little smirk of an expression on her face, and before I'd even finished she was shaking her head. So I got so pissed off, and I just couldn't control my temper, you've seen my temper, it's not me, okay? It's not who I am. You know that now, right, Cassie?

Sure you do.

Anyway, a little voice in my head was saying, "Matthew! Shut up! Play it cool!" but I was using every four-letter word in the dictionary, and I guess those are not actually dictionary words. But I used them and I added strawberry flavoring as well, and the upshot is that I'm not allowed to take trumpet lessons anymore.

As in, I do my trumpet lessons at school with the music teacher because my parents can't afford to pay for them, my dad's just a factory worker and my mum just does some telephone sales from home, and now it's like the world's slammed the door in my face. I'm like hammering on the door with both my fists and the world is behind it, shaking its head.

Ah Cass, I don't know what to do. I'm screwed up, mixed up, messed around, dive-bombing, crashing, and burning. You know. I'll never be a pilot.

I'd kind of like to hold your hand.

Matthew

* * *

Hi Matthew,

Well, you've changed a lot. I'm kind of freaked out.

I wish I could help you. I mean, that's so terrible that you can't have trumpet lessons anymore. I can't believe they would do that to you.

Maybe you should go and apologize to the principal or something? I mean, I know I wouldn't want to do that, because of the indignity and everything. But maybe it's worth it to suffer some indignity for the sake of your trumpet playing?

Best wishes,

Cassie

* * *

Dear Cassie,

Okay, here's what happened. I went and apologized, like you told me to, and the principal was like a witch and said, "Nice try, Mister." As if she could tell I was only doing it to get my trumpet lessons back. She made me hand my trumpet in, so now I don't even have that anymore, and maybe if I hadn't gone back to apologize she wouldn't have recalled that it was a school trumpet.

My parents got divorced awhile back, and my mum hates my dad's guts, but actually I'd prefer to be living with my dad than my mum. My mum's never home because she goes to work in her factory, and my dad has to go around the country looking for work. It's not his fault that he lost his job, and he can't afford new shoes so his feet are all blistered and chafed. My mum wants me to change my name because it makes her want to spit when she remembers that I have my dad's surname, and she can't stand to see me walking around her house knowing I'm half my dad. She wants me to tell the judge that I hate my dad which I can't bring myself to do because it's like lying in a courtroom. That's like blasphemy. There's nothing I hate worse than a liar.

The only person I really liked having around is my nan, but she went and died last year, of a weak heart, and it's, like, as lonely as a drip of water now. As lonely as one single drip of water in a laundry, falling *DRIP* into a rusty sink.

You're a nice person, I guess, and I'm an arsehole the way I kept threatening you when you first started writing. So, okay, step up closer to the mike for a moment, and I'll say I'm sorry. But I only say that word in a whisper.

Matt

* * *

Hey Matthew,

So now you've got me feeling kind of guilty. Talking about how I'm a nice person and everything, when I don't really think I'm that nice.

I didn't take those threats of yours seriously and I just liked messing with your mind. You seemed to hate getting letters from me, so that's the reason why I kept writing. I just liked how mad it got you.

You know, my mother is a lawyer, and I think I maybe mentioned that she used to do a lot of work with kids and protecting their rights and so on. So, if you want, I can ask her for some advice about your situation with the trumpet and all that.

Best wishes,

Cassie

P.S. I thought you said your dad was the factory worker and your mum did telephone sales?

* * *

Hi Cassie,

Yeah, the reason my dad lost his job in the factory was that my mum went along to the factory and told all these lies about how he's not a trustworthy guy, and so they fired him, and then my mum got his job. So now she's the one making the little plastic letter-candles that go on birthday cakes, instead of Dad.

I've been thinking *a lot* about this situation between you and me. How it's kind of changed so sudden and sharply like that.

Like, okay, if an airplane banked as sharp as that, the passengers would tip out of their seats.

I guess it seems weird to me that you can forgive me for all that violent imagery (as you would say in your crazy way). How do I know you're not just messing with me so you can get your revenge sometime? Like stick in the knife. As everyone else seems to do?

No one has ever been honest with me like you've been. I like it.

I get turned on when I see your handwriting on an envelope.

Cannot effing believe I just said that.

It's just that you seem complicated and cool at the same time, and way more fascinating than any other girl I ever heard of, and I cannot believe you're an Ashbury girl. Plus, my friends here kind of hate me a bit these days, because I was being an arsehole to them just like I was to you, lately. On account of that girl from your school breaking my heart and ruining my life and everything.

You're kind of lucky having best friends who you've known since you were five years old or whatever. I bet they'd forgive you if you went through a bad phase like I did.

Okay, I've thought about it, and I'd really like it if you got some help from your mum about my trumpet-playing situation.

It would be so great if I could get to play again, and play in the School Spectacular. You know, it gets televised? So, maybe someone will see it and ask me to be in their band or whatever. Plus my nan would be proud of me. Though you probably can't get ABC in Heaven. You'd only be able to get Foxtel Sports and the porno channels.

Tell me what she suggests, okay.

Love,

Matthew

* * *

Dear Matthew,

Can you tell me if you have a science teacher called the Rattler or the Rattlesnake at your school, and if so, what his actual name is? Also, can you tell me everything you can about him, including what kind of car he drives? Thanks.

In actual fact, I haven't been friends with Emily and Lydia since we were five years old, as you said. Although I did meet

Emily in first grade, but then it wasn't until second grade that we became friends with Lydia, and that was only because Em and I gave her special permission to become our friend. You want to know why Em and I were best friends? BECAUSE WE BOTH HAD GLASSES WITH PATCHES. Everyone else in the class wanted to be our friend because of our eye patches. It was like a kind of secret society. And we made the others do auditions to be our friend. We said no to everyone except Lydia because we both liked her and she made up this really great story about fairies and witches and stuff as her audition, and she made Emily and me the fairies in the story, so we were happy.

Interestingly, it turned out that most of our parents already knew each other because they went to law school together.

I'm sure your friends still like you. You could just explain to them about how you weren't being yourself, on account of going through the difficult time, and apologize, and promise not to do it again? But then again, I guess listening to my advice hasn't been all that helpful so far. I feel bad about that.

But I hate it when people are lonely. This girl in my year named Elizabeth, who I'm kind of half friends with, well, she's got this best friend who used to run away all the time. Last year she even ran away to the circus, and then she disappeared completely for ages. I used to see Liz walking around trying to pretend that she liked the other people she was hanging around with, but I could tell she didn't.

I just can't imagine how it would be if I didn't have Lydia and Emily. Or if they kept disappearing.

I've told my mother about your issue with the trumpet playing and everything, and she got angry on your behalf. She has suggestions to help you. Do you want me to send them?

Don't forget to tell me about your teacher called the Rattlesnake, okay?

Thanks,

Cassie

* * *

Dear Cassie,

How come you want to know about the Rattler? Yeah, we've got a teacher called Mr. Rivers, known as the Rattlesnake, and he happens to drive a very nice little silver Audi, which makes you wonder what he's doing teaching at a hellhole like Brookfield. He's parked it in this special place behind the admin block ever since this moron took it for a spin last year when it was in the parking lot. Now it's under the trees so the birds shit on it, but at least it's shady, I guess.

Apart from that, I don't really have anything to say about the Rattler. Hope that helps.

It would be so great if your mum could help with my situation. I would just love you forever.

Matthew

* * *

Dear Matthew,

Thanks for the information about your teacher called the Rattler. It was very useful.

My mum's got this huge amount of information she wants me to send to you, but I don't really know if I can put it into the Ashbury-Brookfield mail system. I mean, it's like a foolscap folder worth of material, including the United Nations Convention on the Rights of the Child and the European Human Rights Convention, etc., and all kinds of cases about kids' rights to express themselves by playing the trumpet. Or anyway, practically that. One thing you've done is get my mother excited about something, which is a real change for her, so congratulations. But how do you reckon I should get this information to you? I should send it to you soon, I guess, because it's almost the holidays and I guess we won't be in contact until next term.

See ya,

Cassie

* * *

Dear Cassie,

Why don't we meet so you can give me the material? I'd kind of like to ask you out anyway. I think my broken heart has been healed by your handwriting on the outside of envelopes.

I think you are a sweet, kind, mad human being, and I'd like to get together with you and see what happens. I hope you don't mind me saying things like this. I wish I could fly a plane already because I'd take you for a spin, because I think that's where you deserve to be: up there with the stars.

Do you want to meet somewhere? Maybe this Friday after school? I was even thinking we could have a kind of after-school picnic at the reserve at the back of your school, to break the spell of the bad memories and, like, a symbol of a new start: you and me. Start of the winter holidays. Start of something fresh. I know it's cold but I could bring blankets.

I hope I'm not making a fool of myself here.

Matthew

* * *

Dear Matthew,

I don't think you're making a fool of yourself. I think you're pretty weird, and I think this is the strangest way to get to know someone ever. I made a lot of a fool of myself writing you all those stupid letters earlier this term, when you were telling me to get lost. I can't even explain why I kept writing.

But now, you seem like a really strange and interesting person, and I guess I'd like to meet you.

I don't know about meeting in the reserve. It's practically winter, and it's getting dark fairly early each day.

But I suppose if you need to get rid of your bad feelings about the reserve, I can meet you there.

Best wishes,

Cassie

* * *

Dear Cassie,

Thank you for believing in me. I can't tell you how much that means to me. One day I'll play a beautiful trumpet solo for you.

Let's meet just inside the first gate of the reserve — just before the trees get too dense so at least we'll have moonlight if it gets too dark.

Let's make it four, okay?

Last day of term.

I'll bring something to celebrate with.

See you Friday.

Matthew

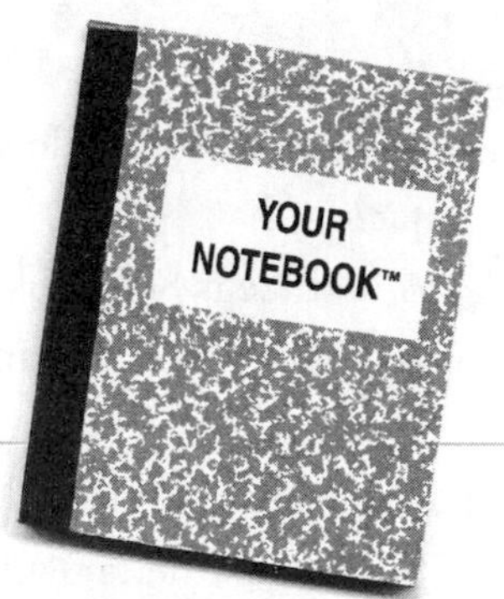

13. Lydia's Notebook

Hey! Things are really hotting up! Your literary skills are on *fire!* Go, you writer!

Which is why the theme of this Part of your Notebook™ is going to be *heat!!* Start by telling us the hottest thing you can think of right this moment.

Seb Mantegna.

Ouch! You've scalded our fingertips! Nice description. You're really getting the hang of this. And now, for a 360-degree rotation, how about the coldest things!

Why?

I saw Seb last night for exactly three seconds.

It was the last day of school and we were meeting at the Blue Danish. Cass was supposed to be there too. She said she had to meet someone else, but then she'd come and find me there.

But she didn't show up. The traitor.

So I'm sitting in the corner armchair, trying to look around without looking like I'm looking around, the loudest noise being the fast-paced tapping of my heart.

Then there's a shadow in the café doorway and a sunflower in my face.

And there is Seb, looking dead serious, handing me this flower, turning round, and walking out the door.

I hardly even saw what he looked like, except for the wicked spark in his eyes.

So how did he know it was me? Do I look like my letters that much? I don't even think I'm being myself in my letters, so how could I look like them?

I did notice that he had dark hair and ~~pale beautiful creamy transparent transluccent milky coffee hazelnut~~ lighter skin.

Well, it's the first day of the winter holidays, so I could talk about "cold" like you want me to. OH LOOK, I'VE RUN OUT OF SPACE. Sorry.

Back to HOT again! Tell us some cures for sunburn! Ask your family for ideas.

I should just let you know that I'm not at home with the family at the moment. I'm at Em's place, sitting at her kitchen table, eating crumpets.

Em's parents are about to go away for a few days. Em is standing at the open fridge looking for honey. Her dad is sitting at the table opposite me, leaning over a notepad and writing in a frenzy. Her mum is walking in and out of the kitchen carrying a Dictaphone which she's talking to in a mystery language.

I will now ask everyone here for a sunburn cure.

Me: Who can tell me a cure for sunburn?
Mrs. Thompson: *(calling from the laundry)* Aloe vera!

Mr. Thompson: *(looking up from his notepad and narrowing his eyes)* You're sunburnt? How interesting. I wonder if you might tell us how you got sunburnt, Lydia? Considering it's been raining these last three days! *(Chuckles to himself as he returns to his notepad)*

Emily: Do you want to know anything else about Charlie, Lyd? Just ask a question. Any question.

Mrs. Thompson: *(wandering into the room and talking into her Dictaphone)* semicolon new line bullet point get a Mixmaster semicolon new line bullet point read The Wind in the Willows. *(Switches off the Dictaphone and looks around with her eyes wide open, as if in shock.)* Benjamin? Why did I want to read The Wind in the Willows?

Emily: Did I tell you what Charlie did when I bought the popcorn, Lydia? It was SO SO funny.

You should always try to offer some advice in your stories. Throw in a sunburn cure and you'll make at least one reader happy!

Describe what it's like being sunburnt.

Barney and Maribelle were riding on a merry-go-round. Barney on the antelope, Maribelle on the zebra. This reminded them that their youngest child, Eloise, had not phoned lately. (Eloise had a pet zebra.) She would be turning four next week.

"Remember when we taught her to fly?" said Barney tenderly. "On her third birthday?"

"Ah yes," recalled Maribelle wistfully. "It was a sunny day and her nose got sunburnt! She felt a stinging sensation. Later, the sunburnt nose itched."

QUICK FLICK! Time for some flexing of your memory muscles! Tell us about some *really* hot days from your past.

I remember Cass in Year 8 holding an ice block against the back of my neck to cool me down on a 104-degree day.

Cass is supposed to be here already, actually.

She's extremely late.

We'll let you in on a secret. Another thing that readers love to hear about is food. The reason people read is so that they can get *recipe* ideas. Tell us some piping-hot foods that are perfect on a cold wintry day.

I'll let you in on a secret: Sometimes you get on my nerves.

The reason people read is so they *can travel without leaving home!* Do a little research on a very hot country for us.

I thought they were reading because they were hungry.

Grab a thesaurus, look up the word *hot,* and write down the first five words that it gives.

Mr. Thompson just got a thesaurus from his study for me, even though his taxi is waiting outside. Mrs. Thompson is still talking in her strange language and doesn't seem to notice the taxi horn, which is blaring.

Warm, humid, sultry, sweltering, simmering, steaming, scalding, burning

Actually, where *is* Cassie? It's almost lunchtime and we were supposed to have breakfast here together.

Okay, we're almost done here, and it's time to let you in on a secret. Are you listening?

Hot, as you know, can refer to the temperature. But did you know it also means a whole heap of other things?!

What do you think this is:

It's the box!

Now — *tattatattatattatatta* (drumroll) — where *should* you be thinking?

That's right!!!!

OUTSIDE the box.

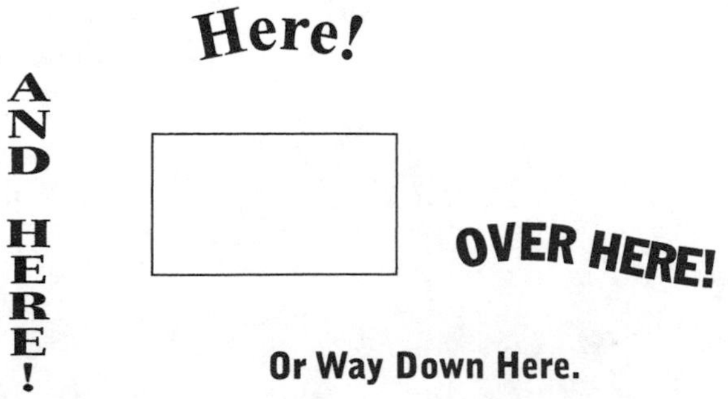

If you think *outside* the box, what does *hot* mean besides a hot temperature?

FINALLY, Cassie's at the door. She's calling out that there's a taxi waiting outside if anybody wants it, and Mr. and Mrs. Thompson both just jumped to their feet, knocking their chairs over in shock.

I'll leave you to play with your boxes and find out where she's been.

Yep. That's right! But don't be embarrassed.

The main thing is — you've got the idea. Take a break, and we'll see you next time.

14. Cassie's Diary

Monday, late afternoon, cannot see the moon

Well, hello there Diary, it's me again. Cassie.

It's the third day of the holidays, and I'm at Em's place, and Lyd and Em are downstairs doing experimental cooking, and they've been trying to make me tell them what's wrong.

Nothing's wrong. I was supposed to meet my Brookfield penfriend on the last day of school, and he didn't show up, and I waited for about five hours like a stupid idiot, and then I was too late to go meet Lyd at the Blue Danish. So, see, there's nothing to tell.

I'm still not the kind of person who writes in diaries so I don't know what I'm doing here. Only, for some reason, I've been thinking about the time when I tried yoga.

I was maybe six years old, and my mum and grandmother were doing yoga in the living room, watching a yoga video so they'd know what to do.

I decided to try it myself (secretly, so they wouldn't laugh at me), and I came up to my room and I was lying on the floor trying to get my feet behind my neck. I did that fairly easily and I felt proud. Only then I got this idea that my feet were stuck there. Like I suddenly forgot I could just take them down. So I started

SCREAMING, and Mum and Grandma came running up the stairs, opened my bedroom door, saw me on the floor with my feet behind my neck, and burst out laughing.

Dad came downstairs from his studio to see what was so funny. He ignored Mum and Grandma, who were now falling against the wall hurting themselves, they were laughing so hard, and he sat down on the floor beside me.

He looked at me carefully, looked at my feet behind my neck, looked at his own feet, and swiveled his own neck, as if he was trying to work out how it all fit together. Then he carefully took my feet from behind my neck and put them back where they belonged on the floor.

Then he kissed the top of my head and said, "*Now* you're cooking with gas."

Afterward, in the kitchen, I heard him tell Mum and Grandma they had a pair of hearts as cold as vanilla ice cream, and Grandma said, "*Pfft!*" and flicked a pea at him.

15. Emily's Weekend

I, Benjamin Albert Thompson, **Lawyer**, of 52 Hunting-down Circle, Cherrybrook, in the State of New South Wales, do solemnly and sincerely declare:

1) My most treasured possessions are my Wife, my two Children ("**Emily and William**") and my wine collection.
2) I keep my wine collection in the cellar of my family home at 52 Hunting-down Circle, Cherrybrook (my "**Home**").
3) Emily and William usually spend their days at school, but they are currently on vacation from school (the "**Children's Holiday**").
4) Two weeks ago, on the first Saturday of the Children's Holiday, my Wife and I left the Home to attend the Law Society Annual Symposium in Brisbane (the "**Symposium**").
5) I left my daughter ("**Emily**") at Home, together with her friends, Cassie and Lydia ("**Cassie**" and "**Lydia**").
6) Upon returning from the Symposium, four days later, I played a game of Pictionary with my Wife, Emily, William, Lydia, and Cassie.
7) I recall that I felt very cheerful, at that time.

The Missing Wine

8) Yesterday evening, I came home from work feeling happy, as it was a Friday. I went down to my cellar to say hello to my wine collection.
9) I noticed that two bottles of 1962 Penfolds Grange Hermitage (the "Wine") were missing from my collection.
10) One bottle of the Wine has the value of approximately one of Emily's horses. Therefore, two bottles of the Wine have the value of approximately two of Emily's horses.

Conversation with My Wife

11) Upon discovering that the Wine was missing, I proceeded to the kitchen, where I found my Wife eating a small chocolate helicopter. I had a conversation with my wife which was to the following effect:

Me: Have you been drinking any wine lately?

My Wife: Do you feel all right? You look strange. Have some chocolate.

Me: Amelia? Have you opened any wine from the cellar lately?

My Wife: No, Benjamin. Not for months, remember, I'm in a no-alcohol phase. Are you sure you're okay?

Conversation with My Son

12) I then proceeded up the stairs, passing my Son, William (aged ten) on the way. William was carrying a chocolate

airplane. I had a conversation with William which was to the following effect:

Me: Hello there, William. Listen, how often do you drink my wine?
William: Huh?

Conversation with My Daughter

13) I then knocked on Emily's bedroom door. Emily was sitting on her bed eating a chocolate giraffe.

Me: Emily, there is no reason why you would drink my wine, is there?
Emily: No. I don't even like wine. I like bourbon and vodka.
Me: Ah. That's a relief. I just thought there was some missing from my collection.
Emily: You must have dislocated it. Try looking again.
Me: Okay. Good idea.
Emily: Oh, hang on. Wait a minute. We made a chicken casserole for dinner when you were away at the start of the holidays! Remember? At your conference?
Me: Did you? Lovely.
Emily: No. It wasn't very good in the end. Anyway, we thought some wine would make it better.
Me:
Emily: Lydia got a couple of bottles from the cellar, but I told her to get the older, dustier ones 'cause you probably wouldn't miss them. That's okay, isn't it?
Me:

Emily: *(suddenly sounding annoyed)* Well, if it's <u>not</u> okay, it's <u>your</u> fault; if you want to go away with a bunch of nerdy lawyers instead of spending time with your <u>children</u>, these kinds of things are just <u>inimitable</u>, aren't they, Dad?

Me: *(murmuring)* Inevitable?

Emily: Exactly.

Gerald at Work

14) Yesterday, I had a chat with Gerald, one of the lawyers at Work. Gerald told me he had been to a seminar on Bringing Up Teenagers and that he found the seminar "super."
15) At the time of this chat with Gerald, I believed I had an excellent relationship with my teenage daughter, Emily. Therefore, I did not pay too much attention to Gerald.
16) However, I do recall that, in the course of our conversation, Gerald said words to the effect:

    "The thing with teenagers is, you have to remember to tell them how you *feel.* Most of us just *react,* you know? We act out our *emotional response,* without *expressing* it."

17) At the time, I thought this was stupid, and I told Gerald to go review a contract.
18) However, since the episode relating to the Wine and Emily (see above), I have decided to express how I feel.
19) I have therefore prepared this Statutory Declaration, to express how I feel.

How I Feel

20) I believe that the use of the Wine in a chicken casserole has broken my Heart.

And I make this solemn declaration conscientiously believing the same to be true and by virtue of the provisions of the *Oaths Act 1900 (NSW)*.

Benjamin A. Thompson

16. Letters from Ashbury

To
Brookfield High School

Dear Charlie,

Hello and welcome to the winter term. ☺ I hope you had a happy holiday. Me too. Even though it was only two weeks. Mostly, Lyd, Cass, and I hung out together and stayed at each other's homes. Just talking, whiling through the rain, and sometimes shopping or seeing a movie. Plus doing each other's assignments. We sometimes exchange assignments, to add flavor.

Cass was kind of eerie and silent for the first few days, like she was keeping something secret. We tried to make her tell us by bribing her with Cherry Ripes, telling her she couldn't use Lydia's massaging chair anymore, and spiking her Coke with bourbon. None of it worked, and anyway, she knew there was bourbon in her Coke.

You would know, wouldn't you, because it tastes different.

It's immortal, keeping a secret. I always tell everybody everything.

I have prepared an assessment report for your Date with a Girl, which, as you know, took place on the last day of term before the holidays. You made me promise to give you one, but I have a question, which is: Are you kidding around? As you will see from the Report, you are a fairly high standard to begin with.

ASSESSMENT REPORT: *CHARLIE TAYLOR*

It was a pleasure to go on a Date with Charlie Taylor. At first, I was a bit surprised to see that he had not obeyed my instructions about what he should wear, but upon consternation, it is good to see that he has some character of his own. And Charlie dressed very well and intriguingly.

Charlie should work on his humor. He was fairly funny when he told jokes, but he should tell them more often, and they should be a bit funnier.

Overall, Charlie was a delight to have in the cinema. He seemed unconsciously nervous at first, but that is a pleasure to see, as it makes him human, and he very quickly became cockled, which means he had a relaxed and funny way. He was kindhearted with the popcorn, etc., and asked unexpected questions. He told some lively stories about his family, but he also asked questions about my family. He did not seem dismayed about my extensive life.

Most importantly, Charlie was very expressive in the impression he got on his face when he first saw me. He was waiting outside the movies and I bore down on him.

This was important because it would have been a shame if Charlie had got a disappointed impression, or a shocked and mollified expression. Instead, Charlie got a big, happy smile as if he was glad.

It might be that he was pretending but, if so, he is excellent at pretense.

Well done, Charlie.

A+

Assessment prepared by Emily Thompson

* * *

Hey Seb,

Thanks for the sunflower. It lasted the whole holidays because I cut the stem at an angle and changed the water every day. This, on the advice of Cass.

She's full of surprises, that Cass, eh?

Very smooth performance at the Blue Danish. How'd you do it?

Lydia

* * *

Hi Matthew,

Hope you had a nice holiday. I did — mainly we took turns staying at each other's places.

I just wanted to write and let you know that I still have the folder of material from my mother if you need it. I waited for you at the reserve, but I guess you must have got held up somewhere, or decided not to come. So it got fairly cold and dark and in the end, I had to leave.

Are you still interested in the information? I can just stick it in the Brookfield mailbox at our school if you like, and see if it gets to you. Or else, I can mail it to you in the regular way if you give me your home address.

Take care,

Cassie

17. Letters from Brookfield

Dear Emily,

Thanks for the Report. It rocked. I had a great time with you that night, and I thought about it a lot in the holidays, wondering what grade I got and how I could have improved.

I think you should have been more critical, though, because how am I supposed to learn? Don't forget that the goal is to steal Christina Kratovac away from her arsehole boyfriend. He stole her from her previous boyfriend, so he deserves to lose her. But I need to be pretty trained up for it.

If you want an assessment of your own behavior on the Date with a Boy, you just say the word.

Love,

Charlie

P.S. My smile when I saw you was real, not pretend.

* * *

Dear Lydia,

Special Covert Operation Report

Agent: AKA

<u>OPERATION</u>

Operation Recognize Lydia First

Assigned by Agent Lydia

Result: Successful (see sunflower with diagonally cut stems/fresh water in Lydia's house)

FIELD NOTES

AKA confirms that Lydia is gorgeous (as AKA originally predicted).

AKA has been questioned about top-secret surveillance techniques/explanation for how he achieved success at Operation Recognize Lydia First.

AKA cannot believe anyone is asking this.

He will respond only with rank and serial number.

Rank: NUMBER 1

Serial No.: 01010101010101010101 (can't remember but it was something like that)

QUESTION

What happens now?

* * *

Dear Cassie,

Where was I?!?!?

You mean, where were *you*? I hung around at the reserve until, what? Nine o'clock? I really wanted to meet you. I went home with blue balls, and I don't just mean from the cold.

One of us must have screwed up and got the wrong place. Sorry to hear you were also on your own there. Bet ya didn't wait as long as I did.

How was your holiday? Get some time in with your friends Lydia and Emily? Been back to see Claire the Retarded Shrink?

My holiday kind of sucked the bag 'cause I was pissed off with you. I was thinking I'd been stood up by another Ashbury princess. I guess I'm kind of bitter about it, but I'm stoked now to see it was just mischance.

So I'm going to give you a second chance to cock it up, I guess.

Kidding with you, Cass. I know it wasn't your fault.

Then again, I've probably messed up my chances in respect of my trumpet playing, because what hope have I got of your mother helping me, now she thinks I left you hanging around the reserve like that? It's not a safe place for nice little Ashbury girls.

You want to give it another shot? We should be more specific about exactly where in the reserve to meet this time.

Matthew Dunlop

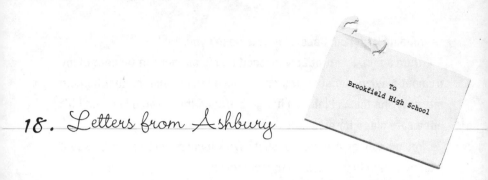

18. Letters from Ashbury

To
Brookfield High School

Dear Charlie,

I am happy to be more critical of you, but I think you should ask yourself a question first: Are you *sure* you want to go out with this Christina? Maybe you should just leave her where she is with this arsehole boyfriend of hers, where she is happy?

I had a nice conversation with Cass today. She is so secretive sometimes, like you wouldn't believe, about personal things, but chatty about impersonal things. Lydia and I always feel like a high five when we get her to tell us something personal. Today she told me that she might be going to meet with her penfriend from Brookfield and he is a guy and she thinks he might be nice in an intriguing kind of way. His name is Matthew Dunlop, apparently, and he must be in your English class, as it is an exchange of letters between our classes that is going on here.

It is so amazing because that will mean all three of us have met with our penfriends from Brookfield.

Did I tell you that Lydia met her penfriend from Brookfield on the same night as I was seeing the movie with you? I can't remember if I mentioned that on our Date, because we were mainly talking about us. Anyway, his name is Sebastian. Do you know him? What's he like and is he good enough for my friend Lydia? I doubt it.

Best wishes,

Emily

* * *

Hey Seb,

You're not in a prisoner-of-war camp.

It was me who gave you the assignment, so you have to tell me how you did it.

What happens now? I'll let you know as soon as Ms. Yen shuts her mouth about parabolic equations.

See ya,

Lydia

P.S. Hey, what can you tell me about a guy in your English class called Matthew Dunlop? Cass got him as her Brookfield penfriend.

* * *

Hi Matthew,

I'm sorry you were waiting there at the reserve. That's pretty stupid that we were both there and didn't see each other. It's kind of weird.

You don't need to worry about my mother quitting on you, because I didn't tell her that you didn't show up. Actually, I didn't tell her where I was meeting you. I don't think she'd have let me go there.

Plus, I was okay in the reserve — a girl from my school, Liz Clarry, turned up and hung out with me for a while. She was training there, only she couldn't stay long because her mother was waiting to collect her.

She tried to make me leave the reserve with her, but I thought I should keep waiting in case you showed up.

Do you really want to try and meet at the reserve again? Em and Lyd would kill me if they knew I was meeting you there.

Cassie

19. Letters from Brookfield

Dear Emily,

Seb Mantegna is a buddy of mine and you should feel relaxed about him seeing your friend Lydia. He's a good guy. I'd be happy if he went out with my sister or my daughter, for example, which is saying something.

But which is not saying I have a daughter. I know that's exactly what you're going to respond with: "Do you have a *daughter*?" is how you're going to respond. I know you, Em. So I'm getting in first here.

Matthew Dunlop, I couldn't say. I've never heard of Matthew Dunlop. Are you sure he's in my English class?

Charlie

* * *

Hey Lyd,

Send me another assignment which involves meeting in person, is my suggestion for what happens next. This time it might involve actual talking.

Seb

P.S. There's no one in my English class called Matthew Dunlop. Actually, I asked around a bit and nobody's heard of him. I don't know who your friend Cassie has been writing to, but he's not at Brookfield High.

* * *

Dear Cassie,

Okay, new meeting place coordinates.

Four-thirty P.M. next Thursday — the third gate along from Pennant Hills Road — the fourth eucalyptus tree inside the reserve (there are *only* eucalyptus trees in the reserve).

All is forgiven from this end for messing up last time. I hope all is forgiven from that end too. And once again, I can't wait to meet you.

Yours,

Matthew Dunlop

20. Letters from Ashbury

Dear Charlie,

Well, there has been a strange and possibly catatonic development here. And I will cut to the chase which is:

We think Cassie has gone crazy.

Okay, so you know I asked about a boy at your school called "Matthew Dunlop"? And you said you didn't know him. At which point I thought:

"It is clear that Charlie does not concentrate. Matthew Dunlop must be in his English class, and yet Charlie has not noticed this. That is an aspect of Charlie's character to work on. Concentrating."

Only then Seb wrote to *Lydia,* and *said he ALSO does not know Matthew Dunlop*!

So then Lyd and I looked at each other in the following way: IF THERE IS NO SUCH PERSON AS MATTHEW DUNLOP, WHO IS CASSIE WRITING TO?

And we got a secret fear in each of our hearts that Cass was writing to NOBODY. Which would mean that either:

(a) she's pretending she's writing to somebody, just to trick Lyd and me, or
(b) she's writing to an *imaginary* nobody and *she thinks that he exists.*

Lyd and I have grimly deduced that it is (b) because why would she do (a)? She has no reason to trick us, so far as we can see, and it would not be like her.

What do you think we should do? We are at a loss, as our first inkling was to go straight to Cass and say words to the effect: "What the hell is going on?"

But then on the reverse hand, we are afraid that she might be in a fragile state and we could send her insane forever. Like when you wake up a person who is sleepwalking.

So we are giving it time.

And in the meantime, we are going to ask you boys to check again, and make CERTAIN there is nobody at your school called Matthew Dunlop.

You could begin by breaking into the administration office and checking the school records.

Thank you very much.

Yours sincerely,

Emily Thompson

* * *

Hey Seb,

Are you sure there's no one there called Matthew Dunlop? I'm kind of freaked out by that because Cass has been writing to him. Also getting letters from him. And now she even says she's meeting him.

Do you think it's possible that a person can have an imaginary penfriend? I'm fairly sure it's not normal.

Lydia

* * *

Dear Matthew,

Okay, thanks for the meeting place coordinates. Hopefully they'll work out better this time. And maybe we can go and get a coffee or something? We won't exactly hang around the reserve for long, will we? It's pretty cold.

I have to say I'm looking forward to meeting you because my friends are being weird at the moment.

Anyway, see you tomorrow afternoon.

Cassie

21. Letters from Brookfield

To Ashbury High School

Dear Emily,

Well, I didn't need to break in to the administrative records as per your suggestion, seeing as I'm a buddy of the school secretary.

This is on account of the times when I'm sitting in the admin block waiting to see the principal. I've told you about those times, right? Yeah I have, because I told you about the gas explosion incident, and that chick who I will never forgive since she defrauded me into the belief that there was gas in my school. You remember that incident.

Anyway, the short story is that I asked the secretary to type the name "Matthew Dunlop" into the computer, and as she is a kind-hearted lady, she checked every conceivable spelling she and I could come up with, lasting pretty much the entire maths period, on the variation of Matthew, Mattie, Matt, *maths,* etc., Dunlop, Doneloghp, Dunhill, Doneliving, etc. And zero result.

I won't write anymore because I know you need this info pronto. Good luck with it, and I hope you girls figure out what to do about your friend. It's a weird situation, I agree, and I don't envy you, and I think we should probably have another Date with a Girl and talk about it face-to-face.

See you,

Charlie

* * *

Dear Lydia,

You should trust me upfront. We figured out that we trusted each other last term, recall, so we've taken the first step in forming the perfect team. You can now pass the ball to me, knowing you can count on me to score. Or to give it my best shot anyhow.

There's nobody at our school called Matthew Dunlop, Lyd.

I can confirm it's not normal to write to someone who doesn't exist. But you told me that your friend lost her dad last year, so I ask myself: Is it so abnormal? If my old man snuffed it, I'd go lunatic on you. I'd watch football 24/7 and I'd look at the chair where my dad sits and I'd hear his voice telling the ref to get himself a day job, and I'd go psycho.

From what you've said about Cass, she's maybe not over it? A year isn't long. Plus, you and Em both got penfriends at Brookfield who you like (sorry to be assuming things here), whereas maybe Cassie's own penfriend didn't work out? Maybe she got lonely. So she had to invent a new penfriend of her own.

I don't know, I've never even met her.

You never introduce your friends to me, Lyd.

You never even introduce yourself, in point of fact.

Whatever happens, I think you're pretty smart, and you'll figure it out.

Though I've got to say, you should let me help you, up close and personal.

Seb

* * *

Dear Cassie,

You know, I saw your name in lights last night. It's the middle of the night, and I can't sleep, thinking all my trumpeting thoughts, and I get out of bed, and I open the curtains, and I look into the night sky full of stars, and you know what I saw?

Your name.

It was like the stars joined up and spelled out the word for me.

It was like a sign. You're somebody special, Cassie. I can tell from your cursive handwriting, the way you join up the *s*'s in your name. The stars had trouble with that pair of *s*'s, but you make them flow like sand on a desert wind.

I'll see you this afternoon.

Matthew

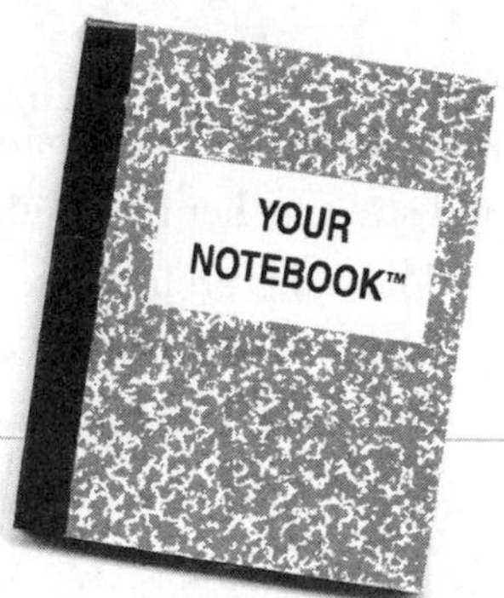

22. Lydia's Notebook

Okeydokey! We will now leave a few blank pages for you to write a first-person, present-tense account of a *significant* event from your life!

Think *way* back into your past now. You ready? When did your event take place?

Yesterday.

Great! Now put yourself in the *space* of the event and go for it. . . .

It's Thursday afternoon, and the bell is ringing for afternoon roll call. It's been raining all day.

Everyone's getting ready to go home, and the girls who had to run across the oval at the end of last period are wringing the water from their hair and getting checked out by the guys. (Their uniforms are see-through from the rain.)

Em and I are trying to act excited for Cass because she's meeting her penfriend tonight. We're smiling these exaggerated smiles which we can't get off our faces.

"What do you think he'll look like?" Em tries.

"I haven't got a clue." Cass tips her chair back, almost falls, and straightens back up again. Em and I grin at her like crazy people, and she tilts her head sideways, like to check that we're okay.

We hang around the balcony for a few minutes to see what she'll do. "Where are you meeting him?" I say.

"None of your business," she says.

We're planning to secretly follow her and see what she does. But then she says, "What are you guys doing?"

"Going to Castle Hill," Em says (improvising), and Cass says she'll walk us to the bus stop.

Em wants to get off at the next stop and go back, but Cass has already disappeared into the rain, so we decide we may as well go have a coffee and figure out what to do.

It's wet and loud in Castle Hill: everyone going to a movie and Thursday-night shopping, shaking umbrellas and stamping in puddles, and we find our way to the corner couch at the Blue Danish. At the table next to us is a girl from our school, Liz Clarry.

We get coffees and Em starts going through it again, as if she can work it out like one of those trick logic questions. (*Bill gets home from work. He finds Glenda lying dead on the floor. He sees a puddle of water. Some broken glass. How did Glenda die?*)

"Cass has been writing to Matthew Dunlop at Brookfield," Em explains. "We find out that there is no Matthew Dunlop at Brookfield. Cass says she's going to meet Matthew Dunlop. What's going on with Cass?"

Glenda is a goldfish!

"She's a goldfish," I try.

Em frowns like she's considering this.

"Maybe Matthew Dunlop's a real person but he doesn't go to Brookfield," she says, "and he somehow got hold of her first letter on its way over to Brookfield and he's been writing to her ever since?"

"But then he would have had to keep finding ways to get to the school mail all the time," I say, "to keep getting Cass's letters and replying."

So now we start saying crazy things, like maybe Cass has been pathological all along, and imagining that every story she ever told us has been a lie, and then Em gets serious and says: "I don't think she's ever lied to us. And I think this is our fault. Instead of being there for her, we've just been going on about Brookfield boys. So she had to invent her own."

I look around the café and notice Liz Clarry at the table next to us and realize she's with a girl in a Brookfield uniform. So I think I'll check one more time.

"Is there anyone at your school called Matthew Dunlop?" I say to the Brookfield girl.

"Not that I know of."

Then Liz says something weird. "How's Cassie?" she says. Like she knows something.

"What do you mean?" pounces Em.

Liz shrugs and says, "I saw her on the last day of term before the holidays, and she didn't seem like herself."

"How do you mean?" I say.

"I don't know," Liz starts pulling on her ears, like to make herself remember. "I was running in the reserve and I saw her sitting under a tree, and it was cold and dark, and I just thought it was strange to be sitting there like that. But maybe I imagined something wrong because the reserve at night makes everything seem sinister, you know?"

"I know," says Em, getting chatty now, "I hate the reserve at night, it's like a graveyard, it's so sinister, it's omnivorous."

"Ominous," agrees Liz, calmly. Cass and I are never brave enough to correct Em's vocab mistakes.

Then Liz introduces the Brookfield girl and it turns out they're waiting for some Brookfield guys. The Brookfield girl, whose name is Christina, says, "When Paul and Jared get here, we can ask if they know Matthew Dunlop if you like?"

And I say, "No, that's okay," because I think it's pretty clear that he doesn't exist and I'm sick of having it confirmed.

Then we all go back to our own conversations, and Em and I keep talking about what we should do, like how it's not Cassie's fault, and we have to be gentle but make her admit it, so then she can start getting better, and maybe we should tell her mother, or even call up the counselor she's been seeing?

And then it hits me suddenly, out of nowhere:

The reserve.

Liz said she saw Cass in the reserve on the last day of school before the holidays. And that was the day that Cass was supposed to meet me and she didn't show up. She told me she was meeting someone. And that's where she was? Sitting under a tree at the reserve?

"What if she's at the reserve right now?"

Em looks at me and looks out the window at the dark sky and pouring rain.

"Maybe that's where she goes," I say, "to meet her imaginary friend?"

Em shakes her head and whispers, "She couldn't be that crazy."

But she's reaching for her mobile, and phoning Cass at home, and getting no answer, and trying Cass's mobile, but it's switched off. She sends a text message to Cass: "R U OK?"

But there's no answer to that either.

Then we both realize right away: We have to go to the reserve. And we can't believe we've been sitting here wasting time.

It's pelting down and the wind is so strong that the rain slants right under our umbrellas and into our faces. We get a taxi back to the school and run into the schoolyard: The wind tries to yank my umbrella out of my hand, and Em's umbrella is turning inside out.

It's so black, we can hardly see into the trees when we get to the reserve. I expect Em to hesitate because she's scared of the dark, but she just swings open the gate, runs straight through, and hits her head on a branch.

Then we're standing there, with the rain drumming on our umbrellas, and slapping against our bare legs, and the mud squelching up around our shoes.

My eyes start to adjust to the shadows, and I see shiny trees and spindly branches waving in the wind.

Then Em says, "She's there."

Em is tripping along through the mud, and finally I see it too — a blurry blue figure sitting underneath a tree.

As I get closer, I see that it's Cass, and a terrible coldness digs into my shoulders like fingernails because she's hunched over, and rocking in such a strange way.

I realize it's because she's crying. There's a closed umbrella lying at her feet, and all around her are little fragments of torn paper. We crouch down on either side of her. We're both trying to hold our umbrellas over her, so they're getting tangled, and there's no point anyway, she's already completely drenched. Her face is streaming with rainwater and tears.

She's clutching a black folder to her chest, and I have this feeling we have to get that off her, but her fingers hold it tighter.

We help her to stand up, and kind of jog with her out of the reserve, and flag down a taxi.

Em tells the driver Cass's address and explains how to get there. Cass just leans against the door, dripping rainwater onto the seat.

At first there is silence except for the taxi's windscreen wipers.

Then Cass says: "I didn't think he was coming."

"Who?" says Em.

"Matthew. My penfriend. I didn't think he was coming."

So now it's time to tell her.

"He wasn't coming," Em says slowly, "because there's no such person as Matthew Dunlop."

Cass laughs a bit and says, "Well, I met him tonight." She gives us a strange smile.

Em and I both say: "He was there?" Then, before Cass can answer, Em leans forward and tells the taxi driver to get into the right lane.

"Cassie," Em says, leaning back again, and forgetting to switch from her bossy voice: "There's no such person as Matthew Dunlop. There's no one at Brookfield with that name."

"Yes there is."

"We know that there's not." She tries to be gentle again. "Charlie and Seb both confirmed it for us."

Cass opens her eyes for a moment, and then she smiles again and says, "Of course. He wouldn't use his own name."

Em and I glance at each other.

"Are you saying that he's a real person?"

"Yes, Lydia, he's a real person."

Then Em and I ask the same question, in a whisper, "Cassie, what did he do to you?"

Just as the taxi turns into her street, she straightens up her shoulders, turns to us, and says, "He didn't hurt me or anything, okay?"

We wait, and she stares at each of us for a moment, like she's making up her mind. And then she says, "He just wasn't all that kind."

And then she is silent.

Cass's house is pitch-black because her mum is still at work.

We take her inside and straight into the bathroom, and Em starts filling up the bath, and I find some bubble bath and all three of us watch as I pour in half the container. Cass is sitting on the edge of the bath, still dripping rainwater onto the floor, shivering.

Em and I come out into the living room, and Em starts talking at a hundred miles an hour, but I hardly even listen to her.

I'm thinking about Cass's dad using his favorite expression: *"Now you're cooking with gas!"* It didn't sound nerdy like it would from my dad. In his Croatian accent, and the way he really meant it. Like when Cass came home with a better report card than usual. Or like when she'd been working on her gymnastics secretly. She called her dad downstairs and made us all stand back, and she did a double back flip right in the middle of the living-room floor.

And all I can think now is this: How can a person take such a long journey from the day she finds out that her father is dying, and end the journey, all this time later, alone in the dark, crying silently, her whole body hunched against the rain?

I hate myself for letting it happen.

23. The Secret Assignment

Secret Assignment

to Emily Thompson and Cassie Aganovic

1. Take a blank piece of paper.
2. Write your Greatest and Most Secret Fears on the paper.
3. Fold your piece of paper into a tiny square.
4. Meet at lunchtime today and hand in your Secret Assignment.
5. The Secret Assignments will not be read by ANYBODY.
6. Instead, they will be sealed into the back of Lydia's Notebook.
7. Each Secret Assignment will be taken out and read by us all in TEN YEARS.

This may seem like a Simple Assignment but it is the most Significant Assignment you will ever have to do. Your Secret Master will also perform this Secret Assignment. As usual, the Secret Assignment is Compulsory and Obligatory and No Correspondence will be entered into.

* * *

Emily's Secret Assignment

Well, okay.

Hi you guys of ten years from now. I just hope that we are now sharing an apartment with views of the Harbour Bridge. On New Year's Eve, we can sit on our balcony and dangle our legs over the edge, swinging our painted toenails, and drinking our piña coladas.

Also, I hope our apartment building has a *connoisseur* and carpet that feels soft under bare feet, and I hope we are always calling out, "Oh Cass, Matt Damon wants to know why you never call him back? Are you afraid of the long-distance phone bills? Ha! Isn't he funny, when he knows how rich we all are?"

My mind is like the streets of Hong Kong.

Well, this is very strange, writing to the future, and I would like to say thank you to Lydia for giving us this Significant Secret Assignment. It will hopefully lead to Cass telling us what happened to her. I don't know how it will lead to that, I only know that Lydia's Secret Assignments always lead us in the right direction.

Most of all I would like to send a special message to Cassie, which is to say it broke my heart when I saw you in the reserve last night, all by yourself in the rain.

Hey Lydia, I bet you are a best-selling world-famous author by now.

Well, okay, I think we have to do something to help Cass, and the assignment is to say: What am I afraid of?

I know.

My auntie June has developed an allergy to chocolate, so that now it gives her migraines. It's my greatest fear that I will get an allergy to chocolate like that.

You guys, just excuse me while I talk to myself for a minute: EMILY OF THE FUTURE! DON'T YOU DARE BE ALLERGIC TO CHOCOLATE. AND IF YOU ARE, JUST EAT IT ANYWAY.

JUST EAT IT AND TAKE A PAINKILLER FOR YOUR HEAD!!

Good.

Okay, well, I only want to say that I love you two a lot, and I think we will be best friends forever and I don't think we need to worry about that. The fact is, girls of the future, if we're not best friends today, then we may as well just throw ourselves off the balcony instead of sitting there swinging our toenails.

I don't really know how I can have anything to say here since the real problem is

I will now try to figure out what the real problem is.

The real problem is obvious, that Cass should tell us everything and then we can look inside her head. Then maybe she would not have ended up alone in the reserve like that. I just think that if everyone is *completely themselves,* then we will all be okay. I am trying my hardest to be myself, and concentrating, etc., but I don't really know if myself is myself or if myself is good enough or

Wow. Suddenly I am crying. I can't believe it. I'm in a German class and I am secretly crying.

That's what that mark is: a tear from me. In the future they will be able to make a little baby Emily out of the DNA in that tear mark.

Okay, I am now going to try harder to do the assignment: What am I afraid of? I'm afraid that Charlie doesn't like me. I'm afraid that he doesn't really like the way I look. I saw a photo of him before I met him, so I knew the way he looked, he's cute. He has hair the color of crème brûlée.

Sometimes I accidentally catch a glimpse of myself when I think I look pretty, and I realize that my face is too round. I don't think I'm fat, but I think I might be on the *verge* of it. I do exercise every now and again, to hold it off.

I used to sometimes think that Cassie would never be unhappy because she's skinny, but I have learned that this is wrong.

I'm afraid that Charlie likes this girl at his school called Christina. And now I have a message for you guys of the future: FIND CHRISTINA AND KILL HER.

Something amazing just happened in my mind.

Listen to this. We met a girl called Christina from Brookfield at the Blue Danish last night.

"Christina," I just this moment thought. *"Christina!"*

Because WHAT IF THAT CHRISTINA IS THE CHRISTINA WHO CHARLIE LIKES?!?!?

It could be, you know. She was beautiful, there is no denying it.

And there we were, wasting time talking to her when we should have been going straight to the reserve to rescue Cassie, my poor little Cassie, sitting under the tree in the rain, I am going to start crying again.

It is all Christina's fault that Cassie was in the rain there.

Finally, thank you, Cassie, for sending back an answer to my text message this morning. If you remember, I had sent you a message yesterday asking "R U OK?"

And today, you sent back a smiley face. And I know you hate smiley faces, so I know you did that just for me, and that's how kind you are.

Cassie: You deserve nothing except kindness and the following smiley faces. Even though you hate them. But you might have changed in the future.

☺ ☺ ☺ ☺ ☺ ☺ ☺ ☺ ☺ ☺ ☺ ☺ ☺ ☺ ☺

Signed, Sealed, and Delivered,

Emily M.A. Thompson

Emily Melissa-Anne Thompson

(Sorry it was more than one page.)

* * *

Lydia's Secret Assignment

My greatest fear is losing my friends. I feel like we're losing Cassie and I want her back.

Mostly, I want to know what that guy said to Cass to make her stay in the rain and cry.

I want her to tell us so we can help her.

And so we can find the guy and kill him.

* * *

Cassie's Secret Assignment

Hey Lyd and Em. Nice to see you in the future.

Thanks for coming to find me last night. Maybe I would still be there now if you hadn't. You guys are mad.

I know you don't actually want to hear what I'm afraid of. You want to hear what happened with Matthew in the reserve, and I'm really sorry that I can't tell you out loud. And I think probably Lydia, you set up this whole Secret Assignment so I would write out what happened, and then maybe it would break my not-talking spell, and I would tell you. But I don't think it's going to work. Sorry.

I'll tell you now on paper, though, because I guess in ten years it won't seem so important.

But right now, I feel stupid. For letting myself get so badly fooled.

Matthew Dunlop was my Brookfield penfriend. Which you already know. And I guess he was using a fake name, since you guys have found out that there's no one at Brookfield of that name.

He was kind of strange at first, but then gradually he became friendly and honest. Ha-ha.

I felt grown up when he wrote to me. Like he was someone I could help, and maybe one day he would help me. I think I had a kind of crush on him, even. He was definitely flirting anyway. And I thought about him late at night. I imagined our conversations, and how he might touch my arm while he talked.

We actually arranged to meet before — on the last day of school before the holidays, and Lydia, I'm sorry I didn't turn up at the Blue Danish that night. I felt bad for letting you down, but for some reason, I couldn't leave the reserve. He didn't show up that time, and I think a part of me was saying, *"Uh, Cassie, can you really trust this guy?"*, but the rest of me wanted to believe he was my new friend.

Maybe even a boyfriend.

I am such a loser.

Anyway, so I hung around at the reserve until some stupid time like eleven o'clock when it was pitch-black and freezing.

Okay, I'll keep writing fast and maybe the pen will write the words for me.

Matthew, or whoever, told me he was there but that we must have missed each other. Now I realize he was probably planning on doing what he did last night, but I was there talking with Liz Clarry at the meeting time, so he must have seen me with her and turned back.

Yesterday, I was so excited about meeting him. I don't know if you noticed, I was kind of jittery and stupid.

I forgot to take an umbrella with me, that's how jittery I was, I just had my raincoat, but I had the idea that we would probably meet and then just get on a bus right away to go into Castle Hill.

I was standing there, with this file of material from my mother under my arm, trying to stay sheltered under branches, thinking what an idiot I'd look when he saw me, standing there getting drenched.

I heard him calling in a low-down, lethargic sort of friendly voice, "Cassie Aganovic, or am I mistaken?" and I started looking around but I couldn't see anyone.

And then there he was, a few meters away from me — he'd come from an unexpected angle. He was taller than I expected: His letters made me think of someone short, for some reason. But he had the hood on his jacket over his head, and pulled down almost to his eyebrows, and he was carrying a black umbrella.

I said, "Hey, so I guess you're Matthew."

It was dark, and noisy with the rain on his umbrella and the trees all around us creaking in the wind.

I guess I had a feeling right away that something wasn't right, because he could see I was standing there getting drenched and he didn't offer to share his umbrella. In actual fact, he seemed to be holding the umbrella really low over his head, and it was making it really hard to see him. But at the same time, he was kind of chuckling, and I thought maybe he was just shy.

Ha.

Then he put one hand flat over his mouth, with a finger tapping kind of thoughtfully on his nose, and he said, "It is so cool to meet you, Cass."

I just smiled and said, "I forgot my umbrella."

"I mean," he said, as if he hadn't heard me, "I feel like I know you so well. All those funny letters of yours — I just *love* those letters. Your crazy therapist with her tapes of applause. And your funny lawyer mother accusing the therapist of copyright breach. Remember? And the way you drive along and you mouth the words, *'Are you, by any chance, a Volvo driver?'* And the other drivers are going, *'What? What?'*"

He was doing a kind of exaggerated pantomime of one of the stories I'd told him in my letters. I thought: *I guess he really did like my letters, to know them so well.* But I felt even more embarrassed.

I said, "Yeah, I liked your letters too."

He nodded a bit, thoughtfully, and then started again, "And that story about how you and Lyd and Em — I mean, Lyd and Em, I feel like they're *my* best friends — Cass — they're the coolest. That story about how you guys cut class to go to the movies? And your teacher? Ms. Spew? Or what was it? Ms. Chunder?"

"Ms. Ralph."

"Ms. *Ralph*!" he laughed loudly. "Ms. Ralph! She was waiting for you there in the classroom, with the pizza and the chocolate crumble or whatever it was, and you guys were at the *movies* and then you felt *guilty*, and you baked a cake for her!! I *loved* that story."

So now I'm thinking he's going a bit far. Like my letters weren't *that* good.

I shook my head and bits of rain splattered around, and then I shivered and said, "So, should we go somewhere a bit warmer? You want to have a coffee or something?"

"And Claire, the psychiatrist? She wears colors that are too bright for her, Cass! And you want to put your *hand* in the air, don't you, Cass. You want to put your hand in the air. You feel like you're drowning, eh? You kind of are drowning in this rain, huh? You want to put your hand in the air right now? Go ahead. I won't laugh."

So then I knew something was wrong.

But I thought I could fix it. I said, "What are you doing exactly?" and tried to make my voice sound kind of cool/tough.

"Well, Cass, I guess I'm just trying to share with you what it's like getting to know you. I guess I'm just trying to give you a little hint of exactly how much I want to be talking to the biggest nerd on earth. You understand, Cass, how I tried to stop you from writing in the beginning? But you just kept going, so I had to try a different strategy. You put yourself in my shoes, maybe, and think about getting letters from a girl who wears glasses with a patch over one eye?"

I just whispered, "That was in first grade," but he was looking right into my eyes, and went on: "A girl who plays the piano, and she squeezes a squash ball, and recommends that I do the same so I can play the friggin' *trombone*."

And then I just stared at him, and he laughed and said, "Sorry. Trumpet. I play the trumpet, don't I?"

I felt stupid with the shock.

I also have to say I was scared out of my mind. Seeing as you want to know what I'm afraid of, Lyd.

Then he put his hand in his pocket and took out a piece of paper and said, "And you know how much I want to read a letter that your *mother* wrote to your *father* all about what you were like when you were a *baby*," then he held up this letter that I'd sent him for some reason, back when I first wrote to him, and he ripped up the paper into little pieces, saying, "This is how interested I am in *that*."

Then he finished up by leaning in close and saying, "I've got a girlfriend at my own school, thanks. Besides which, I'd prefer to have a cockroach crawling around in my ear than to hear one more word in your snooty, patronizing, private-school voice. *Now* do you get it?"

Then he stepped away, put this manic smile back on his face, and said in the friendly voice again, "Hey, Cass! You're getting wet in the rain there! Here, take my umbrella!"

Then he closed his umbrella, put it down at my feet, and walked away.

So that's what happened.

That was fun, writing that down.

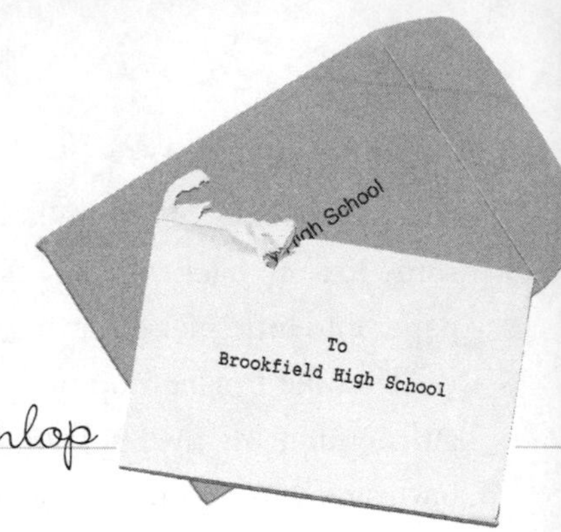

24. Finding Matthew Dunlop

Monday

Hey Seb,

Stand up straight and pay attention because you are about to receive the most important challenge of your life.

You ready to hear what it is?

Find Matthew Dunlop.

You know how we thought Matthew Dunlop was a figment of Cassie's imagination? Well, wake up and smell the coffee grounds and lavender stalks which my mother just put down the insinkerator. (It's breakfast time.)

He exists, and he goes to your school, and he was *using a false name*.

(Slap your forehead and say, *"Of course!"* Go on.)

Em and I found Cass in the reserve behind our school on Thursday night, sitting there in the rain, crying her eyes out. Because, guess what, this guy thought it would be funny to do the Pen Pal Project in the following way: Use a fake name, act as if he likes Cass, set up a meeting, and then tell Cass he hates her.

Yeah, it's pretty funny, isn't it. Why didn't we all think of doing something like that? Because seriously, I can't think of anything more hilarious than leading on a girl and then TEARING HER TO SHREDS.

IT IS SO SO FUNNY.

You want to know the two things I hate most in the whole world? (A) People who are liars, and (B) people who treat my friends badly.

I hope you'll help us find out who he is. He is the excrement of a maggot which lives with other maggots in the excrement of a sheep. So he should be fairly recognizable.

Em and I have given ourselves two weeks to find him. I think you understand the importance of this challenge.

Thanks.

Lydia

* * *

Charlie!

I will cut to the chase, which is: There IS such a person as Matthew Dunlop, but Matthew Dunlop is not who that person is.

Lyd and I feel stupid because we never even thought of the possibility. Instead, we thought that Cass was crazy and this is because we see too many movies.

Cass didn't want to tell us the details, but Lyd did this excellent thing where she made us write out our secret fears, with the plan being that we read each other's fears in ten years. *However,* when she was just about to ceremonially staple these fears into the back of her notebook, you know what she did? She looked up and declared: "At this point, *one* of us can *volunteer* to have the others read her assignment."

Cass just handed hers over, like she knew that was what she was supposed to do. Or maybe it was what she really wanted to do. I'm not sure.

So Lyd and I read it, and it was about Matthew Dunlop, and I tell you, it made my blood freeze over. He acted like Cass's friend and then was totally emotionally vicious. I do not know why anyone would do this. To a girl whose dad died last year in particular.

Therefore, we are going to find out who Matthew Dunlop is, so he can be eviscerated.

I'm hoping that you might be able to help with this search. As you know, whoever he is, he must be in your English class. So therefore, perhaps you could do the following: Arrange a lineup for us.

You will know what a lineup is from watching *Law and Order,* or possibly from your own criminal past, which you have not yet disclosed to me.

In any case, will you please gather the boys from your class and ask them to walk past the front gates of our school in an orderly procession? I will, in turn, arrange to have Cass stand in the shadows and say: "That's him! That is the boy who was cruel to me!"

So, I will now close, looking forward to your response.

Emily

* * *

Tuesday

Hey Lyd,

That's one screwed-up guy, whoever he is.

Where do we meet to discuss strategy? Name a time and place.

Ciao, bella.

Seb

* * *

Dear Emily,

I'm sorry that someone from this school was mean to your friend. Maybe it's something to bring up with your English teacher? Because I've gotta say, I always thought the penfriends-with-Ashbury idea was a catastrophe waiting to happen.

Similar to giving my sister Jessica lessons on how to ride a motorbike. What did Kevin think was going to happen? But that's just incidental.

I'm happy to help, but I don't think I can get the guys in my English class to walk past your school gate in a procession. To be honest, Em, you seem smarter in real life than you do in your letters.

No offense.

Anyhow, what if I sent you last year's form photo?

Catch ya,

Charlie

P.S. I know you're busy finding Matthew Dunlop, but do you have a free moment to continue training me to be hot? I don't think one Date with a Girl was enough.

* * *

Dear Charlie,

I know! I thought the same thing! About the catatonic nature of the Pen Pal Project? A disaster waiting to happen? Me too! I was going to organize a protest at the beginning, but then I thought better of it. But still, it was only under duress and I really thought: THIS WILL NEVER WORK! THEY ARE CRIMINALS AT THAT SCHOOL!

Okay, that's a good idea if you send us the form photo. Please hurry up and send it. Also, why don't you take some Polaroids of your English class, to narrow it down? Although "Matthew Dunlop" might notice you taking photos, and he might think we are on to him, and that would be a shame. We need to cook on the element of surprise.

Okay, we can do a bit of training of you, so you can win Christina's heart; we can do that on the side.

And to begin, I would like to see how you Say Hello to a Girl You Meet by Chance.

I am thinking that you might just lean against the front gates of our school tomorrow afternoon, and I'll be walking through the gates, let's say around four-thirty if that's enough time for you, and we will spot each other *as if by chance,* and you will say, "Hi Emily, how are you?" Or something more lively than that.

Great.

But don't tell me whether you plan to come: It must be a great unknown.

Love,

Emily

* * *

Dear Seb,

I was thinking I'd send you some samples of Matthew's letters so you could compare the handwriting with that of the guys in your English class. But Cass says he typed all the letters.

She also said a strange thing. She wants to write to Matthew again. I said, "Kid, let me take your temperature." But she explained that, while he was being mean to her in the reserve, she just stood there and took it, so he got the last word.

She said she wants the last word. Which I understood. And which also made me think of a strategy.

Let's say Cass writes to him, and let's say he reads the letter, and let's say the letter has some kind of strong perfume on it, so strong that the person reading the letter is likely to get the scent onto his hands, and let's say —

I think you see where I'm going with this!

Do you?

If I tell you when Cass sends her letter, can you watch out for a guy in your English class who smells like freesias?

Thanks.

Lyd

* * *

Wednesday

Dear Lyd,

Okay, I will sniff out the scoundrel for you. But I don't know what freesias smell like.

You'll have to spray the perfume onto yourself, then swing by the Blue Danish sometime and find me sitting at a corner table, where I will lean forward and breathe deeply of your neck and your wrists.

That way I'll recognize the smell.

When?

Seb

* * *

Hey Seb,

I'm enclosing a sachet of the perfume, which Cass is going to spill all over her letter to Matthew Dunlop today. I was hoping writing the letter would make her feel better. But she doesn't look better to me.

Whoever he is, he should get the letter in the next couple of days, depending on how often he checks his mail.

See ya.

Lyd

* * *

Dear Matthew Dunlop,

Did the words of my letters really hurt your eyes that much?

I'm just writing to let you know that your plan didn't work. If you were trying to make me fall for you or something? I didn't. Matthew Dunlop wasn't all that attractive.

Anyway, I won't write again, and I'm guessing I won't hear from you. Now that you've gone ahead and carried out your ingenious plan. It makes me wonder why you would bother, but I guess, whatever turns you on.

Bye then,

Cassie

* * *

Thursday

Dear Emily,

Well, it was nice chatting with you near the school gate yesterday afternoon. It's a shame you couldn't come have coffee with me, as per my suggestion, because bugger me, it was cold. But you were cute as ever, and I hope I did well at Saying Hello to a Girl by Chance.

I'm enclosing the year photo from last year. Sorry it took me a couple of days to track it down. I don't have the type of family who put photos in frames on the mantelpiece. We have a coffee table made out of hubcaps, and on the coffee table there's a humorous picture of Jess being chased by a rooster. That's it.

Anyhow, I hope the photo helps. As I said to you yesterday, I'd like to meet your friends Lyd and Cass sometime, and maybe let Cass know that there are good guys at Brookfield as well.

You will see that there are names underneath the photo, so if Cass figures out which face is his, she can match him up with a name.

I notice that there are a few guys in my year with the initials "M.D.," and maybe that's a clue. This guy might have been using his own *initials.* See Mario D'Angelo and Malcolm Dong, for example.

Love,

Charlie

* * *

Friday

Dear Lyd,

Here's an update.

Matthew Dunlop: 1

Seb Mantegna: 0

As of today, I can see no letter addressed to Matthew Dunlop in the Ashbury letter-box here.

I'm guessing Cass sent it on Wednesday as you said, and I'm guessing Dunlop's taken it. And I've been sniffing out the guys in my English class (to the extent that this is possible without getting my throat cut), but they smell the same way they always do: like feet and testicles. As opposed to freesias.

I don't want to keep sniffing them, Lyd.

I did think I could be a kind of goalkeeper for you, and just guard the letter-box until "Matthew" showed up. But I had to go to classes. Also, goalkeepers tend to be stupid people.

It could be he chucked the letter away without reading it, before the smell got a chance to infiltrate. Or it could be that he ingeniously took a shower while he read it.

Whatever he's done, it was a nice maneuver and you've got to admire his footwork. Me? I hope you have a good weekend and I am very sorry I have failed you.

Seb

* * *

Dear Charlie,

I would like to begin by giving you full marks for Saying Hello to a Girl by Chance. When I saw you standing there at the gate, you got such a genuine surprised look, but on the other hand, it was restrained. I mean, it was kind of a private yet penetrating look. In particular, you stayed very still, leaning against the fence, and allowed your eyes and your little smile to provide the look.

Now, furthermore, I liked your conversation, which was relaxed, and I only wish I had thought of things to talk about in advance, as I suddenly got tongue-tied, as you may have noticed. And this would have surprised you perhaps as I am not normally tongue-tied, am I? No. And I'm sorry we didn't have coffee as you suggested. It would have been jumping the gun. And I was a bit scared of continuing tongue-tied, to speak the truth.

I would like to continue this letter by expressing my gratitude to you for tracking down the photo and sending it over. That is real thoughtfulness, and Cass also says you must be a nice guy to do that. Although she wishes I hadn't told you about "Matthew Dunlop" (M.D.) as she is embarrassed about it, and poor Cass, there is nothing to be embarrassed about. But she is. ☹

Now, the sad thing is that Cass looked at the photo and she didn't recognize M.D. ☹ ☹

(You know, that makes me think: "M.D." means doctor, I believe. So maybe it is a clue in that way? Is there a hopeful young doctor in your English class? Someone who likes blood, for instance, or sewing? Do you know such a person?) I was a bit amazed that she didn't recognize him, but then I looked at the photo closely and I couldn't even see YOU. Not for AGES. I had to find your name in the list of names, and match it up with the face, and your face looked so teeny and your mouth was curious. It did not do you justice, I am sorry.

The next thing to do might be to create an Identikit photo. I will find somebody artistic in my year, and Cass can describe M.D., and the person will sketch him and I can send it over to you.

Cass is a bit dubious, but I am sure you agree it is just the idea.

Best regards,

Em

* * *

Cassie,

You're a psychopath. I ask myself: Why would anybody write *another* letter to me (a *perfumed* letter)? Is she retarded? And then I realize: She must have the hots for me so bad it's sick.

You must have one of those diseases where you get obsessed with a guy and you can't stop liking him even if he tells you you're a stupid slag.

You're so deranged in the head, I feel sorry for you.

Get over me, Cassie.

Yours faithfully,

Matthew Dunlop

* * *

Monday

Dear Seb,

Thanks for the update. Don't feel bad. It's not your fault the plan didn't work.

It's the fault of the plan.

I thought about it over the weekend and I realized it was stupid. This is why: The perfume from a letter wouldn't hang around in a noticeable way for longer than thirty seconds.

This is also why: You could find a guy who had that perfume smell, and it wouldn't prove a thing because maybe it's an innocent guy who's been getting it on with his girlfriend, and the girlfriend wears the perfume.

So don't lose sleep over it. I'll come up with another plan soon. There's no way this guy's getting away with what he's done, and if he thinks he's gotten away with it, he's as stupid as a goalkeeper.

Why exactly are goalkeepers stupid?

Hello, it's me again. I had to stop writing to play a game of squash. Now the pen is slippery because of my sweaty hands.

Cass has just finished her game and is leaning back in the chair beside me, with her feet on the table, not sweating at all. She's an athlete. I'll ask if she wants to say hi to you.

She said no thanks.

Then you know what she said? (She's gone to buy a drink so she can't see me telling you this.) She said she's planning to write to Matthew Dunlop *again*. She says he *replied* to her letter (but she didn't want to show me what he wrote), so now he has the last word again.

I gave her a lecture about last words. Specifically, about how they are fine in the short term, but if you keep on hitting last words back and forth, the words get out of control and spill all over the squash court.

She said I made no sense and went to get us drinks.

Anyway, if she's writing to him again, then I'm going to fill the envelope with crushed glass and all you have to do is look out for the guy in your English class with bleeding hands.

No, in fact I've decided to put a lot of colorful glitter in the envelope. I'll pick some up at the newsagent. If you've had any experience with colorful glitter you'll know that at least one or two bits of it stick to your hands or your face and stay there for days, even if you have a shower. Also, that it glints when the sun hits it.

See you,

Lydia

* * *

Tuesday

Dear Lydia,

I will now watch with hawklike vision for a guy in my English class with specks of glitter on his cheeks.

Lydia, are you interested in meeting me for a game of squash this weekend?

Seb

* * *

Dear Em,

My good buddy Seb Mantegna is an artist. He's like Van Goff or someone, he's that good. He just got chosen to be the one person from the whole school district to take some of his art along to a contest in Newcastle. Plus, as we know, he is friendly with your buddy, Lyd.

So maybe we should get HIM to draw up the Identikit photo for Cass? All five of us could meet someplace and watch him sketch while Cass describes, and it would be a hoot and a blast, as my mother would say.

Think about it.

Another thing, maybe the so-called Matthew Dunlop said something useful in his letters to Cass? Maybe he told her some identifying details/clues etc., which you could pass on to me? Then I could track him down?

I just realized it's Wednesday tomorrow. Do you want to make Wednesday a regular Meeting a Girl by Chance kind of a day?

Charlie

* * *

Hey Charlie,

Yes! I know. It was a good idea asking Cass about clues in the letters.

But what she has disclosed to me is that she thinks EVERYTHING that this "Matthew Dunlop" said in his letters to her was a LIE. He is a real piece of work, as *my* mother would say.

Respectfully,

Emily

P.S. It is clear that we need to work on Meeting a Girl by Chance, as you do not understand it. You don't ARRANGE a REGULAR Meeting by Chance. It must happen by chance. Certainly, I will be leaving school around four-thirty tomorrow afternoon, but what of it?

P.P.S. I am pretty sure it is not "Van Goff" but "Van Go." But there is no need to be embarrassed.

* * *

Wednesday

Matthew,

I wish I knew your real name. I sometimes think that if I just wrote out that name, in a slow, careful way, I might be able to reach the person inside your head.

Here's what I think: that you decided to use a fake name in your first letter, trying to make me go away, and the fake name became a whole character. And then you couldn't get out of character.

Don't worry — this is going to be my last letter. I won't write again — and please don't write to me. I don't want your fingers typing my name.

I'm not a lunatic, it's just that my dad died around this time last year. I never told you that. I've been trying to get better because I think it's been long enough, but sometimes I think it was easier last year, just crying on Lyd's and Em's shoulders. Whereas this year, I'm trying to stand up on my own.

The counselor told me the way to do that was to find a perfect stranger and tell them about myself, and guess what, I chose you.

It's funny, because you're such a perfect stranger, Matthew Dunlop, that you don't even exist.

Anyway, I'm writing now to let you know that you don't know me. You think you got into my head — you think all that gabbling in my letters was the real me. But it wasn't, it was only words.

You only saw a crazy me. Or you only saw lots of tiny pieces of me, like an envelope full of glitter.

Yours truly,

Cassie

* * *

Thursday

Dear Charlie,

Well, you have improved even more on Meeting a Girl by Chance. In particular, I liked your addition to the small smile, which was when you raised one finger in the air to say hello.

I don't know what to do about tracking down Matthew Dunlop. The Identikit idea seems to be of no enthusiasm to Lyd or Cass, which, go figure.

I do think that the solution is for you to walk around to every guy in your English class and whisper *"Matthew Dunlop"* into each guy's ear.

Now, I *know* you laughed heartily at me when I suggested this yesterday afternoon. I know you kept pretending to take it seriously and trying to rehearse by whispering in my ear. I know it was very humorous as I get ticklish when someone whispers in my ear, especially when they whisper nonsense such as "*Toblerone*."

Yes, hah-dy ha, Charlie, very hah-dy ha.

But I don't know what to do. I am at a loss, and so is Lyd, and Cass seems sadder than ever.

Love,

Emily

* * *

Dear Seb,

Cass just told me she sent the letter yesterday afternoon. I was starting to think she wouldn't send it and I didn't know what to do. I hope you're watching out for a glittering boy.

I guess we should be careful to make sure it's him. Glitter gets around.

Cass also told me she's had enough of letters, which is a good thing, because even though I wanted her to send this one, I was going to put her in a straitjacket if she tried to write again.

I hope we find him soon.

Lydia

* * *

Friday

TO: Lydia Jaackson-Oberman

Special Covert Operation Report

Agent: AKA

<u>OPERATION</u>

Operation TRACK DOWN MATTHEW DUNLOP

Assigned by Agent Lydia

Result: Successful (See below)

FIELD NOTES

Suspect was spotted by Agent AKA in the school admin block. Suspect was requesting new bus pass from school receptionist and reaching out to sign form.

Suspect had one pink glitter speck on knuckle of right hand.

Suspect is in AKA's English class, so AKA's heart began to beat quickly.

AKA proceeded to skip next class in order to break into Suspect's locker and search contents of locker. Contents of locker included approximately five hundred glitter specks (scattered over books, rotting fruit, etc.) and the remains of one envelope addressed to Matthew Dunlop.

The envelope seemed to have been ripped into five pieces, probably while standing at open locker (and it looked like he hadn't even opened the envelope, just gone ahead and ripped it up). Suspect must have got a shock when glitter specks went all over the shop. That'll teach him to not open his letters.

DISCOVERY

Matthew Dunlop is PAUL WILSON.

REACTION

Discovery is a shock and a half to me and Charlie, for reasons which I should tell you in person.

QUERY

What do you want me to do to him?

QUERY #2

Charlie tells me he's meeting your friend Em after school every Wednesday. You and I should give that a shot.

* * *

Hey Em,

Seb just told me he's tracked down Matthew Dunlop. It's a guy called Paul Wilson, which has hit us for a six.

I've mentioned him to you before, is the thing. He's the Year 10 Captain, star of the school drama, and boyfriend of the beautiful Christina.

See you,

Charlie

25. Winter Term / Emily and Charlie

Dear Charlie,

THERE ARE SO MANY SURPRISES!

Friday was astonishing. I was just taking a little break from history in the library, downloading some mobile ringtones at the computer there, and Lyd came skidding in, breathless and shining-eyed. She had just got the letter from Seb disclosing Matthew's identity, and she also handed me *your* letter, which she'd found in the mailbox.

There was so much to talk about! Lyd and I had to leave the school grounds: They were too small to contain our many thoughts.

We did not rush straight to Cass with the news: Lyd thought she was too fragile. So Cass still doesn't know. However, Lyd herself is all of one response: She is on fire with revenge. She wants to figure out the PERFECT REVENGE. It might take her a couple of weeks, as she wants to think it through, and then I will participate.

In the meantime, I will just philologize on the surprises.

One surprise is that the evil Matthew Dunlop has a name like *Paul Wilson.* It is so forgetful! It is such a plain, ordinary, *non d'scrip* name! Strange.

Another surprise is that Paul Wilson is the boyfriend of your Christina. And it makes me think: Are you sure this Christina is a nice person, choosing such a horrible boy as that? Christina may not be that great.

You may like to set her aside.

Anyway, I'm glad the search is complete, as I am now free to do homework, etc., and most important, continue with your training program. Would you like to continue?

THANK YOU VERY MUCH FOR ALL YOUR HELP WITH FINDING MATTHEW DUNLOP.

Love,
Emily

* * *

Dear Em,

It was a pleasure.

And yes, please continue with the training.

Great.

You're right about the surprises, but maybe some are not so surprising as they seem. As I said before, I was bowled over when I heard it was Paul Wilson, but now I've thought about it, it kind of makes sense. He's one of those charming types who all the girls giggle about, like girls do, and even teachers attempt to flirt with him. Being form captain, actor, etc., is where he gets his magnetism from, I'd say. Even our deputy principal Anderson, who is very smart and teaches Design & Tech in a way that makes you want to take Design & Tech for all your subjects, thinks he's good value and laughs at all his stupid nancy-boy jokes made during class. Anderson's also the drama teacher, which is part of why he likes Wilson. Arsehole knows how to act. So it's not actually Christina's fault that she got pulled in by him too, eh?

But I've always thought he might have an evil marrow. Seb agrees.

He thinks maybe Paul used the penfriend thing to release his evil self in an anonymous way.

Love,

Charlie

P.S. I don't think you meant *"non d' scrip"* when you said that Paul Wilson is a "*non d' scrip* name." I don't think that's a French expression, but the English word: nondescript. That's just a feeling I have.

* * *

Dear Charlie,

Okay, I have thought about this training program and it's going to have to take several weeks, even years. It may be that you will not even know Christina anymore by the time it's finished! Who knows? The point is: There are so many aspects of being a boy that we have to cover! There are things like the hair, the shoes, the talking, the walking, the dancing, the getting ahold of alcohol without difficulty, etc., etc.

We will be very busy.

To begin: One thing that all boys should be able to do (in my opinion) is to walk along beside a girl, occasionally kicking a pebble. So, I'm just wondering if you want to see me after school one day this week and walk to Castle Hill, kicking a pebble?

Love,

Emily

* * *

Em,

Sure, let's meet at your school gate again tomorrow, same time, and take a walk. I guess the important question is: Do I bring the pebble with me, or do I choose one lying on the road?

Charlie

* * *

Dear Charlie,

For your interest, Cass was mixed in her reaction when we told her we had tracked down Matthew Dunlop. She was quiet and said she didn't really want to talk about it. She asked us to leave it alone, and said she didn't want any revenge.

But she doesn't know what she means.

I await Lydia's suggestions for the revenge, with interest.

See you tomorrow for the walking-along lesson. And please do not bring your own pebble, as that would be funny.

Love,

Emily

* * *

Hey Em,

How did I do at kicking the pebble? I thought I rocked.

Charlie

* * *

Dear Charlie,

Well, to be honest, you are not much good at kicking a pebble. However, you redeemed yourself by being very funny in your conversation as we walked, and I just wonder why you hid that great humor from me on our first date?

One interesting thing is that I just tried to list some examples of when you were humorous, but I found that I could not explain *why* I was laughing half the distance into Castle Hill. I wonder if there is a lesson here, but what?

Now, changing the subject.

Here is something very annoying. Cass told us this morning that part of why she believed in Matthew Dunlop at the start of their letter-writing was that a girl in our year, Bindy Mackenzie, told her that she RECOGNIZED THE NAME. Bindy said that Matthew Dunlop PLAYED THE TRUMPET AT THE SCHOOL SPECTACULAR LAST YEAR.

Oh, puh-lease.

So therefore Cass said to Matthew, "How is your trumpet playing going?" and Matthew just played along and agreed he played the trumpet. Which meant that Cass was more likely to trust him, as she herself is musical.

Lyd and I have had a stern talking to Bindy Mackenzie, to follow up on this, and do you know what she says? She says, "Actually, maybe it was *Michael* Dunlop who played the trumpet?"

So, you can imagine, we wanted to kill her. Why did she tell Cass she was certain it was Matthew Dunlop when she CANNOT HAVE BEEN SURE. What an IDIOT SHE IS.

It now hurts my eyes even to look at Bindy Mackenzie, and the worst thing is that she is apparently SMART. She always comes first in English. The idiot. And when I stay back to do assignments in the library, she is always there with her laptop computer, sitting at a window desk, typing away like the wind. She is one of those touching typists, who makes a lot of clattering to show off how fast she can type, and also she LOOKS AROUND AND OUT THE WINDOW WHILE SHE TYPES. This is so we will all realize that she knows the keys off by heart. What a loser. I can't stand her.

Anyway.

How was your weekend? Mine was of some note. On Friday night, my Uncle Christopher and Auntie June were at our place, collecting my brother William because my parents had to go away for the weekend. It was very unpleasant: Uncle Christopher has breath, as I have told you before, and won't stop talking; Auntie June is a very garrulous woman and hardly says a word.

It was good when they left and Cass and Lyd took their place.

Love,

Em

* * *

Dear Em,

Let's have another training session to talk about all your issues.

Love,

Charlie

P.S. You said that your Auntie June is a "garrulous" person who hardly says a word. I don't see how that works. I didn't know what "garrulous" meant so I asked my mum, and she said it means a person who talks a lot. Like you in your letters.

* * *

Dear Charlie,

Okay, now listen here, Charlie. There is no need for you to correct my language. I notice that this is getting to be a habit, and I think it is very strange that "garrulous" means talkative. To me, the word "garrulous" has a nervy, shaky feeling, matching Auntie June to a T.

But that is as it may be, and I am going to tell you a story that I learned in German today. Frau McAllister even showed us a video of it happening, so we know it is a true story. Well, what happened was, a former president of the United States went to Berlin, Germany, and he shouted at the crowd: *"Ich bin ein Berliner!!"* Now, for some reason which I cannot fathom, he was trying to say, "I am a resident of Berlin!!" (He wasn't.) But, for some reason which I also cannot fathom, he was actually saying: "I am a jelly doughnut!!"

Now, I believe that Frau McAllister was showing us the video to teach us a little lesson about how you can make a fool of yourself when you speak German.

HOWEVER, I will tell you the lesson that I took from the story.

It is this: After the president shouted, "I am a jelly doughnut!!", well, the crowd CHEERED.

They SHOUTED AND CHEERED. Did they just become quiet and embarrassed on his behalf? Did they laugh and scorn him? Did they say, "P.S., Mr. President, you have that word wrong?" No. I don't think so.

Because they knew what he meant.

And the thing is, Charlie, you know what I mean when I get mixed up, and more important, *I* know what I mean.

So shut up.

It is so cold today that I cannot put this pen down. It is frozen to my fingers.

Love,

Emily

P.S. Will we continue with the program? Yes, I hope so. I would like to do Gazing into the Girl's Eyes next. When can we do that?

* * *

Dear Em,

Don't you think that at some point somebody told the president about his doughnut mistake? Maybe the next time he was eating a jelly doughnut, someone said, "Hey, Mr. President, how does that Berliner taste, eh?"

Because if nobody told him, he might have kept coming back year

after year saying the same thing and in the end they would have stopped cheering.

I dropped by your school yesterday arvo, just in case I might bump into you and get to practice Saying Hello to a Girl by Chance. Anyhow, it was earlier than normal as we got out of sport on account of the rain. I didn't see you, but I did hear the bell ringing for the end of the Ashbury schoolday, followed by a lot of announcements from your school P.A. system.

And when I heard *one* particular announcement, well, VERSHOOM (that's the sound of my amazing memory). VERSHOOM went my amazing memory.

You recall that chick who called my school about a gas explosion last term, and I made a total arse of myself by ringing the alarm and everything? And then missed out on the car show of my dreams? You recall that I could hear an announcement in the background of that prank call, which I took note of, and which I took to be as follows:

"Would all [something something] who are [something] on the inside of the Balkans, please devout immediately [something] *and the lives of others.*"

Well, I'm standing outside your school and I hear the following over your P.A. system there:

"Would all those students who are climbing on the inside of the balconies please get out of there immediately. You are endangering your own lives and *the lives of others.*"

VERSHOOM, as I said, goes my memory, and hyperlinks the two announcements.

The chick was calling from your school, Emily. I know it. And for some reason which I cannot fathom, the kids at your school are regularly climbing on the inside of the balconies.

But the question is: Why would someone at your school want to make a prank call to my school?

Maybe YOU could help track down the evil witch who made this phone call, just as I (tried to) track down the evil Matthew Dunlop to help you? Interested?

Catch you,

Charlie

* * *

Hey Em,

I haven't heard from you for a couple of days. Is everything okay? I was at your school again yesterday afternoon, hanging out, but maybe you're tired of the training course? Maybe you're avoiding me? I swear I will not hang out at your school gates anymore if you don't want me to. It's f/n freezing, anyway.

I will spend my time at home instead, kicking the pebble around.

Catch ya,

Charlie

* * *

Dear Charlie,

Well, Lyd and I have had a secret meeting to talk about the revenge on Paul Wilson. It went on for several hours and the *apchotte* of it was that:

1) Lyd has been thinking that the best way to get revenge on Paul Wilson is to discover the thing that he loves most in the world, and take it away from him.
2) Lyd has confirmed that the thing Paul Wilson loves most in the world is his beautiful girlfriend: Christina Kratovac.

3) Therefore, we must steal Christina away from Paul Wilson.
4) It is clear that you are a person who likes Christina, and (in my professional opinion) you are ready to steal any girl from anybody.
5) Therefore, I invite you to go ahead and steal Christina.
6) Please let me know when she is your girlfriend.

Also, Charlie, listen, I would be very happy to help you track down the girl who made the prank call about the gas explosion. You know what, now that I think about it, it was almost certainly Bindy Mackenzie. She is that type. I will be really mean to her for you, and you will forget all about it and get on with your life. Okay? Great.

Best wishes,

Emily

* * *

Dear Emily,

I know you don't want to be corrected, but I swear to God you mean "upshot," don't you? Not *ap-chotte*? It is not always necessary to translate things into another language, you know.

Are you sure you want me to go after Christina? Lately I've kind of thought I might just give up on that. Plus, didn't you and I need to gaze into each other's eyes first? How will I know how to gaze at Christina? And my pebble kicking? Disaster.

Love,

Charlie

P.S. What makes you think it was Bindy Mackenzie who made the prank call? It sounds like you just kind of generally hate her, the reason being that she made a mistake about the trumpet playing of "Matthew Dunlop." Is it really Bindy's fault she made a mistake? Maybe she just wanted to be friendly with Cassie?

* * *

Dear Charlie,

Can you stop lecturing me please? Thanks. It's really morally resplendent. And besides, it is as if you don't want me to be ME.

Plus, Charlie, you get a lot of things wrong.

E.g., you say that the only reason I don't like Bindy is that she made a mistake. But no! There are plenty of reasons not to like Bindy: She has a very high-pitched voice, for one. And today, furthermore, she has a pimple under her nose, and she doesn't seem to know about it. Or at least she hasn't squeezed it, even though it is like a tomato seed, and therefore I get the impression that she doesn't know about it.

Second e.g., you say that "it is not necessary to translate things into another language." Well, BLEEP (as in the sound of an incorrect answer). It is ALWAYS NECESSARY TO TRANSLATE THINGS.

And I know this because just last night Lyd and I were at Cass's place, and Cass's mother was on her treadmill there. She was running along on her treadmill, yet standing still, as is the nature of the treadmill, and she had many little rivulets of sweat on her face and her neckline.

Cass's mother is freckled and large-bosomed, and her name is Patricia. Therefore, I will now call her Patricia for this story.

Anyhow, Lyd, Cass, and I were just watching TV with the background thud-thud-thud of Patricia's feet on her treadmill. Then this ad came on, which maybe you have seen, in which a man in a suit comes home and his wife leans out of the kitchen and says, "Just making you a *divine* Diamante dinner, darling," and the husband says, "You can make *me* dinner *any* day, my Diamante darling."

"Make your own dinner," Cass said hostilely.

"That ad is so sexist," contributed Lydia.

From her treadmill, Patricia said, "Well, of course, the ad is sexist. But that's just one of the ways you can interpret it."

Cass was a bit surprised as it is her mother who is always trying to make us into so-called feminists. I try to refuse her attempts, as it is not needed in our generation.

"For example," Patricia continued, hardly puffing at all, as she is very fit, "for example, how might a Socialist interpret that ad?"

We all turned around from the floor and looked at her.

"A Socialist might point out the conspicuous consumption in all that luxury furnishing and the man's designer suit and the unimaginable waste of a packaged Diamante meal while most of the world's population is starving."

"Huh," said Lydia.

"But an advertising executive might say, 'nice product imaging,' because they've got cheap microwave meals and associated them with a young professional lifestyle. And a trade-practices lawyer might say, 'Hmm, is that misleading and deceptive to call those awful meals "divine"?' And a Christian might say, 'Well, that is a beautiful, loving marriage, and marriage is based on sacrifice.' Or some tosh like that. And now, tell me what might a Muslim or a Buddhist say?"

We all continued to stare at her.

Patricia's feet started moving faster while drops of sweat scattered from her hair. "Come on! Didn't you girls take comparative religion last year?"

We explained that the comparative religion class was cancelled, so we did liturgical dance instead.

"The point is," said Patricia, the pounding of her feet slowing down as the treadmill let her have a break, "the point is, that there is no right or wrong; there is no one truth, there are lots of truths. And you girls should *translate* the world into as many different languages as possible. If you see the world in just one language, your world becomes too small. Okay?"

We did not answer as we were translating the TV ad into liturgical dance, which was making us laugh too much to talk.

See you,

Emily

P.S. You are definitely ready to ask Christina out. I don't really feel like giving you advice on how to do it, I think you should just go ahead and be funny, etc., like you are with me, and give her that little wave by raising one finger in the air. Please go ahead and hurry up and just make it happen.

* * *

Dear Emily,

Well, you should maybe listen with care to your friend's mum and her theories about looking at the world in different ways. Because it might make you calm down a bit. As my brother Brian often says to Mum when she's in one of her moods, you seem to be a person of EXTREMES and HYPERBOLES. You are a bit whacked out and crazy, and I have used those capital letters in the previous sentence as an echo of all the capital letters you often use.

No offense.

When can we meet up again?

Love,

Charlie

P.S. Sometimes the right thing to do with zits is not squeeze them and maybe that's what your buddy Bindy is up to there?

* * *

Dear Charlie,

I will now translate the criticisms in your letter into a variety of languages:

Sexism: Boys always think that girls are too extreme and emotional. They think that girls are crazy, whereas they think they themselves are level as a head. They are WRONG.

Socialism: It is wrong to use long words like "hyperbole" because that is the way of the rich classes.

Mathematics: Hyperbole is something to do with graphs. What is it in particular? I don't know. I hate maths.

Christianity: You should not throw stones until you learn how to kick a pebble.

Stupidity: What you say in your letter is fairly stupid.

I might check with Cass's mum whether I am playing this game correctly.

Well, Charlie, you are exasperating me. I hear no word of you pursuing Christina. She will be wrapped in you. I know it.

Emily

* * *

Dear Emily,

I don't know. I still think Christina is gorgeous, and she's a really nice girl and you were fairly wrong back when you said she must be a bad person if she's going out with Paul Wilson. It's not her fault that Paul tricked her into falling for him.

I mean, think about it: Paul Wilson tricked your friend Cass too. He's just good at taking people for rides, clearly. The teachers here slobber all over him and he doesn't even *do* that well. He's just a smarmy bastard

who thinks he was put on earth to take the next plane to Hollywood and *perform* for the girls, is all.

This is all incidental, leading me up to the point: that maybe I'm not interested in Christina anymore. Maybe I have changed.

Remember what you were like when you wrote to me last term? You were a bit of a loser. You were always going on about "Secret Assignments," I recall, and you really wanted to get your English teacher into bed.

So maybe we have both changed since then.

I just need to check with you *one more time.* Do you really truly want me to go for Christina?

Yours,

Charlie

* * *

Dear Charlie,

Lately I have been thinking a lot about the idea of *hurting yourself*, and I have some conclusions, which are:

(a) It's okay to hurt yourself in little ways. For example, it's okay to scrape your knuckles on a brick wall and make yourself bleed a bit. It's okay to bite the middle part of your thumb as hard as you can and leave sharp tooth marks. It's okay to slap the palm of your hand against a mirror until it cracks, and maybe you get a cut. Those things are okay.

(b) It's not okay to hurt yourself a LOT, e.g., suicide or eating disorders.

This girl in our year jumped off a cliff last year, and I would put that in category (b). People said she was trying to kill herself, something to do with her boyfriend. Maybe he broke up with her or something? Anyway, I was so angry with her.

Because this was happening around the same time as Cassie was going to her dad's funeral, and I was scared it would make Cass think of doing the same thing, and I thought, *What a stupid idiot that girl is. If Cass can get through this without jumping off a cliff, then I think you can get through a breakup.*

And NOW THIS PAUL HAS DONE EVEN WORSE, AND WHAT IF IT MAKES CASSIE WANT TO KILL HERSELF?

So it is extremely important that Lyd and I do our best to help Cass. It is what we do, we help each other.

E.g., this last year we were criminals fairly regularly (shoplifting, etc.) as our means of distracting Cass from all her sadness.

Second e.g., just today I got so upset because I got forty-two out of one hundred in a history exam, and that's practically failing. Anyway, I came out at lunchtime and sat down and just started crying. And Lyd said, "Wait right there," and she went to the canteen and got me a Toblerone, whereas Cass started French braiding my hair. So before you knew it, I was feeling much more cheerful.

You see how we fix each other?

I therefore really need you to steal Christina away from that horrible boy and break his heart.

Thank you.

Love,

Emily

* * *

Hey Em,

I'm not so sure it's okay to hurt yourself, even a little bit. Could you not scrape your pretty hands along the wall and cut the skin, please? Because that makes me feel upset.

Also, it's never okay to break a mirror as that's seven years' bad luck. Right there.

I get the point of your story about how you all help each other, but I wonder if distracting Cass by getting her into crime is all that mature? Maybe you could have distracted her with some action-packed DVDs?

In relation to the exam, I myself have never cried about failing an exam. You did fail, by the way: 42/100 is not practically failing.

No offense.

Em, is it really so serious to fail a history exam? In the grand scheme of things?

Charlie

* * *

Dear Charlie,

You might not think it to look at me, but my greatest fear is that I won't be able to become a lawyer or any other profession because I'm not smart enough. So, yes, in the grand scheme, it *is* that bad.

We are supposed to be choosing our subjects for Years 11 and 12, as you are too probably, and I happened to ask Mr. Botherit about what books they read in 3 Unit English and he gave me this funny look. And I realized he was thinking, *"I hope she doesn't think she's good enough to do 3 Unit English!"*

It is strange that I tell you this, because I think I told you that we had Secret Assignments from Lydia, in which we had to write out our greatest fears. And they are now sealed in Lydia's notebook ready to read in ten years' time. Although of course we already read Cassie's once.

Go figure.

But the terrible thing is, I don't actually think I was honest. Even with my two best friends. I didn't write my *real* fears which include: a sudden outbreak of bad acne right before the formal (or at any other time), weapons of mass destruction, any of my family getting sick.

It sounds terrible, but when Cassie's dad died I got so frightened that my own dad or mum or brother would also get sick, almost like awfulness was contagious.

You know, Cass is so quiet these days that it reminds me of when her dad died — it was stupid, but I felt really angry with him for that. It was like he took a piece of Cassie with him when he left.

And now I think Paul Wilson has taken another piece of Cass.

She started skinny to begin with, I don't think you can take any more of her.

Lydia and I get annoyed with Cass (not to her face), because we wish she would be verbally angry with Paul so we could give her therapy. But the only time I ever saw Cass lose her temper was once in primary when I told her she couldn't ring the school bell properly. Also once last year, when the doctor came out of the hospital room and told her that her dad wouldn't be able to leave. We were there with Cass because it was the day her dad was coming home. Cass became very stern and angry with the doctor, as if he was a rude shopkeeper. "Don't talk to me like that," she said. "Don't you *dare* talk to me like that."

Anyway, never mind.

Dad just issued me with a summons to attend dinner. I was planning on skipping it as I understand from a recent magazine that it is no longer a required meal. Dad got William to serve the summons on me. "Are you Emily Melissa-Anne Thompson?" William said, and I said, "Yes," and he threw a paper on my bedroom floor and said (as in the movies), "Consider yourself served."

William is now making the summons into a paper airplane, and Dad is standing in the stairway chuckling to himself.

Love,

Emily

* * *

Dear Emily,

There were a lot of sad stories and interesting things in your letter, and I would like to see you again and talk about them. I'm not good enough at letter writing to talk about them by pen. Can we please go out again soon? I could just swing by your school and we could take a walk into Castle Hill. Any day next week?

I have many questions, e.g., are you saying that Lydia is the one who gives you Secret Assignments? Why? Are they connected to your criminal conduct? Let's meet up, eh.

Charlie

* * *

Hey Charlie,

I didn't actually mean to give it away about the Secret Assignments, but I guess I wrote without thinking. The Secret Assignments started in primary when Lyd, Cass, and I had this huge fight. It was the first fight we ever had and I can't even remember what it was about. Well, it was about how you ring the school bell properly. Anyway, all three of us stopped talking to each other for like ONE WHOLE WEEK.

Then Lydia solved it by inventing this thing she called the Significant Secret Assignment. She wrote out this assignment on three different pieces of paper, one for each of us, and she used different colors for each one and burned the edges of all of them.

The assignment was to go over to her place for a slumber party and have a midnight feast and never have another fight again.

After that, Cass and I became a bit obsessed with Secret Assignments, and we made Lyd give them to us all the time. So she would give us assignments to do scary things such as sneak into the principal's office *while the principal was in the office having her afternoon nap*. We almost never got caught.

So! Then they faded away, but Lyd brought them out again to solve a fight we had in Year 7.

And then? Last year? When we needed some wild and criminal distractions?

Again.

They have faded away lately, except that Lydia always brings them out as a way of solving problems.

Anyway, Charlie, that is a nice idea about meeting up, but I don't think we should do that. The fact is, I am going cold turkey on you, as our parents did with marijuana a few years ago. If I keep seeing you, I might miss you a bit when you start going out with Christina.

On that note, could you please give me an update of how it is going with Christina? Lydia is getting impatient with the revenge.

It is SO COLD it is like the coldness has my head in a headlock.

Love,

Emily

* * *

Em,

I am going to lay this on the line here. I am not interested in Christina anymore. This is because I am interested in somebody else. Do you actually need me to tell you who the somebody else is?

Charlie

P.S. Can you give examples of what you've done for criminal Secret Assignments in the last year? Out of professional interest.

* * *

Dear Charlie,

Well, actually, I think you had better tell me who the person is in whom you are now interested. Thanks. Or just give me a clue or two. Thanks.

Yes, I can give you examples of Lyd's Secret Assignments. She gave Cass an assignment to break into the car of a teacher at YOUR school last term and steal some exam papers. This was actually to help Seb avoid doing his exam.

You know, it's strange that you and Seb are friends, isn't it? Don't you think that's a coincidence? That Lyd and I ended up writing to Seb and you?

Love,

Emily

* * *

Dear Emily,

Well, Seb and I were kind of distant buddies, but we became friends when this letter-writing scheme began. This was because Seb received a letter from Lydia and he started asking around if anybody knew her name, because he thought, you know, the level of effort he put into his reply would be dependent on whether she was cute.

That is Seb's style, not mine, by the way. I knew you were cute from your handwriting.

Anyway, I recognized Lydia's name because of my supersonic memory. Her mother is Marianne Jaackson, the former star of the excellent soap opera *The Tall and the Blooming,* and her father's a big-time judge. So I acknowledged Seb's request for information, and he and I spent a bit of time trying to track down a photo of Lyd. We found an old story about the family which had been in the *Woman's Day,* got ahold of the photo, and got confirmation that your friend Lydia is gorgeous. So he stepped up his letter writing.

Meanwhile, in the process, Seb and I became buddies. It was inevitable anyway, as we are both the type of people to get in a fair bit of trouble at school. Through no fault of our own. We would have run into each other in the principal's office at some point.

Catch ya,

Charlie

P.S. I will give you a clue about the person I'm interested in. She gets a very cute dimple in her right cheek when she's trying not to smile. She has a very cute way of pronouncing *th,* and she wears a cute hat on cold days, which is like a French beret. I once had an appointment with her to Gaze into the Girl's Eyes, which she went and cancelled on me, and I've been waiting all term for a chance to Kiss the Girl.

* * *

Dear Charlie,

News flash! We have cancelled the revenge idea. You do not have to pursue Christina!! REPEAT: Do not worry about pursuing Christina! Leave her! Lydia and I are going to work on something new. We don't know what yet. We will do something, though! We know that!

And I will just be honest with you here, so there are no tricks or betrayals between us, and say that I actually knew what you looked like a fair while before I knew you. It was because Seb sent a photo of his own foot to Lydia, as part of a game they were playing (which now turns out was a dishonest game), and you were also, coincidentally, in the photo. Playing soccer. This happened just before I suggested we go on a Date with a Girl.

So, listen, you and I can go out on another Date with a Girl, if you like, sometime. You say the word.

Emily

* * *

Emily,

It is the middle of the night. The most weird thing has occurred to me. My supersonic memory just gave me another hyperlink in the void.

I was lying in bed here, thinking that it's nice that you saw a photo of me early and still wanted to go out with me, that is a very nice story and I'm glad you told me. And then I was thinking about all the various cute things about you. Including the cute way you say the letters *th*. And then there was this VERSHOOM and I remembered: that chick who made the prank call about the gas leak? She had a funny way of saying *th* too.

And *then* I got to thinking — well, you know, when I set the alarm off, as a consequence of the so-called gas leak, well, that meant I didn't have to do a history exam. Which also meant that Seb didn't have to do a history exam.

So my question is this: Is this something to do with Seb and Lydia? Did Lydia maybe tell Seb she'd get him out of the exam, and then give YOU the secret task or whatever you call it of arranging for the alarm to go off?

Can you please tell me, Emily, that you are not the person who made that prank call? As we are getting into being honest with each other at the moment?

Charlie

* * *

Charlie,

Well, I do not see why we need to be quite as honest as THAT.

I am very sorry but I cannot tell you that it was not me who made the prank call. Because, actually, it was me.

Please, will you forgive me and put it in the past as I have been trying to get you to do? Okay? It will just be left alone now. Okay, I am sorry that it was me who made the prank call. It was necessary, as it was a Secret Assignment, and we HAVE to do them.

I am very sorry you felt embarrassed, as that was not my intention.

And when you think about it, it is fairly unfair because WHAT ARE THE CHANCES THAT IT WOULD BE YOU, my PEN-FRIEND, answering the phone? That is so unfair, the odds being against me like that.

So therefore, let us forget that.

Love,

Emily

* * *

Well Emily,

I think maybe I can't forget it. I see now that you've been laughing at me this whole time, and that doesn't make me feel all that happy.

So we'll just take a break, okay?

Thanks,

Charlie

P.S. By coincidence, Christina just broke up with Paul Wilson. I guess she saw through him all on his own. Paul seems to be moving on to someone else already, without much excess anguish, so that's ironic.

* * *

Charlie,

I HAVEN'T BEEN LAUGHING AT YOU! NEVER, EXCEPT WHEN YOU WERE BEING FUNNY!

PLEASE can we forget it? And okay, great that Christina broke up with Paul, but just try not to move in on her, okay, you'd better just leave her to have a little thinking time. She'll need a break, okay? I am VERY VERY sorry and I wish you would have some chocolate to feel better because I see that you might feel betrayed and so on. I see that maybe I should have told you straightaway it was me, or maybe not even done it! But I had to do it!

And besides which, you are not so perfect yourself, Charlie? Remember? You get into trouble at school all the time? And I don't even know why! And there are things I don't like about you! I don't like the way you say the word *chick*, for an example. I don't like the way you often have something very superior to say to me.

Emily

* * *

Great, Em. Thanks. That's fixed things.

As I said, could we just leave it for now then? Maybe in a couple of months I'll feel like I can look you in the eye again. But I can't just now, okay?

Cheers,

Charlie

* * *

Charlie,

Well, I did not mean to get too carried away with negativity, and please recall with that supersonic memory of yours that I have often been kind to you, as much as I could. And speaking of your supersonic memory, HOW SUPERSONIC IS IT REALLY WHEN IT TOOK YOU THIS LONG TO REMEMBER THAT THE GIRL WHO PHONED YOU HAD A FUNNY WAY OF SAYING *TH*? HOW SUPERSONIC, REALLY? EH?

Not so supersonic, after all?!?!

Besides which, Charlie, come on! It's not like I did anything ILLEGAL, is it? I mean, I just phoned the school and pretended there was the danger of a gas leak! That's not exactly a CRIME!

Emily

* * *

Emily,

Please see below, as provided by my brother, for your information.

Section 93IH, Crimes Act 1900 (NSW)

(1) A person who conveys information:

- (a) that the person knows to be false or misleading, and
- (b) that is likely to make the person to whom the information is conveyed fear for the safety of a person or of property, or both, is guilty of an offense.

Maximum penalty: Five years' imprisonment.

Regards,

Charlie

* * *

Go to hell, Charlie.

* * *

Go to buggery, Emily.

26. Winter Term / Lydia and Sebastian

Dear Seb,

You're the best secret agent in the history of secret agents. You rock.

Thank you. I owe you.

How come you and Charlie were shocked by it being Paul Wilson? Can you tell me anything about him? Thanks for the offer, but I don't need you to do anything to him: I want to figure out something myself. So any information would be good.

Another thing: Your field notes were great. Why don't you send me notes like that explaining how you knew who I was in the Blue Danish? Sometimes I think maybe you cheated. Like asked around to find out what I looked like. I hope you didn't, because I'd have to kill you.

Thanks again.

Lyd

* * *

Dear Lyd,

Okay, got some information for you about Paul Wilson:

Physical Appearance: Tall; lifts weights a bit too much so that muscle tone is kind of obvious; gets a bit too much sun so skin is too brown for his white-blond hair. Fairly stupid looking, all up.

Sex Life: Seems to be pumping. Has had a lot of hot girlfriends the last few years, and latest conquest is girl-of-many-guys'-dreams Christina Kratovac.

Other Points of Interest: Year 10 Form Captain. Smarmy bastard. Thinks he can act. This agent (AKA) has long-standing contempt for Paul Wilson, for various reasons, including Paul Wilson's crap soccer playing (apparently has no respect for the game). Has supernatural powers (see next point).

Supernatural Powers: Has bizarre ability to hypnotize teachers. Example: Our deputy principal Anderson is mad — fairly old, but a big guy with a lot of red hair and freckles, and most important, a mad soccer player when you can get him out there. Also, smart and hilarious guy, who can usually see through any small untruth you might tell and turn it into a joke (he's the drama teacher so knows drama when he sees it); gets you laughing even though you know you're screwed. But guess who Ando's best-buddy-here-let-me-give-you-advice-on-your-career-choices-and-let-you-off-your-Design-and-Tech-assignment-for-extra-drama-rehearsal-time-all-time-favorite student is?

Paul Wilson.

Only drama he can't see through.

Supernatural power is only explanation.

You want to hook up this Friday night, maybe see a movie, and discuss in detail?

Your favorite agent,

Seb

P.S. You think I cheated at Operation Recognize Lydia First last term? You break my heart. You want to trust a guy? Thanks.

* * *

Dear Seb,

Thanks for the information about Paul Wilson. Can you tell me anything else about that girlfriend-of-the-rainbows or whatever you called her? I wonder if she knew her boyfriend was acting out some weird fantasy with Cass? Maybe she hates Ashbury girls and made him do it.

Sorry I didn't get to you before the weekend — I couldn't have met you on Friday anyway because we were staying at Em's. Her parents were going to a conference for the weekend. The conference was called "*Lawyers Are Lovely, Great, and Superb: So Why Does Everyone Think That They Are Liars, Greedy, and Scum*?" and Mr. Thompson was doing a speech called "*Ten Tips to Make Lawyers as Popular as Doctors.*"

I'll give you a sample, in case you ever become a lawyer:

Tip No. 3: Look out for legal emergencies in your day-to-day life. In medical emergencies, people always shout for a doctor — but nobody ever shouts, "Is there a lawyer in the house?" So lawyers need to be vigilant and find the emergencies for themselves. Let's say a lawyer overhears two neighbors having an argument about who owns a lemon tree. The lawyer should sprint right up, calling, "It's okay, everyone, I'm a lawyer! For starters, who planted the tree?"

You want to take a guess how I spent Friday night? Listening to Mr. T. practice his speech. He was also teaching us how to make coq au vin without using any wine. It all makes you think: Would I have had more fun seeing a movie with you?

Difficult to say.

Got to go,

Lydia

* * *

Hey Lyd,

Very easy to say, actually.

But you want to know about Christina. For starters, I seriously doubt she knows anything about Paul Wilson's evil side. She's a buddy of mine, and her best friend happens to be an Ashbury girl (met in last year's Pen Pal Project), so she can't be anti-Ashbury.

A lot of people are, though.

Christina is gorgeous, but also very cool. Wilson stole her from her long-term boyfriend, Derek Turner, which was a scandal around these parts. Everybody saw it happening, except Turner, and we were all waiting to see what he'd do when he realized he'd lost her.

He broke his hand by punching a brick wall, is what he did.

And he's still trying techniques for getting her back, but I wouldn't call them likely to succeed. Example: The last couple of weeks he's been wearing nothing but a singlet, shorts, and thongs, and you'll have noticed that it's winter. He told Christina he'd be happy to get frostbite if she would just realize how much he still loves her.

But no way Wilson's letting her go. I would say she's his greatest possession.

Any-old-how, Lydia-the-beautiful-Lady, would you look at that, I've just received a new top-secret spy-agency assignment. And I need to pass it on to you, as you're one of the participants. What a surprise, eh? The Assignment is called Operation Movie, it takes place this Friday night and is as follows:

- Agent Lydia must go to the Castle Hill movies at seven P.M.
- She must buy herself a ticket to the movie of her choice.
- Agent AKA will stand at the Candy Bar but *will pretend he doesn't know Lydia.*
- Agent AKA will ask for a large popcorn, at which moment, Lydia

will stand beside Agent AKA and *secretly let him see the ticket which she bought.*

- Both Agents will go into the movie and sit next to each other, as if by chance.
- Both Agents will stare straight ahead, but about halfway through Agent AKA will take Agent Lydia's hand in his hand and stroke the palm of her hand with his thumb, *three times.*
- This will be the signal for Lydia to knock over the popcorn, so that both agents can lean forward, like they're picking up the popcorn, and have a secret, urgent, short conversation about *anything at all.*

So, I guess I'll have to see you Friday night. Too bad if Mr. T. needs to give you any more cooking classes: The world needs you. Let me know if you have any queries about the Assignment and I'll take them up with the boss.

Won't it be great for you and I to have a conversation at last? Even if it's just a secret, urgent, short one.

See you,

Seb

* * *

Dear Seb,

Why are guys always punching walls when they're upset? Is it the fault of the brick wall? I don't think so.

It's Friday morning right now, so tonight I guess I'll see you at Operation Movie.

Last night, Em and I had a meeting at the Blue Danish to discuss the revenge plan. I'll tell you my idea: It's to steal his girlfriend from him.

When I said that to Em, she got her ruthless look and said Charlie's the guy to do it.

"It's obvious," she said, "Charlie has always liked Christina, and he knows how to get a girl to like him back."

I actually thought she liked Charlie herself, the way she's been talking about him, but when I said that she got angry and said, "He's just a *friend,* Lydia."

Em has high standards in guys, so if she thinks Charlie can get Christina interested, I guess it's true. But maybe she's got him wrong. Do girls at your school seem interested in him?

See you at Operation Movie tonight.

Lydia

* * *

Hey Beautiful,

I think you will agree that Operation Movie was a success. Nobody would have guessed that we knew each other, and our conversation over the spilled popcorn was a work of art. You're better at keeping a straight face than I am, though.

I thought about the conversation all weekend, and about how I would have continued if we hadn't had to keep watching the movie. You say your friend Em is ruthless. She can't be as bad as you: the way you sat back up, stared straight ahead, and then left the cinema as soon as the credits started rolling.

Anyway, fair enough. It was the "Assignment." Do you want to just meet up after school this week, maybe Wednesday arvo, like normal people instead of spies? When you think about it, how old are we? Me, I'm sixteen. I'm legally allowed to have sex and buy cigarettes. Shouldn't we be having sex and buying cigarettes?

But okay, if you want to play the games. They're pretty cool, Lyd.

You're a crazy girl.

I'm not so sure that Charlie will be able to steal Christina away from Paul W. She's not the kind of girl to cheat on a guy and she seems pretty into Paul.

On the other hand, Charlie does have a way with the women.

The last few years, he just seemed to be in the background, and usually a long way back because he wasn't into the school concept. He didn't come to many classes, and nobody wondered where he was, or if they did, they thought he was probably just smoking up somewhere.

Then they found out where he was. He was taking teachers' cars for a spin.

It turned out he'd been doing this since age thirteen. And he wasn't just taking them for a spin, he was working on them. His older brothers had taught him about engines.

Don't look at me like that, Lyd. This is a true story.

He was so interested in cars, he'd drive them out to Kenthurst, give them a tune-up, and bring them back in time for the end of the school day.

I think the only reason he got caught was that some girl realized what he was doing and talked him into taking her for a ride in the Rattler's Audi. She was so turned on by the experience that she told everyone, and it got back to the Rattler, and it all came crashing down on Charlie's head.

So, Charlie did a lot of time in the principal's office this year.

Which is kind of how he and I have become buddies, as I myself have spent some time there.

But the point is that Charlie's now a bit of a legend, and he doesn't even realize it, which makes him even more alluring to the ladies.

See you Wednesday arvo, I hope,

Seb

* * *

Hey Seb,

Sorry I didn't get back to you before Wednesday. I suddenly had a lot of homework.

I couldn't have met you yesterday anyway because we went to Cass's — her mum wanted us to come over, like in the old days. It was kind of a tradition, that we'd watch TV and eat pasta while Patricia (Cass's mum) worked out on the treadmill and gave us advice for life. And then Cass's dad would sometimes come downstairs from his studio and make microwave puddings for dessert.

Em adores Patricia. I don't know about Patricia's philosophies, but it's true that she's smart, and she's so nice to Em and me, and at the end of the night she got off the treadmill and started talking to us about what we wanted to do for careers. We got so into career talk that we hardly even noticed there was no dessert.

I know exactly what I want to do with my life; I want to be a writer. But you can't just decide that. They keep telling us we have to have a backup career, and maybe I'll never become a writer so I have to choose the backup carefully, but the fact is, I haven't got a clue.

Only that I don't want to be a lawyer.

See you,

Lydia

* * *

Lydia,

Why don't you want to be a lawyer? I hear they're good in emergencies.

I know what you mean about backup careers. Paul Wilson has

been going on about how he has one career goal only, which is World Famous Actor. The teachers are praising him for his "determined attitude," which is like praising someone for being determined to win the lottery.

Paul Wilson is not a smart guy. You've got to have options.

Personally, I plan to play for Man United as my career, but I know that's not necessarily possible. Example: I might get a hamstring injury just before the tryouts.

So I have a backup career choice which is: artist/graphic designer.

I'm fairly confident about that career at the moment, for a reason which I have not told you yet, on account of not wanting to sound as arrogant as a striker. A painting of mine got selected to go in some competition at Newcastle.

I get to take a train trip with my art teacher, who's a buddy of mine, carrying the painting in a canvas bag. And they'll give us these small delicious food items known as canapés.

Please see the below assignment.

<u>Assignment</u>

When: Friday night

What: Both agents go to the Voodoo Lounge at Surry Hills, ten P.M. The agents have to pretend they don't know each other. Agent AKA has to choose a pool table and rack up and then turn around, and *at that moment* Agent Lyd has to step up and ask if he wants a game. They have to play five games of pool. They're allowed to buy drinks and have conversations. After the fifth game, they both have to leave.

Special Note: The bouncer who works there on Fridays is as stupid as a goalie, so it's fairly easy to get in. But let me know if you need help getting ID.

Seb

P.S. Not all goalies are stupid, I need to add here. Mr. Anderson, our deputy principal, is a supreme goalie, and you need brains for that. Especially when you're an old guy like he is.

* * *

Hey Seb,

Congratulations on the art show. We heard about that competition here, and I think the people in our art classes are pissed off that your school got to represent the district. But I think it's fantastic.

On the other foot, I don't think you put much effort into that pool-playing assignment. You forgot to give it a name.

Don't worry about ID for me.

Lydia

* * *

Dear Lydia,

See you tonight at Operation Chalking-the-Cue.

Love,

Seb

* * *

Dear Lyd,

Hello, it's Monday. Welcome to the New Week.

You are a beautiful pool player. Who taught you how to win every game? Also, to do it so fast.

You are beautiful at most things, but you still take the assignments too literally. Example: I was kind of gutted when you picked up your bag and walked right out of the place, without even looking back, at the end of the fifth game. As sexy as it was, it kind of hurt, Lyd.

I'm seriously ready to stop playing games and start being humans.

Also, it hurts my hand, all this writing. I could be getting repetitive strain injury. I've heard of that. It could affect my soccer.

These letters to you add up to more writing than I've done my whole school life.

Do you want to come over to my place sometime and meet my mum and my kid brother? Do you want to maybe go into the city with me one day?

Thanks,

Seb

* * *

Hey Seb,

I like the games.

Yesterday, I got home from school and I was just hanging around with my mum eating lamingtons and drinking tea, and we both knew Dad was up in his study working on a judgment, and I started thinking about Cass. How it must have been for her when we were over the other day, watching TV, with Patricia on the treadmill, how she must have felt the absence of her dad.

Because in the old days, he used to be up in his studio working on his furniture. He liked to make furniture that had secret compartments, and Cass always put tiny locks in for him. Anyway, you could hear his footsteps on creaking floorboards sometimes, and you could hear tins being opened and closed, and you knew he'd come down any moment. Or even if he was too tired to do anything, you would hear his sofa creaking as he turned around on it.

And the other day, when we were over there, Cass must have heard that silence all night. I sure did, anyway. Maybe after we left she went up to the studio and looked around the empty room, the desk in the corner where he used to draw designs, and the old pool table where he taught us all to play.

And I was thinking how, right after he died, it was almost easier for Em and me, because Cass just collapsed, and we took care of her. She sat beside me in the car on the way home from the hospital, with her head on my shoulder. On the day of the funeral, her hands trembled so much she could hardly get dressed, and Em and I helped her do up the buttons of her shirt.

But then a few weeks later, she was acting like everything was fine, except she was quieter than before, and sometimes you'd be talking for a while and then realize she hadn't been listening to you. And Em's mother said what Cass needed was for Em and me to just be ourselves. Em says she stamped her feet on her bedroom floor each morning for a while, trying to stamp herself back in to herself.

And what I was thinking, while I ate the lamingtons with my mum, was that I don't understand what it's like to be properly sad — nothing nearly as bad as losing a father has ever happened to me. Which means I can't really understand how Cass is feeling. I can't get inside her sadness.

I kind of wish something terrible had happened to me before, so I could know how to help.

Anyway, I decided I should talk to Cass right then, and Mum agreed that it was a good idea and she drove me over.

So, Cass was home by herself and we made ourselves cold Milo and hung around in the kitchen eating the Milo straight out of the tin with dessert spoons, the way we used to when we were kids. So then, we're standing in the kitchen and I said, "Do you prefer not to talk about your dad?"

And she just blows me away. She says, like she rehearsed it: "A year is a long time, Lyd. And besides which, it wasn't a shock." And she explains, in this practical voice: "I looked up some stuff on the Internet one time, and I read these stories about teenagers who lost their parents suddenly, like unexpectedly in car accidents. They were all talking about how it would have been better if they could prepare themselves and say good-bye and everything. So, see, look at me."

Then she put the lid back on the Milo tin and put it away in the cupboard.

I was standing there, staring at her, figuring out something to say which would break through that crap without breaking her at the same time.

"Cass," I said, "you know there aren't rules for being sad, don't you?"

"But I had a whole year to prepare," she said again. "It was pretty clear he wasn't going to get better this time."

"Well, *I* thought he was going to get better."

I started getting a thumping heart then. Like I had said something too harsh to be said.

But it was true. Even with all the medical facts in the world, I never thought he'd actually *die*. How could he stop existing?

Cass gave one breath of laughter, and said in an ordinary voice, "So did I."

Anyway, I won't go into more details, except she started crying, and then she said more stuff, and I was trying so hard not to start crying too, because I couldn't believe the things that had been happening inside her head.

All I can say is, I feel like killing Paul Wilson, like breaking his arms or crushing his bare feet under my mother's sharpest stilettos.

He has to be punished, Seb, and I can't stand how powerless I am. I mean, I seriously think he could have killed Cass — if you're that cruel to a person who's trying to pretend she's strong, you could push them over the edge.

Long letter, eh.

Sorry Seb.

Love,

Lydia

* * *

Dear Lydia,

Thanks for your letter — it took me most of the afternoon to read it, and then I had to reread it because there were a lot of issues there. I will have to hand in your letter as an explanation for why I didn't do my French assignment.

Just kidding, Lyd, I would never hand in your letters. They're precious to me. I would never show another human being a single word.

There are a couple of issues I would like to focus on in this letter. The rest we should talk about in person, because Lyd, you are beautiful, and I would like to help if I can.

Issue Number One is about Paul Wilson. Can you not talk too much about what a prick he is, please? Because it makes me feel like beating him up, and I have to clench my fists to prevent that happening. I've got a confession to make, which is that I've had a bit of trouble at school in the last few years. The trouble is my tendency to beat people up when they're being arseholes.

So I was on the verge of getting thrown out of school earlier this year, which was breaking my mother's heart, which was not good as she was fairly pregnant at that time. But I got put on probation, and I've controlled this temper of mine ever since, which has been hard labor, I tell you.

Plus, I started tae kwon do. That might seem like a strange way to stop yourself from beating people up, but the point of tae kwon do is NOT to beat people up. Which is why I did it.

So, in relation to Paul Wilson, I know exactly what you mean when you say you feel like breaking his face, but you're lucky in a way because you're a girl and you can't do that. It must be a relief.

Issue Number Two is about how you wish something bad had happened to you in your past. You don't really wish that, Lyd. You don't want to wish tragic events on anyone, and that includes yourself. As the Mighty Mighty Bosstones like to say, it's bad to have tragedies happen. Knock on wood.

Or words nothing like that, but which mean the same thing.

Issue Number Three is about how people can be so cruel that they cause another person to do themselves in. In actual fact, I heard of some girls in Canada who bullied another girl so much that she killed herself. And I think the bullies got done for it. As in, convicted of manslaughter. So you're right about that possibility. The principal told me this story because she thought I was beating people up like a bully. But that's not what it was: It was just people who deserved it. She didn't get the distinction.

Anyhow, maybe your friend Cass is not so weak as you think — I have this feeling, from what you've said, that Cass has a fair bit of strength of character. Plus, she's got you and Em.

So I don't think that the risk was all that real.

Issue Number Four, and the final issue, is about feeling powerless. You seem like a girl who likes a lot of power. My suggestion is to think of ways of feeling powerful that also make you feel good. Example: I am excellent at burping my baby brother. This is a powerful yet good thing to be able to do: *MAKE HIM BURP.* It means he doesn't have a pain in his little baby tummy.

You come over to my place and I'll teach you how to do it.

Yours sincerely,

Seb

* * *

Dear Seb,

You put a lot of thought into that letter. Thanks. You're a good guy.

And Em says Charlie's going to steal Christina any minute. So he's a good guy too.

I'm sitting in the lower courtyard, leaning against the brick wall. That's why the handwriting is wobbly. It's freezing. Is it freezing at Brookfield too or do you have different weather there? This is the only place in our whole school where there's any sun at lunchtime. But the sun moves, so we have to follow it along the wall.

Em just gave me her woolen gloves because she's worried about me getting too cold while I'm writing, and I said I couldn't write wearing gloves so she took them back and cut off the fingers. Which seems excessive. Sorry, I mean which shows how nice Em is, and I'm just going to write about what a wonderful, beautiful, amazing, smart, generous, compassionate person Em is, as she is reading over my shoulder and dictating to me.

Okay, she seems satisfied.

Now Cass is trying to give me her scarf so she can get the same kind of praise. TOO LATE, CASSIE.

Hey Seb, I've been thinking about a new Assignment, and it can take place a week from Saturday if you're available. We have to pretend we don't know each other again, and it goes like this:

1) Get the 2:37 City via Strathfield train, third carriage from the front, upstairs, and then change to the Circular Quay train.
2) Get the ferry to Taronga, then the bus to Balmoral Beach.
3) Get off at Balmoral Beach, buy fish and chips.
4) Sit on the sand and eat the fish and chips.
5) Go home.

Somewhere between items (2) and (3), I have to get a message to you, without anybody seeing it, and you have to tell me what it is in your next letter. Somewhere between (4) and (5), you have to get a message to me.

I see you shaking your head, a frown slowly creasing your forehead. Smooth the frown away, Seb, you look like a turtle.

Thanks again for your nice letter.

See ya,

Lyd

P.S. Except for one thing — it's not a "relief" not to be able to beat someone up, Seb. That's wrong right there.

* * *

Dear Lydia,

Okay. See you at Balmoral Beach a week from Saturday. Why so far away? I'm ready to do an Assignment today. It seems like a well-thought-out program, Lyd, and I'm proud of you. You forgot to give it a name though.

You know what I remembered the other day, which might make you feel a bit better? I once beat up Paul Wilson. It was in Year 7, and the early days of my beating people up. He deserved it because he was being a prick to my art teacher (the one I told you about — I loved her a lot in those days, whereas now she's my buddy).

This was in the days before Paul Wilson developed his smarmy personality and started getting teachers into bed with him.

So, anyway, when we left the art room, I started a fight with him. Actually, I think I even knocked him unconscious.

No, I didn't. Now I remember. He took a dive. I hardly touched him, and he threw himself down writhing, like the snake that he is. I got two weeks' detention on account of that little piece of performance art of his.

I shouldn't have remembered that story. I'm starting to lose my temper again. The little arsehole.

See you,

Seb

* * *

Dear Seb,

I was just peeling some potatoes for dinner and they all looked like crisp white potatoes until I cut them in half. Every single one had a rotten, gray core. Like a circle of gray reaching almost to the edge of the potato.

So I came up to my room to write to you.

You know what I feel like? I feel like the whole world is black, rotting, and evil. Even when it looks crisp on the outside, that's a lie, because you can't trust anything — on the inside it's nothing but mold.

Like that Paul Wilson — acting like a good guy so all the teachers love him.

And like my mother, she used to be an actress on this daytime soapie that no one has ever heard of now, and she was kind of famous, and she thought she was heading for Hollywood.

But the show got axed, because it was crap, and she never got another acting job, and now she just owns a production studio, but she hardly ever goes there, and she gets more wrinkled every day. And the only thing left to make her think she's a celebrity is sometimes they call her to go on a charity telethon, and once, a couple of years ago, the *Woman's Day* did a crap "Where Are They Now?" story in which she got photographed with her happy family.

And Cass's dad — I used to think when people went into remission, it meant they got cured. It doesn't mean that, it means they've got the cancer to go down for a few years, but it'll come back for sure.

Today at lunchtime Em was upset because she failed a history exam. And I hate to confess this, but it just made me feel scared, like the darkness is about to envelop all three of us. That's my greatest fear.

I didn't say that to Em, of course. I told her that she'd get one hundred on the next exam. But how long can you keep lying for?

Because secretly I thought she's never going to get good enough marks to get into law school, even though that's her dream. And Cass is never going to be able to be a singer, like she really wants to, because she'll never be able to sing in public. And I'll never ever be a writer because practically nobody gets to be a writer, and there's no way I'll ever get published, and I can't even finish the novels that I start.

So, see, nothing good is ever going to happen, and anyone who says it is, is lying to you.

I remember the day when I came home and told my parents that Mr. Aganovic's cancer had got into his brain. I was secretly hoping it wouldn't be important, like they'd just have to give him a lot more chemo. But Mum said, *"Oh Lydia,"* as if I'd just told her I'd got caught shoplifting and she was really disappointed in me.

And Dad scraped his chair back from the table and walked out of the room. Dad and Mr. Aganovic were pretty good friends — they went sailing together, and Dad was always buying chairs and coffee tables from Mr. Aganovic.

Okay, so this has been a fairly happy letter, eh. Just to cheer you up for today.

Sorry.

I should go back downstairs and see if I can find some unrotten potatoes for dinner. Mum must be wondering where I am.

Best wishes,

Lydia

* * *

Dear Lydia,

The world is not a dark place, okay. I'm fairly certain of that. Maybe it's dark over in your Turramurra mansion there, but over here at Penno Hills, we've got north-facing windows, so we get plenty of sunshine. Come over and let me show you the sun.

Plus, if you came by my place, I could show you something of exquisite beauty: my video collection of the best goals in World Cup history.

I could also play you a particular Tom Waits song in my room, and you can kick back on the bed there, and I'll let you know when a line of music is about to happen that'll get into your soul and cure every inch of that darkness of yours.

And I could introduce you to my little baby brother, Nathaniel, and you could take a look at those cute little toes and have a little conversation with him — "De de de," he'll say, all thoughtful. "Is that so?" you can say, with interest.

If you let me do these things for you, Lyd, you'll see that the world is honest, and not full of rotten potatoes at all.

Love,

Seb

* * *

Dear Seb,

I didn't remember telling you that I lived in a Turramurra mansion. We moved here a few years ago, and Dad wanted me to change schools and go to Abbotsleigh or Loreto, but no way was I going anywhere different from Em and Cass.

I liked those examples you gave of things you find beautiful. Thanks, buddy.

Well, I need to think of a new punishment for Paul Wilson. If I can just make him see what an arsehole he is, I'll feel better. But the plan has just collapsed.

You want to know what happened?

We went over to Em's place last night to work on a joint presentation that we're giving in history, and Em was acting weird. Mrs. T was lying on the couch with cucumbers over her eyes — she said she'd been working until midnight every day this week — and Em started telling her about this theory of Cass's mum. Something to do with there being no right or wrong, just a lot of different ways of looking at the world. It was strange, because she was telling her mum in this hostile way, like she almost wanted her mum to disagree. And Mrs. T just lay there listening and then she said, in a reasonable voice, "Well, I agree, but maybe she's being a bit too postmodern for me. I think there are *some* absolute truths."

"Like what?" Em demanded.

"Well, I think you should never hurt other people, and never hurt yourself. Maybe Patricia agrees with that, anyway. But you could look at the way certain cultures treat women, and you could interpret it as cultural differences, but I say if the women are being mistreated, then I say that's wrong. That's all. Just wrong."

"Oh, that's *ridiculous,*" said Em.

"In what way?" asked her mother.

"Well, you *can't* have absolutes. You can't say that you should never hurt other people or hurt yourself, because maybe you *have* to hurt yourself because someone else has been hurt and they're your friend, and *hurting yourself* is the only way to stop your friend hurting, and —"

"Give me an example of that situation," said Mrs. T.

But Em stamped her foot and ran upstairs to her bedroom.

Cass and I went up there, and she was getting out the stuff for the assignment, slamming books down, and kicking things aside, and making *tch* noises and sighs, while Cass and I opened our eyes at each other until finally we said she had to tell us what was wrong.

Then Em started crying and said she was in love with Charlie.

She said she'd been trying not to notice it because she knows Charlie has to steal Paul Wilson's girlfriend, but she really, really likes him and she just can't stop.

We hadn't actually told Cass about our revenge plan. When she figured out what Em was going on about, she just shook her head and threw her hands in the air, the way her grandma Matilda does.

She said we should forget Paul Wilson and get on with our lives. She said she would like to see him suffer, but not if Em has to suffer. And not if it means stealing a girlfriend. As if a girlfriend was like his wallet or something, instead of a human being.

That was a good point, actually, which I should have thought of.

And then I agreed that I didn't think Em should give up Charlie if she liked him.

But anyway, Em stopped crying while Cass and I talked, and then she started crying again but in a happy way and gave us both hugs, and we didn't do the assignment, we just listened to Em saying all the things she likes about Charlie for the rest of the night.

I'm not supposed to be telling you this, Seb. Em would kill me. But I know I can trust you.

If you think of any other revenge ideas, can you tell me? I'm kind of down again, because I can't stand the thought of Paul Wilson walking around like he's allowed to be walking around.

I guess I'll see you next Saturday for the Assignment at Balmoral Beach. Are you still free?

Lydia

* * *

Dear Lydia,

It's a shame about the revenge not working out. But I've been thinking it was a tragic plan, since I also have the impression that Charlie likes Emily. Furthermore, I think Christina's on the verge of breaking up with Paul all on her own, so the plan was destined to take an unexpected turn.

Maybe you should do what Cass suggests and just forget about it? I've had a lot of thoughts about revenge in the last year, what with almost getting expelled and it nearly breaking my mother's heart. If I did one thing wrong last term, then I would have been chucked out. That included even failing a single exam.

That's why I needed you to help me get out of exams, by the way. Just to get myself a bit of extra time to study, so I wouldn't fail.

Thanks for that.

But anyway, during that crisis time, I had a lot of talks with my mum about violence and so on. And my mum is a pretty cool lady, who tries to speak in my own language: that is, the language of soccer.

This is kind of sweet of her because she doesn't really speak the language. Sometimes she sits down to watch a soccer game with Dad and me, and she leans forward trying to figure out what's going on, and Dad and I shake our heads at each other. But after a few minutes, she remembers the rules and then she starts shouting at the TV as much as we do. And she always says, "Who's going to lose?" and we tell her, then she roots for that team.

So, anyway, last term Mum was driving me home from one of the appointments with the principal and she said, "You know when you're watching a Manchester United game, and they keep getting the ball all the way up the field and then, *just* before they get to the ring, they lose it?"

The ring. I told you my mum was sweet.

"No," I said at the time, "that never happens to Man U. They always score."

"Seb," she said warningly.

So I said, "Okay, sure. That might happen sometimes."

"And you get all excited and you're jumping up and down ready for the victory?"

"Sure," I said, to keep her happy.

"And then it's such a disappointment when they lose the ball at the last second, and you know they have to start all over again?"

"Uh-huh."

"Well," she said, "that's how I feel sometimes watching my eldest son." She meant me. I'm her oldest son. "I can see him working away, doing well at school, heading toward the goalposts, and then *wham*, just when he's almost there, he's in the principal's office because he got into another fight, and I'm heading up to the school to try to talk them out of kicking him off the team."

So that gave me something to think about, and then, while I was still thinking about it, she started talking about football hooligans, and it was clear that she'd been planning this speech for a while. She talked about how they ruin the game because they overreact when their team loses, and they start hurting other people, and sometimes people even die.

"And Seb," she said, "you know that soccer is just a game, don't you?"

I got a bit shocked by this piece of wisdom, but she's actually right. Even if you feel like crap when Man U loses, and you feel like you've been taking E when they win, well, it's still just a game.

So all this comes down to Cass and how that arsehole was bad to her, but is it really worth hurting yourself or hurting Em to get revenge?

You've got to get things into perspective, Lyd.

I hope this has helped.

I can't wait to see you this Saturday, and I could die waiting. But that's not what you call perspective.

See ya,
Seb

* * *

Hey Seb,

I like the sound of your mother.

Also, I'm glad I helped you get through the probation last term. But I've been thinking, did you actually skip school to do those tasks that I gave you, like moving the polar bear sign around the shopping center and putting ribbons around trees?

Okay, I take your point about *perspective,* but I don't think what Paul Wilson did to Cass was a game. I think it was serious, and I think he has to be punished.

Anyhow, it's Friday afternoon, so you probably won't get this until Monday. I'm seeing you at Balmoral tomorrow for the assignment.

I hope it's not too cold at the beach. Just go ahead and build an igloo if it is. You can use sand for that. Put in stained-glass windows and a fireplace.

Great.

Thanks.

See you,

Lyd

* * *

TO: Lydia Jaackson-Oberman

Special Covert Operation Report

Agent: AKA

OPERATION

Operation Balmoral Beach

Assigned by Agent Lydia

Result: Unsuccessful

Agent AKA hereby hands in his badge and gun and resigns.

DETAILS OF FAILURE

Agent AKA proceeded through train, ferry, and buying fish and chips successfully, and thinks that Lydia's message was:

Watch out for windsurfers, weddings, and whales.

However, Agent AKA did not complete the next phase successfully. Instead of behaving like a stranger, Agent AKA moved along the sand to sit next to Agent Lydia and kissed her. This kissing kept up for about half an hour or so, until it got too cold to be on the beach, and then continued on the trip home until we fell asleep and missed Hornsby Station. Agent Lydia seemed fairly into this, but I take full responsibility for the failure.

EXPLANATION OF FAILURE

Have you seen what Agent Lydia looks like? Have you ever sat two meters away from her on the beach and seen the way she hugs her knees in the cold? If so, you don't need an explanation.

QUERY

Lyd, do I actually have to make up another assignment before I can touch you again?

* * *

Hey Seb,

You can keep your badge and your gun, etc. I'm okay with what you did. Actually, I liked it. I'll put in a good word with the boss.

But don't you want to keep playing?

Lyd

* * *

Dear Lydia,

I don't want to keep playing, I just want to see you.

A lot of time has passed since we started writing letters, and I feel like I know a lot about you, but at the same time there's a whole lot I don't know at all. It confuses me, Lyd. Example: I don't know what you like and what you don't like. You could even have a boyfriend, for all I know.

If you do, you're cheating on him by spending so much time inside my head.

And, I guess, that was technically cheating, all that messing around at Balmoral. I wouldn't tell your boyfriend about that.

Love,

Seb

* * *

Dear Seb,

Okay, I'll tell you what I like and what I don't like.

I don't like sultanas in cakes, especially in a cake that seems to be sultana-free. I don't like mornings, especially cold mornings, and I don't like stockings, shoes, shoelaces, shoe polish, hair scrunchies, hair dryers, and train passes.

I like socks, pens, nail polish, detective novels, and spy movies.

I like fairy penguins, whales, huskies, and pelicans. I like looking for four-leaf clovers and locket shells.

I like Bacardi Breezers, Kahluá and milk, sangria, and tequila shots.

And I'd like a tattoo of a lizard on my ankle.

And now I'll tell you some things that I liked about last weekend.

I liked the way you took that whole journey to Balmoral without looking at me once. But all the time I felt like you were crinkling the corners of your eyes for me.

I liked the way you ordered fish and chips and a can of Coke, and said no thanks to the special seafood sauce, and then the way you said "Hup" at the last minute and changed your mind and got the seafood sauce. The girl at the register smiled at you when you said "Hup," but you didn't notice because you were getting out your wallet.

I liked the way one windsurfer was out on the cold gray water at Balmoral, and when he fell, he'd stay there patiently in the water, and let the wind pick him up again with the sail.

I liked the way you ate your fish and chips, looking out at the sea, with a big smile like you'd given up trying not to smile.

I liked how you cleared the smile away with the napkin, wiped your hands and took out a drawing pad and pencil, and started sketching without looking back at me once. I liked how you seemed to be sketching the windsurfer or the sea, because you were frowning into the distance.

I especially liked it when you shifted so I could see what you were drawing, and it was actually a portrait of me, and I liked how you smiled when you heard my reaction. And I liked how you wrote a message on the corner of the page: *"There's a whale on the horizon — can you see the spout?"*

I don't think there was actually a whale there. But maybe.

And I liked it a lot when you put the picture away, slid over to where I was sitting, and kissed me. I liked how you did that fast, as if it was kind of inevitable.

I haven't got a boyfriend at the moment. If I did, I wouldn't have let you kiss me, Seb.

I don't think I want a boyfriend. I've had three boyfriends from this school and it never works out. I always feel like I disappear; I always feel like it's just physical and like they never really hear me when I speak.

Last year I was with a guy called Sergio for three months. I thought he was sexy as hell. He's got a burn scar on his face, and people stared at him wherever we went, which he said he liked, but I was always so pissed off at them. Sergio called me his "wild-eyed girl," and the more he said it the more wild I got.

In the end I broke up with him because I was turning into this angry person all the time — like I knew that was what he liked about me, and I couldn't ever smile and be stupid, which is also what I like to be.

Plus I started thinking that "wild-eyed girl" made me sound like a horse.

So, see, I always start to act like someone I'm not.

That's why I want to keep writing letters, okay. And maybe meeting up sometimes if our letters say we can. It's the only way I can stay honest to myself.

Love,

Lydia

* * *

Lydia,

I don't really want to hear about Sergio being sexy as hell. But okay, thanks for the news.

Do you really turn into someone else when you're with guys? I find that difficult to get my head around, because you seem like a fairly strong person, Lyd.

Also, do you really think you are "yourself" in your letters? I remember your first letter to me, you told me you were a fish and your mother was a pinball machine.

I don't want my hand to be holding this pen, I want it to be holding your hand.

Can I phone you sometime?

Love,

Seb

* * *

Hey Seb,

If we're not writing to each other — if we're just kissing and stuff — then why should it be me? Why shouldn't it be any other girl?

Lyd

* * *

Lyd,

You're not making sense.

I love your letters, and I want you to keep writing them, if you want to. But you can't kiss a girl made out of ink and paper. Let's hang out together. Let's talk on the phone.

You have to realize that boys don't write. Girls write. Boys don't.

Seb

* * *

Hey Seb,

Boys don't write, eh? You might want to mention that to William Shakespeare, Charles Dickens, etc. I get the feeling they're boys.

Wait a minute, I get it. Boys don't write unless they can show that they're better at it than girls are.

Is that what you mean?

Can you tell me something? Did you see a photo of me before we ever saw each other? Is that how you knew it was me in the Blue Danish?

Lyd

* * *

Lydia,

You keep asking me that. I didn't cheat on the task, Lyd.

But I looked up your phone number yesterday. Maybe I'll call you tonight. You want to kick a soccer ball around on the weekend? This letter can give us permission.

Love,

Seb

* * *

Seb,

Em told me yesterday that you and Charlie found a photo of me in a magazine when you first got my letter last term.

So I guess you knew what I looked like before you saw me.

So I guess you've been lying to me every time I've asked about that. I thought I'd just give you one last chance. But you lied to me again.

I guess I know what kind of a guy you are — the kind who's only interested in what a girl looks like. Not in what she says.

Lydia

* * *

Dear Lydia,

Okay, I get where you're coming from. I get it: You hate lies, and you think the world is evil like a rotten potato, and now you think I'm part of the evil. I see how you might think that.

But listen Lydia, you're thinking wrong. I'm not part of the evil: Everything else I've said to you is true. You were the one who suggested the competition where we had to recognize the other one first — how could I not use my advantage? And then I didn't tell you because I didn't want you to be mad. But trust me, it was just messing around.

No offense, but it's not like you're full of the truth yourself. You go on about your parents fighting in the breakfast pyramid, and then we hear that your dad's getting your room painted for you, and your mum's kicking back with you and a couple of lamingtons, not to mention driving you around the neighborhood. (And now I've had about three conversations with your mum, trying to call you, and she seems like a good person, by the way.)

Anyhow, why did Emily have to tell you about it? There are too many words coming out of girls' mouths. Why do girls have to talk so much?

Love,

Seb

* * *

Seb,

No, you're right, this is all Emily's fault. All the words coming out of her mouth.

Just for your information, she found out about this a few weeks ago and only told me now because she's got a broken heart and isn't thinking clearly.

And don't suggest that I'm as deceptive as you. Maybe I make up stuff about my parents, but that's poetic license. You lied to me.

Lydia

* * *

Lyd,

Poetic license, was it? Guess what, I've got one of them too. I picked one up when I was down at the license bureau getting my learner's permit. So we're both allowed to exaggerate.

Come on, Lyd. Get over it. You're so into game playing, you forget what real life is. Get some perspective.

Love,

Seb

* * *

Seb,

In relation to "game playing," could I just remind you that you started the games? Remember last term when you needed me to prove I could be *trusted* by passing your *tests*? Which meant doing things to get you out of exams?

I think we should stop writing, okay.

Lydia

* * *

Lydia,

Please stop calling yourself "Lydia." What happened to Lyd? PLEASE DON'T STOP writing to me. I'm SORRY SORRY SORRY. Charlie tells me he and Em have stopped writing now, so I can't even get him to lobby her on my behalf. It's all falling apart. Are you mad at me because I keep ringing? I'll stop, if you promise to write back to me.

I'll write ten-page letters if you like. I'll keep doing assignments. I'll do anything you want. I just want to touch your face again, I just want to see you chalking a cue and narrowing your eyes at the pool table.

Love,

Seb

* * *

Lyd,

I can't stand your silence. What can I do to make it up to you?

Seb

* * *

Dear Seb,

You can't.

Yours sincerely,

Lydia Jaackson-Oberman

27. Winter Term / Cassie

Thursday, 4:30 A.M., half a moon in the sky

Hello there, Diary.

I guess you've been missing me.

Also, I guess you're supposed to write more frequently than this in a diary, like say every day? As opposed to when you can't sleep. And you're supposed to talk about what's going on in your life and what the weather's like and who you've got a crush on, and how many pimples on your face, etc., etc., but you know what I think? I think it's all just

words

words

words

so why don't you write them yourself.

* * *

Friday, 7:30 A.M., cloudy

I wonder if Claire, the counselor, knows that I'm crazy.

I guess my mum keeps her distracted most of the time by giving her imaginary legal advice.

And Lyd and Em are also distracted these days, seeing as they want to get revenge on the perfect stranger, even though I keep telling them not to. They know who he is, even. Lydia tracked him down. From the glitter in an envelope I sent him.

I didn't want to know his name.

But you want to know something, I've been secretly checking the mailbox at school, in case Matthew Dunlop (or whoever he is) replied to my glitter letter. Which he hasn't, of course.

* * *

Wednesday, nighttime, raining

It's cold outside, but we have gas heating. One small gas heater is making this whole studio toasty warm.

Here is my attempt to write a diary like a normal girl who goes to school.

Well, you're not going to believe this, but Mr. Pappo has not been turning up to any classes for the last three days! Everyone is trying to keep this quiet so the school doesn't notice and send in substitute teachers. Mrs. Lawrence broke her collarbone trying out a dance step on top of her desk! Damien Carrol and Helena Wong broke up on Wednesday because Damien needed more space, but then they got back together on Thursday, and then they broke up this morning because Helena wanted to consider her options.

Also, a bird flew into the classroom in my history class, but why would you care about that.

* * *

Later on Wednesday, also nighttime

Sometimes, bits of craziness escape into the outside me. Like, I get addicted to writing letters to a boy who hates my guts.

Plus I forget a lot of stuff. I forget to do homework, or to meet up with friends, or to finish sentences when I'm talking. I'll go into the bathroom to clean my teeth but won't even get out the toothpaste. I'll just stare at my fingernails for half an hour and then come back out again. Once, I came to school without my socks on. Just my shoes. I pretended I did that on purpose.

* * *

Tuesday, afternoon, blue sky outside

Today, Em and Lyd were arguing about a story Lyd wrote for English. Mr. Botherit read it out to the class, and everyone was practically crying at the end because she'd killed off all her characters. She always does that.

So at lunchtime, Em said that Lydia should have let the characters get married and move to a mansion by the sea. But Lydia said that's dishonest because a week later they'd be divorced and the house would be knocked over by a tidal wave. Em said Lydia just had to keep writing until the characters fell in love again and built a cottage in the mountains. Lyd said that was impossible because the man would be dead, drowned in the tidal wave, and the woman would have been left destitute, etc., etc., etc.

Claire can't say the word "dead."

She keeps saying we *lost* Dad, which is stupid because if you lose something, you can usually find it if you make enough effort and phone up all the lost property offices and taxi companies. Unless maybe someone stole it, in which case it isn't really lost.

* * *

Sunday, maybe lunchtime, some sun around

Sometimes when Claire uses the word "lost," I think she's trying to point out that we didn't put in as much effort as we should have. Like, if we'd just tried another herbal remedy or started eating zucchini all the time, then we might have found a cure for Dad.

I don't really think that.

Just like I don't really think that I'm crazy. I know that it's common to forget stuff, and be absentminded, and it's just called SADNESS.

I know for a fact that it's not our fault that Dad died, and I know Claire is not trying to say that.

But it's a lot easier to be crazy or mad than to just get on with living.

* * *

Tuesday, raining quietly

Imagine if my dad was downstairs right now, calling me to come and have breakfast.

Hey, Diary, it's two o'clock in the morning, and you know what? That would be a weird time to have breakfast.

And you know what else? I hate myself. Because in actual fact, I'm lying to Lydia and Emily. They're being so nice, like they came over for dinner last week, and stayed really late talking to us, even though I'm sure they were bored out of their minds hearing my mother lecture them about life and careers, etc.

And they don't even know that the whole thing with Matthew Dunlop was all my fault.

Because I kept writing.

Okay, let's think about what a NORMAL person would have done when they got that first letter from Matthew Dunlop.

A normal person would have said, "Jesus, Brooker kids are psychopaths," and chucked the letter away.

So what did I think I was doing, eh Diary?

Every day I try to make myself tell Lydia the truth, and every day I can't because I don't want her to know that I'm deranged in the head.

* * *

Tuesday after school, eating ginger biscuits

Actually, writing here in Dad's studio, I feel like I should just talk about my dad, really.

It's like when I first came back to school, and it seemed strange that anyone could talk about anything other than my dad. Like we shouldn't have been analyzing *My Brilliant Career* in English, we should have been sitting around chatting about Dad's favorite books. And getting mad about how unfair it was that the leukemia came back after four years. The doctors had said that if it stayed away for more than five years, then it probably wouldn't come back. But it just made the deadline.

After a while I stopped wanting to talk about Dad at school. I just wanted to keep it all in my bedroom, and in this studio, because I didn't think I could carry it outside.

Remember when Dad was feeling bad, and he'd lie on the couch over there and sometimes I read stories to him? His favorite books were Roald Dahl's *Tales of the Unexpected*. When there were bits about sex, he'd tell me to keep reading but cover my ears.

Hey, guess what, I just looked out the window and Lydia's standing at the front door.

* * *

Wednesday, early morning, frost on lawn

I've noticed that in movies there's always just one reason for everything.

Like, it turns out that the guy's a murderer because of this one time when his mother made him wear a pink hat to school and all the kids teased him.

That's it: Bang. He's a murderer.

It would be good if it was as simple as that.

Or maybe not: There'd be too many murderers.

So anyway, Diary, last time I spoke to you it was yesterday afternoon and Lydia was standing outside my front door.

And you know what happened?

I told her about how it was all my fault with Matthew Dunlop. How I kept writing to Matthew Dunlop even when he threatened to break my fingers.

She just blinked once, when I told her, and said, "I wonder why you kept writing back?"

Not like it was a question that I had to answer, but like an unexplained event in a movie we just saw. Like we could figure it out if we talked long enough.

We couldn't figure it out, though.

I said, "Do you think I'm crazy?"

She looked at me and said, "Hmm."

* * *

From: Emily.Thompson@ashburyhigh.com.au
To: Cassie.Aganovic@ashburyhigh.com.au
Subject: Is Cassie Crazy?!

Dear Cassie,

Well! Lydia has given me a Secret Assignment, which is to send you an e-mail explaining that you are not crazy. She has given herself the same assignment, so expect an e-mail from her too.

Her assignments have really changed lately, haven't they? There is almost no shoplifting or "prank calling" or cake baking. It is all about writing things down, and I have to say I'm a fairly different person when I write things down. So, that's interesting.

You are not crazy, Cassie. That needs no explanation.

But you are confused as to why you continued writing to Matthew Dunlop even when he made strange and unlikely threats? You have been keeping that a secret from us because you thought it would make us aghast?

Well! Cassie, no! I am not aghast. I am tilting my head to the side with understanding. And I am glad you gave Lydia permission to tell me the story. For it is perfectly clear to me.

I shall explain it as follows:

I think you were probably looking for a way to feel hurt. Because maybe you can't believe you still feel bad, even a whole year after your dad died. Remember how you used to get so many injuries, Cass? Because you are athletic. And remember that one time when you tried to high-jump a bookshelf in your living room, and somehow a big heavy vase got knocked over and landed on your toe? Lyd and I gasped, but you just looked down at the bloody, mushed-up toe, in true Cass style, and said, "Interesting."

Then I kind of fainted, so I don't know what happened next.

It is my consternation that, by writing to a boy who was cruel, you were looking for an injury which would interest you, and distract you from the hurting of your heart.

That is my theory.

My recommendation for the future is this: If you need someone to be cruel to you, make sure you come to Lydia and me. We would be glad to be cruel.

Now, one final thought for this e-mail and then I'd better go and do an exam. Although you might not know it, Cassie, EVERYBODY loves you. You are very popular here at Ashbury, as is the nature of skinny girls who are excellent at sport (running, high jump, basketball, etc.) and who do not have a single drop of blood.

By "blood" I mean to say "bad blood."

But there is more to this, Cass. It is your gentle and interested way of listening, and your dry and/or musical way of being funny. The point is, Paul Wilson could have had the privilege of you for his friend. If only he had given you a chance.

If anyone is crazy here, Cass, it is Paul Wilson. He, my friend, is a psychopath.

Lots of love,

Emily

* * *

From: Lydia.Oberman@ashburyhigh.com.au
To: Cassie.Aganovic@ashburyhigh.com.au
Subject: Crazy Cassie

Dear Cassie,

Well, just pondering the mystery of why you decided to keep writing letters to a person who belongs in a high-security mental institution.

And what I think is that it was maybe a power thing. Like this counselor, Claire, was telling you what to do. And you knew it was stupid, what Claire wanted, so In a weird way you got power back by going ahead and doing it. It's like when you're little and your mum says you have to eat your vegetables even though you hate them, so you go ahead and eat so many of them and so fast that you throw up.

Which is the sign of an interesting and powerful person, Cass, not a crazy person.

Anyway, that's my theory, and you can take it or leave it, but just keep in mind that I am a genius, so I'm probably right.

Lots of love,

Lyd

* * *

Friday, midnight, full moon with small tear out of corner

I think it was because I was scared of him.

That doesn't make sense, I know.

I'll explain.

See, to begin, nobody knows what causes leukemia — they think there are some contributing factors such as smoking cigarettes, or exposure to radiation, or even some kinds of cancer treatment (brilliant). But my dad didn't have any of those reasons. So he got this idea that it was because he'd always been kind of nervous — all his life, he was anxious in social/professional situations. He said that he bet it was all the fear that got caught up inside him and made him sick.

And one time, he was talking about this idea of his, and he said to me, "You never be afraid of anything, will you, Cassie?" And I said okay.

So, okay, earlier this year they were asking for volunteers for the Spring Concert. And when I saw the notice about that, I thought about how I'd like to be able to sing onstage, and maybe even make a career out of being a singer one day. But then I just said to myself, "Yeah, right," and walked away. Because I'm always too scared to sing in front of a crowd.

And then SUDDENLY I remembered that conversation with my dad — how he told me never to be afraid, and I'd said okay, like it was a promise or something.

I made up my mind I would definitely volunteer for the stupid concert. It would be like a message to my dad, that I was doing what he wanted, and a good example too, because he liked to hear me singing.

But, guess what, I didn't raise my hand when they called for volunteers.

I just left it there by my side. With my heart thumping like crazy. I was so scared even of the *idea* of raising my hand. My *hand* scared me when I looked at it.

I hated myself for that.

I hate myself for it still.

After that I got more and more depressed, wishing I'd raised my hand, and thinking how hopeless I am, and kind of like how I let my dad down because actually I'm scared all the time, like scared of the nighttime, now that it's just Mum and me here. I keep thinking I hear someone breaking in. One day I spent the afternoon putting extra deadlocks on all the doors.

This is a long story, but I'm almost at the end.

The end is this: When this Brookfield guy wrote his first threatening letter, I was really frightened. I'm kind of scared of Brookfield kids to begin with, but this guy seemed like a lunatic.

So I thought, okay, here's where all the being-scared finishes.

And I wrote back to him.

And I kept thinking the whole time that the being-scared was finished, and I kept writing back, *whatever he said,* and it was like, the scarier he got, the better it was for me, and every time he tried to make me go away, I'd think, kind of angrily, "Okay, Dad, you want to see how unscared I can be?" and then I just kept talking like a crazy girl, I guess.

Anyway, that's my long theory for why I kept writing.

I don't know.

Probably, I did it for lots of different reasons.

Probably, my dad got sick because of lots of different reasons too. Not just because he was afraid.

* * *

Sunday, nighttime

Today we were at Lyd's mother's studio because she invited us along to get makeovers. We didn't tell her that we go there all the time on our own. There was no reason for her to know that.

It's strange to think that Mrs. Jaackson used to be a famous celebrity and now she just wears long satin jackets and a lot of lipstick. She's kind of dreamy a lot of the time, which Lyd says is senile dementia or alcoholism, one or the other, but I think she's maybe just dreamy.

Anyhow, while Mrs. Jaackson was doing our makeup, we were having this argument about whether we actually exist or not, because how do you know it's not all someone else's dream? Emily thought it could be her dream.

Also, about whether the color blue is actually blue.

And then Mrs. Jaackson said out of the blue (but what is blue?), that the trouble with us is that we all need to get nose studs.

Lydia and I wanted to do it, but Em went ballistic, so we didn't. We went to a pub instead, because we all looked about twenty-five the way she did our makeup, I swear.

* * *

Sunday, later, raining

Actually, now that I think about it, what Lyd's mum said was that we've all forgotten who we are. We were having philosophical arguments about whose mother was right between my mum and Em's mum, and then *Lydia's* mother said that the only thing that counts is to be true to yourself.

Whatever, I thought. Because people are always telling us to *be ourselves* or be *true to ourselves,* and I always think: *Whatever.* Because who is myself?

"But who is myself?" Emily asked.

Then Lyd's mum said she didn't mean it that way. She meant that we had to listen for the truth inside our heads.

"If you have a thought," she said, "ask yourself why. And then always ask: '*Are you sure?*' For instance: 'I'm angry.' '*Why?*' 'Because he ate my cherry pie.' '*Are you sure that's why you're mad?*' 'Okay, because he often eats the pie.' '*Are you sure?*'"

"Mum," said Lydia, "what are you talking about?"

But Mrs. Jaackson just laughed and finished putting eye shadow on Em. And then she kissed the top of all our heads.

And then she said the solution was to go and get silver nose studs.

* * *

Monday, three A.M., unable to sleep

Am I angry?

Yes.

Why?

Because the leukemia came back.

Are you sure that's why you're mad?

And because Dad didn't fight it hard enough.

Are you sure?

Okay, because Dad wasn't *strong* enough to fight it.

Are you sure?

No. He wasn't weak. He was just scared.

Are you sure?

Okay, well, that's the thing. What if I inherited that? That being scared.

Are you sure?

So I'll never be brave. So he'll never be proud.

Are you sure?

What do you mean am I sure?

Are you sure?

Do you ever say anything else?

* * *

Friday, late afternoon, dark blue sky

I thought I would give you an update, the update being that Lydia and Emily have both got broken hearts.

You never know what direction things are going to go in, do you? One minute they're figuring out how they can bring Seb and Charlie to the formal (even though we're not allowed to bring guys from other schools), and next minute it's all gone down the sinkhole. I'm not clear on why they're fighting with the boys, but it's something to do with letters, and I have to say, I don't know about letters. Maybe talking is better.

I should try and be more decisive like Mum. She always has a definite opinion. An example being that she has had a definite opinion about Claire the counselor from our very first session, the opinion being that Claire is an idiot.

I'll tell you one thing, though, Diary, and it's this: That even though Lydia is upset about Seb, she's been coming over to my place every couple of days lately (ever since I confessed the truth to her about Matthew's letters), like pretending she was just in the neighborhood. Usually, we talk about nothing, maybe watch TV, maybe play a game of pool on Dad's old table, which he built himself, by the way, and which is a work of art.

And since Dad's table is in his studio, it seems normal to chat about Dad, and I just smile to myself sometimes, because Lydia knows my dad almost as well as I do. She even remembers stuff that I'd forgotten, right back to when we were little and Dad used to teach us Croatian words, and make the first ice-cream spider for whoever pronounced the words best.

And I'll tell you something else. This afternoon, while we were playing pool, I accidentally told Lydia my theory about why I kept writing to Matthew Dunlop. About how I felt like I had to write because I'd failed my dad, seeing as I was too scared to volunteer to sing on stage.

So I was just leaning against the wall as I said all this, while Lydia was sinking one ball after another, not looking at me, but occasionally nodding to show she was listening. And then when I finished, she chalked the pool cue, leaned forward, and sunk the eight ball.

And then she narrowed her eyes at me and said, "Well, Cass, do you know how mad I am with you about this?"

Her voice actually did sound angry.

And she said, "You think that your dad *wants* you to do things that might get you hurt? You think your dad's *disappointed* in you for not singing on stage? You've forgotten your dad? Is that what you're saying?"

Then I got a bit mad too, and started talking in a rising voice like, "You think I've forgotten my dad? You think you know him better than I do?" Stuff like that.

Lydia calmed down and said no, she didn't think she knew him better than I did, only that she knew one thing for sure.

"What?" I said.

"I know exactly what your dad would say if he could see you sitting at the assembly, trying to raise your hand to volunteer to sing but feeling too scared of the stage. You want to hear what he would have said?"

She didn't wait for my answer, she just put on a fairly good imitation of my father's accent and his way of speaking and she said, "'Cassie, I'm so proud that you even *think* of singing on the stage, and do you know how much I will cheer for you when you do?'"

Then she looked at me in her fiery way. *"Disappointed?"* she said, kind of to herself and all full of contempt. "Give me a *break*."

* * *

Monday, evening time, in the kitchen, very windy outside

Sometimes I think the trouble with talking to you, Diary, is that everything seems so *serious* when I write it down. Okay, Friday was kind of dramatic, and I was crying half the night, but when I woke up on Saturday morning I felt kind of calm and happy, and Mum and I had pancakes with maple syrup and strawberries for breakfast. And then today, at school, Em arrived wearing her summer uniform and her beret, because someone had told her that all heat escapes out the top of your head. So she thought she could stay warm if she just wore a hat all day. Lydia and I found 127 goose bumps on her arms at lunch while she pretended not to hear us counting, and it was just funny and I thought —

Hang on, I think someone just put a letter underneath the front door. Weird.

* * *

Monday, 6:35 P.M.

Dear Cassie,

Well, you are going to think this is strange, me writing to you now.

My name is Paul Wilson, and I'm at Brookfield. I got your letter last term in the Ashbury-Brookfield Pen Pal Project — and I was pleased to

hear a little about you. And obviously, I was supposed to reply and become your pen pal.

But I didn't reply! (As you probably noticed.) I've just been way too busy — I'm an actor and I've got the lead role in our school drama this year, so I've been rehearsing my arse off!

To tell you the truth, the only reason I'm writing now is that I'm a wreck. I'm ashamed to tell you this, but I was the "loser" in an (unprovoked) fight this afternoon.

This guy in my year (Seb Mantegna) ambushed me as I was walking home from school. I'm walking along, minding my own business, thinking about my gorgeous new girlfriend (sorry to bring her up, but she's never far from the top floor of my consciousness) — what was I saying? I'm just walking along and out of nowhere Seb Mantegna turns up and starts laying into me.

Now, I'm not a little guy, but he's got a black belt in karate or whatever, and the fact was, I was just not interested. I don't believe in violence. So I was trying to calm him down, you know, defend myself.

The result was a black eye, bloody nose, etc., and me lying on the ground getting kicked in the gut.

Wow. Not a pretty picture.

So why am I telling you this?

Well, when Seb kicked me for the final, vicious time, he said, "This is for what you did to Cass Aganovic, you scum-sucking arsehole."

Whoa! "Who's Cass Aganovic?" I pondered as I tried to get my breath (and my dignity) back.

And then I remembered — it's that Ashbury girl who wrote to me way back last term.

So, Cassie, do you happen to know anything about this? Is Seb a great friend of yours? Or are you as lost as I am?

The one good thing is that this guy — Seb — has been in trouble for fighting before.

So this should be enough to get him expelled.

All the best,

Paul Wilson

P.S. I just looked up your address (your last name is fairly unique!), and I think I'll swing by and put this under your door right away. The faster we get to the bottom of this, the better. Hope you don't mind that I now know where you live! Maybe I'll spot you through a window!

P.P.S. You know, it occurs to me that Seb Mantegna is going off to Newcastle for some art show tomorrow. I'll make sure I get to the principal first thing in the morning and stop them from letting him go! Am I wicked to look forward to the disappointment on his face? No. In any case, he shouldn't be allowed to represent the school — he's obviously unhinged. Deranged in the head.

Take care, Cassie,

Paul

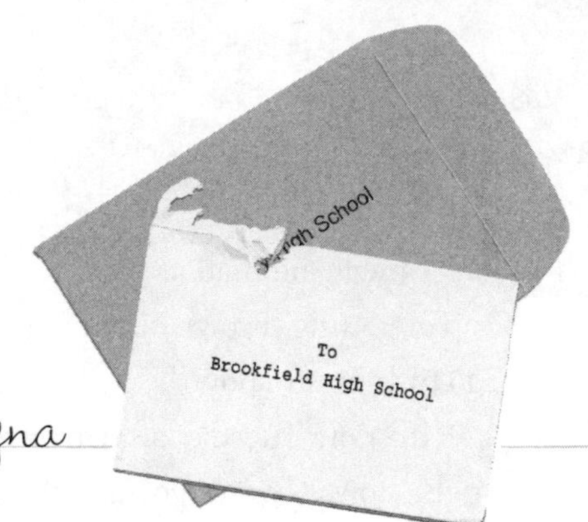

28. Saving Seb Mantegna

Tuesday

Dear Charlie,

GUESS WHAT WE HAVE DONE?!?!

WE HAVE KIDNAPPED PAUL WILSON!

I'm not joking, it's true. (And Charlie, therefore you should speak to me again, and listen to me! And forgive me. Forget all about the gas leak incident, okay, as that incident just fails by comparison.)

We had to kidnap Paul because he was going to tell the school that Seb attacked him, which would have stopped Seb from going to the art show! Which we all know was his dream.

Don't worry, though, it is not an illegal kidnapping, as Paul does not know he has been kidnapped.

Please forgive me now, okay, great, thanks. I have to go as I'm just rushing this at afternoon roll call, which I'm attending on behalf of Cass and Lyd and me.

Love,

Em

* * *

Dear Seb,

I might be mad at you, but I didn't want you beating someone up or getting thrown out of your school. And I really wanted you to go to your art show.

It's now Tuesday afternoon, so I'm hoping you're at your show right now. I won't go into details, but we've been keeping Paul distracted for today. I don't know how we can stop him going to the principal tomorrow, though.

Lydia

* * *

Wednesday

Dear Em,

You guys took care of Paul Wilson so Seb could go to his art show? I just saw Seb, and guess what, he won some prize at the show.

I don't just forgive you, Em, I completely adore you.

Love,

Charlie

P.S. Em? How exactly did you kidnap Wilson without him noticing?

* * *

Dear Lydia,

Okay, I'm writing this with the full expectation that I'll be expelled when Paul gets around to telling the teachers how I kicked his arse.

But I've got a heart full of happiness. Because it's so good to see your words again, and because I went to the art show yesterday. Which was an excellent day, with the canapés as promised, and my art teacher full of canapé-like conversation on the train.

I got to school expecting to be thrown out on the spot, and I couldn't believe it when the art teacher and I just headed to the station, brazen as a pair of cockatoos. I thought maybe God had sent a truck to run Paul down on his way to the principal's office.

I now realize that you are God.

How did you even know I'd attacked Paul Wilson? How did you keep him away all day?

These are the questions that mystify me.

You're right, Lyd, it was a stupid thing to do, attacking the Year 10 Form Captain and star of the school drama. But I swear on David Beckham's haircut, Paul Wilson is the last person I plan to beat up in my whole life. Unless, let's say, it's absolutely necessary to beat someone up.

So you know that I'm not a maniac who lays into people at random, I'll tell you what happened with Paul.

I'm walking home from school, thinking about your beautiful face, and even more beautiful personality, and trying to figure out how I might see them again, and I notice Paul Wilson across the road, walking along with good posture like the arrogant prick that he is.

I started thinking as follows: It's the fault of that guy that Lyd thinks the world is an evil place that you can't trust, and it's the fault of that attitude of Lyd's that she's taking so long to forgive me for a small error of mine.

"Hey arsehole," I said, but in a friendly way, so he thought I was just saying hi.

"Hey cockbrain," he said in response.

Then I crossed over the road, and we walked along for a bit, pretending to like each other. I raised the fact that Ashbury girls are hot. He agreed but added that they're cock-teasing rich bitches, or words like that. I acted like I was interested in this opinion and asked if he'd had personal experience. He said he could tell from the way they looked at him.

So then I asked whether he got a penfriend at Ashbury in Radison's class.

And you know what he did? He told me what he did to Cassie. In shorthand form, but basically it was all there, like a funny story.

Like maybe he'd been waiting to tell someone?

So I said, "Jesus, you really are an arsehole," and beat the crap out of him.

You have to admit, that's an unusual situation.

Love,

Seb

* * *

Thursday

Dear Seb,

I hope you're still at school to get this letter. Sorry we couldn't figure out a way to stop Paul from telling on you ever, e.g., we could have killed him. But I'm happy we got you to the art show — I heard you won a prize, and I'm so proud of you I can't stop smiling.

Okay, I'll now tell you what happened with Paul Wilson.

The night before your art show, Cass found a letter under the front door of her home, which was from Paul. He basically told her you'd attacked him, and that he was going to get revenge by telling the principal the next morning.

He must have thought that Cass had arranged the attack, and he wanted to let her know he was still the winner.

So Cass figured out this plan to make sure he couldn't get to say anything until after your show.

Then she called Em and me around and we worked out the details.

So this is what happened.

Early in the morning, Em phoned Paul Wilson's place and put on a posh voice. She said that she was a casting agent who sometimes went to rehearsals of school plays to scout for new talent. (Okay. Shut up. It was a long shot. But he fell for every word.)

"Now, I've been at some of your Brookfield play rehearsals lately," Em said, "and I've been *extremely* excited by your work, young man."

She was reading from a script which we'd written together.

Cass and I could hear Paul's voice on the other end of the phone. He was trying to be polite, like "Well, that's very kind of you," with this little chuckle.

Then Em says, "I've been meaning to suggest you come in for a photo shoot, but I've got a minor emergency and I'm calling to ask for your help. A local production company is filming the final scenes of a made-for-TV movie today, and they had a young actor lined up for a small part — but, as luck would have it, he's got food poisoning and can't do it!"

"Oh no!" said Paul.

"The filming is way over time," continued Em, "and Heath and Naomi have to fly back to L.A. tomorrow — so it's got to be done today!"

Originally Cass wanted Josh Hartnett and Reese Witherspoon to be flying back to L.A. tomorrow, but then we decided to Australianize it.

"Oh dear!" says Paul, sounding like the biggest nerd on earth.

"So the producers called me, and I was going through my regular list, but I just kept seeing your *face* in my *mind's eye,* and I think you'd be perfect for this role."

Paul goes, "Really?"

"Really. I phoned your school principal, got your contact details, and also got her permission to take you out of school for the day."

(Actually, we got the contact details out of the phone book. We tried three Wilsons in the Hills district before we found him.)

Anyway, Em stopped and Cass mouthed at her, "If that's not a problem for you."

"If that's not a problem for you," Em added.

Paul tried to switch on a professional voice and said, "That's not a problem at all — although" — and he got slightly panicked — "I was in a bit of an — accident last night — and I've got a bit of a bruise around one of my eyes. . . ."

"You clearly don't know the magic of makeup artists, do you?" Em says smoothly, which was some pretty amazing improvisation on her part.

"We'd obviously like you to come by right away so you can learn your lines and get your makeup and costuming done," Em continues, going back to her script.

And Paul says, "No problem."

I think I already told you that my mum is one of the owners of a small production studio? The receptionist, Mary-Ellen, lets us hang out in their makeup section when we don't feel like going to school.

So Em gave Paul the address of the studio.

And we asked Mary-Ellen to watch out for our "friend," Paul Wilson, and send him to the makeup room when he arrived.

That's where I met him, and I pretended I was like the director's trainee assistant, and I gave him this five-page script which I'd written.

He spent all morning practicing his lines into one of the mirrors.

I made him play this boy who's having a mental breakdown in the middle of a disaster scene. So he had these really stupid lines, such as a bit where he had to burst into tears and say, "Mummy? My socks are falling down!" and also another bit where he has to have a sneezing fit.

I kept going in and out of the room, pretending I was doing stuff with makeup, and trying not to crack up at the way he kept trying out different kinds of sneezes.

Then I asked Jerry, the makeup artist, to go in there and give him the most over-the-top makeup job ever. Jerry had a good excuse for it too, because of Paul's black eye (which didn't look that bad to me — he's a bit of a wimp if he calls that getting smashed). Anyway, Jerry did a fantastic job. Paul looked like a vampire.

We sent him off in a taxi into town and told him to meet the film crew in Martin Place. Then we gave Mary-Ellen a message to give him if he called, and we hung out in the reception area of the studio and waited.

He finally called around four-thirty. Mary-Ellen didn't know what was going on, but she knew enough to put it on speaker phone so we could hear.

He asked if there were any messages for him, in this worried voice. Like he probably thought he'd gone to the wrong place and messed up the whole movie.

And Mary-Ellen said, all innocent, "Oh yes, there's a message here for you from Cassie Aganovic. She says she got your letter under her door last night, but she doesn't have a clue who you are."

There was this dead silence on the other end of the phone.

"Hello?" Mary-Ellen said. "Hello? Are you there?"

"There's a message from *who*?" Paul says.

"From Cassie Aganovic."

"Does she — does she *work* there?"

"No, she doesn't."

"Okay, well, what about the movie? I'm supposed to be meeting Heath and Naomi here, and —"

"Heath and Naomi? I don't know what you're talking about. I just have this message for you — would you like me to read it again?"

"No — I just — I thought —"

Then you could practically hear the whole thing tumbling down in Paul Wilson's head as he figured out what had happened. His breathing got heavy and fast, and he was trying to slow it down. And then he said, really quietly, "I'm sorry, I think I have the wrong number," and hung up.

Mary-Ellen put the phone down and looked over at us with her eyebrows raised, like: *Is that what you wanted?* Then she went back to her paperback novel.

I have to tell you, Em, Cass, and I were silent for a moment. We have a capacity for feeling bad, which we always catch from each other. And I know all three of us were thinking about his voice when he said, "I'm sorry, I think I have the wrong number." Like you never heard disappointment so heavy in your life.

And Em said, "That sure got him," in a doubtful kind of voice, and what she really meant was: *Did we go too far?*

Like, to send someone over the moon, thinking they were going to be a star. And then to crumple up the moon in their face?

Then Cass said, really quiet and straight-faced: "Mummy? My socks are falling down."

Mary-Ellen shook her head at us from the reception desk, we were laughing so hard.

I'll tell you what I've been thinking. That Em and I spent all that time trying to take away the thing that Paul Wilson loved the most. Which we thought must be his girlfriend. Whereas Cass figured out exactly what it was that he loved most:

Himself.

Or at least, his idea of himself.

He was so sure of himself that he didn't even doubt it for one single second when Em phoned up, pretending to be a casting agent.

And Cass took all that away. For one day, anyhow.

So, anyway, Seb, I guess you don't want to talk about you and me when you're waiting to find out whether you're going to be expelled or not. But I just wanted to say that I maybe overreacted about the way you tricked me, you know, seeing the photo before you saw me? We were just playing a game, but I turned it into something really serious. And now I sometimes wonder why I got so mad.

I guess the thing is, I thought you were getting to know me on one level, and that you liked me because of my letters. Whereas in fact, you were just interested in the regular way. So how can I trust that you like who I really am?

Yours sincerely,

Lydia

* * *

Friday

Dear Charlie,

Well, I'm so glad we kidnapped Paul Wilson! It was like killing a flock of birds, that kidnapping. Cass got her revenge on Paul; Seb got to go to his art show; you got to forgive me; the list goes on! I will tell you the whole story of what happened one day! Which day?! This weekend, Lyd and Cass will come to my place so we can celebrate everything. Maybe you and I can celebrate on a day next week?!

Love,

Em

* * *

Dear Lydia,

I'm still here, and that was a beautiful thing that you and your friends did for me. Set up a meeting at the Voodoo Lounge, can you, so I can buy all three of you drinks all night?

Furthermore, it seems like you've saved me for a lifetime, not just a day. Paul's scars are fading as we speak, and he hasn't gone to the authorities. He's even smiling at me, in a "*Hey mate, let's put it behind us and move on*" kind of way. At least that's how I read the smiles. Maybe you guys embarrassed him so much you reformed him?

I am grateful to you for the rest of my life. And when I say "you," I mean every part of you, including your mind and your smile and your giggle and the mad look you get in your eyes sometimes. If you don't believe that your words have got into my soul, take a look at the painting which I took to the art show (it's called *The Puppy and the Pyramid,* which is what you might call a clue). But if I don't get to kiss you fairly soon, Lyd, I won't have a soul left to speak of.

Lots of love,

Seb

29. The Battle

Day 1 — Monday

THOUGHT FOR THE DAY:

Spring is in the air! But is it in your step?
And is it in your writing hand, and is it in your chair?
If not, you'd better put it there!

WELCOME TO THE NEW WEEK, YEAR 10!
LET'S HOPE IT'S A GOOD ONE!

THIS HAS BEEN A MESSAGE FROM YOUR FORM MISTRESS.

URGENT NOTICE — Monday, 10:45 A.M.

Due to serious events that have just been brought to my attention, the Ashbury-Brookfield Pen Pal Project has been SUSPENDED, EFFECTIVE IMMEDIATELY. The mailboxes will be removed and placed in safe storage. Any correspondence currently in the mailboxes will be confiscated and may be destroyed.

THIS HAS BEEN A MESSAGE FROM YOUR FORM MISTRESS

From: Emily.Thompson@ashburyhigh.com.au
To: Charlietheengineman23@hotmail.com
CC: Lydia.Oberman@ashburyhigh.com.au;
Cassie.Aganovic@ashburyhigh.com.au
Subject: What's going on?!?!

Dear Charlie,

Thank the Lord it is the modern age and we do not have to rely on cardboard mailboxes to communicate!

What's going on!? Do you know?!

We hear that "serious events" have occurred! What could they be? WHY HAVE THEY SUSPENDED THE ASHBURY-BROOKFIELD PEN PAL PROJECT?! It's such a great and educational project!

The teachers remain tight-lipped.

Love,

Emily

* * *

From: Charlietheengineman23@hotmail.com
To: Emily.Thompson@ashburyhigh.com.au
CC: Sebdavinci@hotmail.com;
Lydia.Oberman@ashburyhigh.com.au;
Cassie.Aganovic@ashburyhigh.com.au
Subject: Re: What's going on?!?!

Hey Em and you others in the CC world. Here is the serious event as I see it: Some Ashbury kids broke into our school over the weekend and used red paint to write DEATH TO BROOKER KIDS and BROOKER BITES all over the walls of the Year 10 homerooms. Way to go, Ashbury.

Buggered if I know why they had to stop the letter exchange, though.

* * *

From: Emily.Thompson@ashburyhigh.com.au
To: Charlietheengineman23@hotmail.com
CC: Lydia.Oberman@ashburyhigh.com.au;
Sebdavinci@hotmail.com;
Cassie.Aganovic@ashburyhigh.com.au
Subject: Re: Re: What's going on?!?!

Charlie! That's ridiculous!! No Ashbury student would be brave enough to break into your school and paint graffiti! Except maybe Lyd or Cass. And it wasn't you, was it Lyd and Cass? Please confirm. I can see you both across the library there, typing your overdue assignments, so please confirm immediately.

Charlie, I'm sure it wasn't Ashbury students.

* * *

From: Lydia.Oberman@ashburyhigh.com.au
To: Emily.Thompson@ashburyhigh.com.au
CC: Cassie.Aganovic@ashburyhigh.com.au;
Sebdavinci@hotmail.com;
Charlietheengineman23@hotmail.com
Subject: No, Em, it wasn't us.

Em, do you really think Cass and I would use the expression "Brooker Kids" in graffiti?

* * *

From: Cassie.Aganovic@ashburyhigh.com.au
To: Emily.Thompson@ashburyhigh.com.au
CC: Lydia.Oberman@ashburyhigh.com.au;
Sebdavinci@hotmail.com;
Charlietheengineman23@hotmail.com
Subject: Another Thing

It should also be mentioned, Em, that we all spent the weekend together at your place. At what point did we sneak away from you to go paint slogans at Brookfield? Why do they think it was Ashbury students anyway?

* * *

From: Charlietheengineman23@hotmail.com
To: Cassie.Aganovic@ashburyhigh.com.au
CC: Lydia.Oberman@ashburyhigh.com.au;
Sebdavinci@hotmail.com;
Emily.Thompson@ashburyhigh.com
Subject: Re: Why do they think it was Ashbury students?

I hear the Ashbury crest was painted after every anti-Brookfield slogan. Listen, I've gotta go, they're locking down the computer room for the night, but take care walking the streets in your Ashbury uniforms, eh? Personally, I'm very happy for you Ashbury kids to paint our walls, but a lot of people here are taking it to heart. There's anti-Ashbury threats being made under the breath (and on top of the breath) of some of the criminal element.

* * *

Day 2 — Tuesday

THOUGHT FOR THE DAY:

Where is the spirit of unity
When intruders behave with impunity?

Students: With regret, I must inform you that intruders smashed the windows of the Year 10 classrooms last night, broke in, and spray-painted unkind words on the walls. The classrooms have been locked so that the police can investigate.

With even greater regret, I must inform you that this incident may have been carried out by Brookfield students as retribution for a weekend attack on Brookfield.

Anybody with information about these attacks should come forward immediately.

THIS HAS BEEN A MESSAGE FROM YOUR DISTRESSED FORM MISTRESS.

From: Emily.Thompson@ashburyhigh.com.au
To: Charlietheengineman23@hotmail.com
CC: Lydia.Oberman@ashburyhigh.com.au;
Sebdavinci@hotmail.com;
Cassie.Aganovic@ashburyhigh.com.au
Subject: ATTACK FROM BROOKFIELD

Charlie! You were RIGHT to warn us!!! We are in danger here at Ashbury! Some of your compatriots have broken into our school and SMASHED THINGS! I feel a bit uneasy. On the bright side, all our classes are now being taken outside, on the squash courts, in the art rooms, etc., so it's fairly leisurely.

But we cannot understand why Ashbury students attacked your school on the weekend! Why? I suppose it was someone from Year 10 here since it was your Year 10 classrooms that were attacked. But none of us can figure out who, even though we have been asking around a LOT!

Lyd and Cass, please confirm that none of us can figure this out.

* * *

From: Cassie.Aganovic@ashburyhigh.com.au
To: Emily.Thompson@ashburyhigh.com.au
CC: Lydia.Oberman@ashburyhigh.com.au;
Sebdavinci@hotmail.com;
Charlietheengineman23@hotmail.com
Subject: Information

That's right, Em. None of us can figure it out.

* * *

From: Charlietheengineman23@hotmail.com
To: Emily.Thompson@ashburyhigh.com.au
Subject: UPDATE

Hey Em, it's lunchtime and I've been trying to call you on your mobile but no answer. Where are you? Give us a call, eh? I've got some interesting information. Very hungry so have to leave computer room now.

* * *

From: Emily.Thompson@ashburyhigh.com.au
To: Charlietheengineman23@hotmail.com
CC: Lydia.Oberman@ashburyhigh.com.au;
Sebdavinci@hotmail.com;
Cassie.Aganovic@ashburyhigh.com.au
Subject: Tell us the information!

Tell us what your interesting information is!

Here at Ashbury, developments have continued all day. You Brookfielders have such mendacity! As you might know, the Ashbury Show Pony Club trains at the field next door to Brookfield on Tuesdays, and they have just returned to school, their faces ashtrays! — because Brookfielders shouted insults (more than usual) and frightened their horses! Also, Lyd just heard that Brookfielders crept into our school grounds through the reserve at recess, and put purple dye in our swimming pool! All this as revenge for some graffiti over the weekend? It is overcompensating!! It boils my blood a bit but is very exciting and who knows what will happen next!! Will Ashbury reciprocate?! I hope so!

Love,

Emily

P.S. Sorry about my phone. Frau McAllister confiscated it after I called you on Monday to get your e-mail address. (How did she know I wasn't speaking to someone in Deutschland?) Why do phones have to be outlawed during school hours anyway? It's a nuisance, as I have to keep slipping out of class to e-mail you, which is detrimental to my education.

* * *

Day 3 — Wednesday

THOUGHT FOR THE DAY:

I cannot think, when I am on the brink.

STUDENTS: As you all know, a dispute has arisen between Ashbury and Brookfield. After yesterday's string of attacks by Brookfield, it seems that, overnight, Ashbury students have reciprocated.

It is not surprising that Brookfielders are conducting themselves in this childish manner. But it astonishes me that Ashbury students could stoop to their level. Please try to set an example to them by *TURNING THE OTHER CHEEK.*

THIS HAS BEEN A MESSAGE FROM YOUR DISTRESSED FORM MISTRESS.

From: Charlietheengineman23@hotmail.com
To: Emily.Thompson@ashburyhigh.com.au
CC: Lydia.Oberman@ashburyhigh.com.au;
Sebdavinci@hotmail.com;
Cassie.Aganovic@ashburyhigh.com.au
Subject: Here is the information

Hey Em, sorry about your boiling blood.

The information was this: I've had a word with my contact in the principal's office (the school secretary). And she tells me something unexpected. She tells me this: They think that the weekend graffiti artists had help from the inside.

See, there were no broken locks, windows, etc., at Brookfield: Someone just walked into the classrooms and painted their messages on the walls. So it's assumed that someone at our school let the Ashbury kids in — maybe someone doing music or drama practice there over the weekend.

That's why they've cancelled communication between our schools. They think it must have started with the Pen Pal Project. Seeing as there was never a single word spoken between Brookfield and Ashbury until letters started flying.

Charlie

* * *

From: Sebdavinci@hotmail.com
To: Charlietheengineman23@hotmail.com
CC: Lydia.Oberman@ashburyhigh.com.au;
Emily.Thompson@ashburyhigh.com.au;
Cassie.Aganovic@ashburyhigh.com.au
Subject: Traitors

Hey Charlo, good police work re: the inside job. You should give Lyd a call sometime — she recruits detectives like you. Meantime, I'll keep an eye out for who the Brookfield traitor might be.

Hey girls, someone from your school must've rigged up the PA system last night so it keeps blasting out mixes of the Ashbury school anthem every ten minutes. They've added techno, jazz, and hip-hop beats to the song to make it more entertaining. Nice distraction, and it's pissing a lot of people off. Is this the work of friends of yours, girls?

* * *

From: Emily.Thompson@ashburyhigh.com.au
To: Charlietheengineman23@hotmail.com
CC: Lydia.Oberman@ashburyhigh.com.au;
Sebdavinci@hotmail.com;
Cassie.Aganovic@ashburyhigh.com.au
Subject: Re: Traitors

I only have two minutes but, I have to say, I don't have a clue who would blast different "mixes" of the Ashbury school song into your corridors. It would need to be someone with audio looping software, wouldn't it? And what is audio looping software? Any ideas, Lyd and Cass?

* * *

Day 4 — Thursday

THOUGHT FOR THE DAY:

The time has come to end this disaster!
Damage has been done to floor and rafter.

STUDENTS: A **STATE OF EMERGENCY** HAS BEEN DECLARED. SCUFFLES HAVE BROKEN OUT BETWEEN ASHBURY AND BROOKFIELD STUDENTS IN THE VICINITY OF BOTH SCHOOLS. OUR SCHOOL IS IN SERIOUS DANGER.

A NOTICE WILL BE SENT TO ALL HOMES TONIGHT INFORMING YOUR PARENTS OF A PUBLIC MEETING WHICH WILL BE HELD TOMORROW NIGHT IN THE ASHBURY ASSEMBLY HALL. THE MEETING WILL BE CONDUCTED BY SENIOR TEACHERS FROM EACH SCHOOL.

THIS HAS BEEN A MESSAGE FROM YOUR CONCERNED FORM MISTRESS.

From: Emily.Thompson@ashburyhigh.com.au
To: Charlietheengineman23@hotmail.com
Subject: Re: CHECK IT OUT! THIS IS A LARF.

Ashbury sux. Ashbury sux. Ashbury sux. Ashbury sux. Ashbury sux. Ashbury sux. Ashbury sux. Ashbury sux. Ashbury sux. Ashbury sux. Ashbury sux.

Click on the attachment for a LARF.

* * *

From: Charlietheneginemann23@hotmail.com
To: Emily.Thompson@ashburyhigh.com.au
Subject: Re: Re: CHECK IT OUT! THIS IS A LARF.

What makes you say that, Em? And why so many times?

I hear there's a meeting on at your school tomorrow night to solve all the world's problems. Are you going?

* * *

From: Emily.Thompson@ashburyhigh.com.au
To: Charlietheengineman23@hotmail.com
Subject: NEVER CLICK ON ATTACHMENTS

SORRY. It was a virus!!! It is believed to be yet another invidious attack by BROOKFIELD upon our school. I have now told everyone in my address book that Ashbury sux. My father was especially distressed to hear this, as he pays good money to send me here.

I doubt we'll go to the meeting tomorrow night, as it has really got nothing to do with us, this battle. Anyhow, it's lunchtime now, and we're just leaving the school to go to the movies as we usually do on Thursdays. Those two are at the door of the library waiting for me, and that's loyalty for you. (Me, I mean, not them, b/c I'm writing to you even tho they're waiting.)

Love,
Emily

* * *

Day 5 — Friday

THOUGHT FOR THE DAY:

It is time to bow our heads in shame.
The end is nigh for this dreadful "game"
Which, indeed, is not a game
At all.

STUDENTS: WE NOW HAVE THE NAMES OF THE ASHBURY INDIVIDUALS RESPONSIBLE FOR THE ATTACKS ON BROOKFIELD.

The individuals in question were observed carrying out a childish prank at Brookfield yesterday after lunch. YOU KNOW WHO YOU ARE. You have until midday today to report to me.

THIS HAS BEEN A MESSAGE FROM YOUR HORRIFIED FORM MISTRESS.

From: Emily.Thompson@ashburyhigh.com.au
To: Charlietheengineman23@hotmail.com
Subject: VERY EXCITING NEWS!!!

Exciting development here! They have found the culprits!! It's on our notice board here! Someone at your school SAW them do some kind of childish prank yesterday afternoon. Stupid. They mustn't be very good at childish pranks, to have got seen.

To be honest, Charlie, I am looking forward to the reinitiation of the Pen Pal Project (which will surely happen now they've got the bad guys). I miss your handwriting on envelopes. I miss opening the envelopes. Just so you know, I wrote a letter to you today, setting out the things that I think are particularly good about you. For the sake of your self-esteem. I will post this as soon as the mailbox returns outside the upstairs staff room.

Love,
Emily

* * *

From: Charlietheengineman23@hotmail.com
To: Emily.Thompson@ashburyhigh.com.au
Subject: Tactics

They put up a notice saying they know who did it? Don't believe a word of it. They're trying to smoke out the bad guys is what they're up to, those crafty teachers of yours. They try that here all the time, and I personally have never fallen for it.

But let me know if anything interesting turns up.

Can't wait to get that letter of yours. I also miss your handwriting.

* * *

From: Lydia.Oberman@ashburyhigh.com.au
To: Sebdavinci@hotmail.com;
Charlietheengineman23@hotmail.com
Subject: VERY URGENT MESSAGE

Seb and Charlie,

You're not going to believe what's been happening here.

At exactly midday, Em, Cass, and I got called to the form mistress's office. And informed that we are the ones behind the Ashbury attacks on Brookfield.

They say they've got some witness at Brookfield who saw us at your school yesterday afternoon, tipping grapeseed oil all over the floor of one of your empty science labs.

As if we would do anything as stupid as that.

But listen to what happened.

We're sitting there open-mouthed with disbelief, and the form mistress (Mrs. Lilydale) says, "As I now have proof that you were at Brookfield yesterday, I have no doubt that you three troublemakers were the people who began this whole sordid affair — I have no doubt that you broke into Brookfield last weekend and painted that dreadful graffiti."

Which we practically started laughing at. But while we're laughing, she gets up and says, "Wait right here."

Then she walks out, and comes back five minutes later and she says, "I'm going to have to read through these, okay?" And she's carrying the following things:

1. my private notebook, which is a book I'm using to learn how to write;

2. Cassie's diary; and
3. an envelope addressed to Charlie, which Em must have written.

You can guess what she'd done. She'd opened up our lockers, gone through them, and got out the most personal-looking stuff she could find. I had to stop myself from getting up and hitting her across the face. And you should have seen Cass; she was practically crying.

I'm so angry I can hardly type.

Mrs. Lilydale reckons that there must be some incriminating evidence in these papers, proving that we started the whole battle. Which there's not. But she wants to read them and prove that for herself. So obviously we said, "Don't you DARE read our private things." So she said, "Well, you'd better just confess then." And we said that we had nothing to confess to. And she said, "Girls, we have a <u>witness</u> who puts you at the scene of yesterday's crime. Of course, you should have been in <u>maths</u> at the <u>time</u> of the crime, so perhaps the witness was wrong." And then she calls in Ms. Yen, the maths teacher, and puts on a show of asking whether we were in our maths class yesterday afternoon, and Ms. Yen looks all surprised and says, "No! They weren't!"

Well, of course we weren't. We were at the movies.

And we couldn't exactly say that. We'd have got expelled, since we got in a lot of trouble for going to the movies last year.

Then Mrs. Lilydale said we have until the last bell today to confess, or she'll read our things.

Then she let us go so we could "make up our minds."

There is no way in hell we're letting her read our things. But what are we supposed to do?

Em and Cass have gone to call their parents, but I seriously don't know how they can fix this. Even if they stop her from reading our stuff, we can't prove we weren't the ones at Brookfield yesterday. The witness, whoever it is, must have made a mistake, or must be lying, but they won't tell us his/her name. They're giving us some crap about how they have to protect confidentiality.

Lyd

* * *

From: Emily.Thompson@ashburyhigh.com.au
To: Charlietheengineman23@hotmail.com
CC: Lydia.Oberman@ashburyhigh.com.au; Sebdavinci@hotmail.com; Cassie.Aganovic@ashburyhigh.com.au
Subject: THE INJUSTICE

Charlie and Seb,
The INJUSTICE! THE INJUSTICE!

This is the BIGGEST DISASTER OF OUR LIVES.

Lyd says she has told you the whole sordid story, and now I am giving you an update, which is this! Cass and I called our parents and MY DAD and CASS'S MUM both came screaming up to the school!

What parents!

They were both very excited about the events, my dad in an unnecessarily jolly way, but Cass's mum in a FURIOUS way.

Cass's mum (Patricia) is excited by children's rights, so she was OUTRAGED at the idea that they were going to INVADE OUR PRIVACY AND READ OUR SPECIAL, PRIVATE THINGS.

She said: "ABSOLUTELY NOT."

And Mrs. Lilydale said: "Then they simply need to confess." (Infuriating!)

And Patricia said, "REGARDLESS of whether they are GUILTY or NOT, I will not have you reading their private things."

She was so fiery-eyed!

It went back and forth for a while, with my dad making excited exclamations of agreement, and Patricia saying she would go up to the Supreme Court right then and get an INJUNCTION to stop Mrs. Lilydale!

So Mrs. Lilydale started to get a bit panicked and said, "BUT THERE'S A WITNESS WHO SAW THEM DO IT. AND THEIR REFUSAL TO LET US READ THEIR BOOKS SEEMS TO CONFIRM THAT THEY ARE GUILTY. WHAT ARE WE GOING TO TELL THE PARENTS AT THE MEETING TONIGHT?!!"

At which Patricia thought fast and then said, "Well, if it's a MEETING you're concerned about, we'll resolve this BEFORE the meeting. Who's running this MEETING of yours?"

She was on fire, that Patricia.

"Senior teachers from both schools," trembled Mrs. Lilydale.

"THEN, they will act as JUDGES and we'll hold a PRELIMINARY hearing, immediately BEFORE the meeting, to DECIDE THE ISSUE!!! It's either that or I'm heading up to Court RIGHT NOW!!"

So, reluctantly, Mrs. Lilydale agreed.

Patricia said she wants the hearing to be done PROPERLY like a REAL LEGAL HEARING, and she even wants a TRANSCRIPT typed up so that she can use that to APPEAL TO THE SUPREME COURT if there is ANY PROCEDURAL INJUSTICE AT ALL.

So that made Mrs. Lilydale look frightened.

And my dad said he would be the LEGAL CONSULTANT at the meeting, to make sure IT IS DONE PROPERLY LIKE A PROPER TRIAL!!!!

And then Patricia said, without even looking at me: "Emily can represent the girls."

And I said, "Can I?"

And she said, "Yes."

I am going to be a lawyer tonight!

I'd better go and prepare.

Cass and Lyd will be depending on me.

Especially because Patricia told me afterward that she was bluffing the whole time with Mrs. Lilydale, and she could never get this up to the Supreme Court and get injunctions, etc., because, for one thing, this is a private school and they wouldn't have jurisdiction.

So it's all up to me!

See you, and wish me luck,

Em

* * *

From: Sebdavinci@hotmail.com

To: Lydia.Oberman@ashburyhigh.com.au

Subject: No problemo

Hey Lyd,

Typing at hi speed as hve to get outta here. I betcha the "witness" is that a/hole, Wilson. Trying to take advantage of this whole Brookfield-Ashbury battle to get revenge for your revenge. Charlie & me will try & get some dirt on him for you, Lyd, but I have to warn you, it's not going to be easy & we probably won't be able to help. He's got a reputation you could eat your dinner off. Let's say his reputation was a dinner plate. I know from personal experience that it sucks bad being in the situation that you're in, Lyd, waiting to get thrown out of school, but you should know that I will love you even when you're an outlaw.

Seb

P.S. Talking of outlaws, you once said you had a contact with a talent for breaking locks. Any chance you could hook me up with that person tonight?

* * *

From: Lydia.Oberman@ashburyhigh.com.au
To: Sebdavinci@hotmail.com
Subject: Thanks

Hey Seb,

I've asked the person with the talent for locks to contact you, so you'll hear from them soon. Why do you need locks broken?

I'm just in the library, waiting for the meeting to start, watching Em throw papers around the room. She looks terrified. I'm not holding out on her saving our private papers from being read.

Even if she does, we're going to be expelled. They've made that pretty clear. Because they believe Paul Wilson (I'm guessing you're right and he's the witness), and we can't prove it's not true.

It feels surreal sitting in the library knowing this is the last time I'm going to be here. And knowing how bad it's going to look on our CVs, getting expelled from Ashbury, and how it might affect things like getting into uni, getting jobs, and basically our whole lives.

It's ironic, because we didn't actually break into Brookfield yesterday, but we've got a reputation as the kind of people who would, and now our reputation has us trapped. (That and our preference for going to the movies on Thursdays, of course.)

But, Seb, the worst thing is this: Our bad reputation is all my fault. These kinds of things are always my idea. So I haven't just ruined my life, I've ruined Em's and Cass's lives as well, and I am now too depressed to type another word.

30. Transcript of Proceedings, Typed by Bindy Mackenzie

HANDOUT

(FOR DISTRIBUTION PRIOR TO MEETING)

NOTE THAT A PRELIMINARY MEETING IS BEING HELD AT 5:30 P.M. PARENTS AND FRIENDS NEED NOT ATTEND: IT IS A SPECIAL "HEARING" TO DECIDE IF TEACHERS CAN READ THE PRIVATE PAPERS OF CERTAIN ASHBURY STUDENTS WHO HAVE BEEN INVOLVED IN THE DISPUTE.

THE "REAL" MEETING BEGINS AT 6 P.M.

DISCUSSION POINTS FOR 6 P.M. MEETING

- Attacks have been carried out by BOTH schools (see next page for "Breakdown of Major Attacks").
- Has been random violence between students in after-school hours.
- Is the dispute gang-related? What can we do about "gangs"?
- What can parents do to help?
- Do "student leaders" have any suggestions?
- Long-standing tension between our two schools — Why? How to stop it?
- DRASTIC SITUATIONS CALL FOR DRASTIC MEASURES. What measures?

TEA AND COFFEE SERVED IN UPPER STAFF ROOM BEFORE AND AFTER MEETING.

BREAKDOWN OF MAJOR ATTACKS

Ashbury attacks on Brookfield:

- Graffiti attack on classrooms using red spray paint (last weekend).
- Ashbury school anthem played over P.A. system (Wednesday).
- Grapeseed oil on science lab floors (Thursday).

Brookfield attacks on Ashbury:

- Windows broken, lewd graffiti spray-painted (*Monday night*).
- Verbal assaults on the Ashbury Pony Club; swimming pool dyed purple (*Tuesday*).
- Ashbury computer network infected with virus (*Wednesday*).

Transcript of Preliminary Meeting

The Preliminary Meeting is taking place in the Ashbury Assembly Hall, which is already beginning to fill with anxious parents and excited Year 10 students, all of them here for the 6 P.M. Meeting, but interested in the Preliminary Meeting (word having got around). All are scraping their chairs, chattering like budgerigars, and rustling the handout. (I will insert a copy of the handout at the start of this transcript.)

In the front row, the Year 10 student leaders sit, straight-backed and proud. The Brookfield Year 10 Captain is striking to look at, a tall, blond young man.

A table has been set up on the stage. The table is laid with a pretty lace cloth. Judge Anderson (the Brookfield deputy principal; freckles, red hair) and Judge Koutchavalis (the Ashbury headmistress; darting eyes; curly gray hair) are sitting side by side at the table. Emily Thompson's father is alongside them and is wearing a suit.

A row of chairs has been set up across the back of the stage for the many teachers from both schools who are attending. Ms. Lawrence and Ms. Yen keep whispering to each other and giggling like schoolgirls.

The defendants, Emily Thompson and Lydia Jaackson-Oberman, are sitting over there, but where is Cassie Aganovic? It is interesting to note her absence.

I (Bindy Mackenzie) am sitting at the end of the judges' table and typing on my laptop. I just went "shhhh" and frowned at Ms. Yen and Ms. Lawrence; they looked at me with surprise. Ms. Lawrence raised her eyebrows archly.

Judge Koutchavalis is clearing her throat. She is about to speak —

Judge Koutchavalis: Ladies and Gentlemen. This is a preliminary meeting and relates to three Ashbury students. The meeting will be conducted as if it is a "legal hearing." As this issue is not of interest to you, you may like to partake of the refreshments in the staff room, and we shall let you know when the real meeting has begun. *(There is some shuffling in the audience, but* *nobody leaves.)* Very well, I shall proceed as quickly as possible. The issue is this: A witness saw three Ashbury girls carrying out a prank at Brookfield yesterday afternoon. Some people now think that these girls must have started the whole dispute. *(Clears her throat and looks to Mr. Thompson, who nods wisely.)*

The Year 10 Form Mistress at our school believes that she should be allowed to check through the girls' personal papers for evidence to this effect. The girls themselves deny the charge and seek an order that she not be allowed to look through their papers. The Year 10 Form Mistress will speak first, on behalf of the teachers, and then Emily Thompson will speak on behalf of the girls.

Please thank Mr. Thompson, on my right, who is our legal consultant today, and also thank Bindy Mackenzie, who is typing up the transcript.

Mr. Thompson: She types very quickly, doesn't she?

Judge Anderson: She types like the wind!

Emily: She's not that fast.

Mr. Thompson: Yes she is. Look at her.

Pause as the people on stage watch Bindy Mackenzie, typing like the wind, typing like a tidal wave, typing up a storm — while parents and students in the audience talk amongst themselves.

Judge Koutchavalis: *(talking into the microphone again)* We will begin by inviting Mrs. Lilydale, the Year 10 Form Mistress, to address us. *(More quietly, to Mr. Thompson)* How's it going so far?

Mr. Thompson: Excellent. *(Mrs. Koutchavalis smiles proudly.)*

Mrs. Lilydale stands up, coughs, and says an experimental "ahem." A small pause.

A couple of students in the audience begin applauding and making loud, ironic comments such as, "What a speech," and "That was a great point, that second thing she said?" and "You tell 'em, Lily," as if to indicate that the speech is over now. Parents frown and say "Shhh!"

Mrs. Lilydale: *(ignoring students) I will be very brief. Your honors (turning to the two judges and putting on a sort of little-girl's voice)*, your honors, I am the Year 10 Form Mistress.

Judge Koutchavalis: You certainly are.

Mrs. Lilydale: *(clears her throat again)* As such, I have responsibility for the physical and emotional well-being of the students of Year 10.

Student in Audience: *(putting on sincere voice)* Thank you, Mrs. Lilydale.

Mrs. Lilydale: *(ignoring student)* In the last week, the education of Year 10 has been in serious jeopardy.

Students in audience break into spontaneous applause, cheering, etc., presumably in support of the detriment to their education; parents tch! at their children.

Mrs. Lilydale: *(over the cheers)* It is vital that the people who are organizing these attacks be apprehended. We have a witness who saw three girls at Brookfield carrying out a prank. We have the same three girls missing from their maths class. Yet the girls themselves refuse to confess to this! What are we to think? Are they guilty or not? One way we can make sure is to look through their personal papers — if there is no mention of their attacks on Brookfield, there may be some doubt! If there is mention, then the issue will be resolved. The girls refuse to allow us to read their papers. This makes it even more likely that they are guilty and gives us even more reason to read their papers. *(She holds up both hands and looks around the audience, as if waiting for applause. There is silence; some parents are nodding.)*

Judge Koutchavalis: Well, thank you, Mrs. Lilydale. Do you have anything to say, Mr. Anderson, excuse me, Judge Anderson?

Judge Anderson: As deputy principal of Brookfield, I'm obviously keen to track down the culprits. But Mrs. Lilyfield, what do you have to say about these girls' right to privacy?

Mrs. Lilydale: It's dale, actually. Not field. Lilydale. *(Judge Anderson tilts his head to the side, as if he finds Mrs. Lilydale a little curious. She continues.)* Privacy is well and good. But the time comes when the safety of two entire schools must be put ahead of three students' privacy in whatever they might have scribbled. Now is that time.

Judge Koutchavalis: Thank you, Mrs. Lilydale. You may sit down. I am sure the people here are considering your words carefully.

She looks to the audience, where some people shrug slightly. Others frown. Somebody sighs, deeply. A sniff from the audience. A single cough. Someone says "ow," and someone, somewhere, whispers that they are very hungry. Another voice offers some chewing gum. The first voice says, "That won't help." Another voice says, "There's a spider on the wall." Another voice says, "No, that's just the tassel from the curtain." "No, it's not"; "Yes,

Emily: *(standing in her place)* Before Mrs. Lilydale sits down, I want to cross-examine her.

General shouts of approval and some of unexpected sexual innuendo from the students in the audience. Is cross-examining Mrs. Lilydale something sexual? I cannot understand it.

Mrs. Lilydale: Is that allowed? Can she cross-examine me?

Mr. Thompson: Absolutely.

Judge Koutchavalis: All right, I don't see why not.

Emily: Mrs. Lilydale, you want to read our private diaries and letters, right?

Mrs. Lilydale: Right.

Emily: And you think you should be allowed this because you have evidence that we went to Brookfield yesterday afternoon, right?

Mrs. Lilydale: Right.

Mrs. Lilydale: And the only evidence you have against us is a Brookfield student who says he saw us there yesterday afternoon, right?

Mrs. Lilydale: All right.

Emily: And you won't tell us this Brookfield student's name?

Mrs. Lilydale: That's right. We agreed to protect his identity.

Emily: Why?

Mrs. Lilydale: Well, obviously, there is much hostility between the two schools, so we need to protect him from that hostility and —

Emily: Because Ashbury students could not be trusted to be nice to this Brookfield student?

Mrs. Lilydale: Precisely.

Emily: Ashbury students are so mad at Brookfield students that they might <u>attack</u> this boy, if they know he has told on Ashburians?

Mrs. Lilydale: Exactly.

Emily: Ashbury students might <u>attack</u> this boy <u>physically</u>, or they might, let's say, <u>insult</u> him, or they might even start <u>telling lies about him</u>?

Mrs. Lilydale: Right.

Emily: They might, even, let's say, <u>accuse him of doing something he didn't do</u>?

Mrs. Lilydale: I suppose — well, hang on there —

There is a ripple of excitement from the audience as people realize where she is heading.

Emily: Mrs. Lilydale! Don't Brookfielders hate us as much as we hate them? WHY SHOULD ANYONE BELIEVE THIS BROOKFIELD BOY WHEN HE IS SAYING SOMETHING MEAN ABOUT ASHBURY GIRLS?!!

Mrs. Lilydale: *(Nothing; gaping a bit.)*

Judge Anderson: *(aside, to Judge Koutchavalis)* She makes a good point, but our witness is fairly reliable, you know.

Mrs. Lilydale: Well, this so-called Brookfield boy knew your names and described you in detail!

Emily: And yet we are not allowed to know anything about him! How did he know our names, for example, when we hardly know anyone at Brookfield! Why did he see us if nobody else saw us? How is his eyesight? IS HE BLIND? FOR ALL WE KNOW, HE COULD BE BLIND!?!?!

Mrs. Lilydale gives a little frowning shrug, as if all of this is silly — but Emily is correct, what if he has some sort of perceptual shortcoming? The audience is really excited now, leaning forward, whispering, listening, nodding to one another.

Emily: Another thing, would you agree that yesterday, you put a message on our Year 10 notice board that said, "OUR SCHOOL IS IN SERIOUS DANGER"?

Mrs. Lilydale: I wouldn't have a clue.

Emily: Well, would you have a look at this, please? See where it's highlighted in pink?

Mr. Thompson: *(leaning forward with interest)* Let the record show that Em is showing Mrs. Lilydale a piece of paper.

For the record, Em is showing Mrs. Lilydale a piece of paper.

Emily: It's the notice from yesterday.

Mrs. Lilydale: All right then, I see that I did say that.

Emily: And would you agree that people who read that the school was in serious danger might be afraid that the school was in serious danger?

Mrs. Lilydale: Excuse me?

Mr. Thompson: The question was perfectly clear.

Mrs. Lilydale: All right.

Emily: And do you think that someone spray-painting our classroom walls puts the school in serious danger?

Mrs. Lilydale: Well, no, but —

Emily: *(fiery-eyed)* Just answer the question, Mrs. Lilydale!

Mrs. Lilydale: You can't talk to me . . . ! . . . Okay. No.

Emily: *(dramatically)* So wasn't it <u>false</u> for you to say that the school was in <u>danger</u>?

Mrs. Lilydale: Of course not.

Emily: Did you have any <u>evidence</u> that the school was in danger?

Mrs. Lilydale: Well, but —

Emily: So it was false!

Mrs. Lilydale: Oh, for heavens' sakes.

Emily: *(lowering her voice to a dramatic whisper)* What would you say if I told you that, under section 93IH of the Crimes Act 1900, New South Wales, it is illegal to say that a school is in danger if that is not true *(long pause)* — and what would you say if I told you that the maximum penalty for this crime is <u>five years in prison</u>!!!!

There is a great uproar of cheering, applauding, stamping, hysterical laughter, from, I should say, both parents and students — offers from students to phone the police — offers from humorous parents to make a citizen's arrest —

Once it has quieted down a bit:

Mrs. Lilydale: Emily Thompson, that is nonsense. I had every reason to believe that the school was in danger and —

Emily: *(interrupting her and walking away theatrically so that she can read the transcript over Bindy's shoulder)* But, Mrs. Lilydale, didn't you just say — hey, Bindy's putting all kinds of adjectives in the transcript.

Mr. Botherit: *(leaning forward from the back row)* What do you mean when you say adjectives?

Emily: She's putting things in there like "lowering her voice to a dramatic whisper" and "walking away theatrically."

Mr. Botherit: I don't think those are all adjectives.

Ms. Yen: It can't hurt, can it? It will make the transcript more entertaining.

Judge Koutchavalis: Well, I don't know if that's normal is it, Mr. Thompson?

Mr. Thompson: I'm pretty sure it's not normal. Of course, just between you and me, I'm a tax lawyer. I haven't been in a courtroom for years. But I'm pretty sure it's not normal.

Judge Koutchavalis: (bossily) Bindy? Can you stop typing in those descriptive bits?

Mr. Pappo: They're adverbs, aren't they?

Mr. Botherit: I would call them adverbial phrases.

Mr. Thompson: *(looking over at Bindy)* She's really a very fast typist.

Emily: She's not that fast.

Judge Koutchavalis: You should get on with your cross-examination, Em.

Emily: I've finished, haven't I? I proved that Mrs. Lilydale is a criminal.

Judge Koutchavalis: Order, everyone! Order! *(The general clamor begins to subside.)* Please show some respect, Emily.

Emily: Sorry. But I've got more to say.

Judge Anderson: *(enjoying himself)* Go ahead.

Emily: And to conclude, I will now read out a short declaration which I have written this afternoon in some hastefulness.

(*reading*)

We were dismayed to be accused of a crime which we DID NOT COMMIT. We bet a million dollars that if we could just find out who the so-called witness was, we could prove that he is making it up.

But, let me tell you, we were even MORE dismayed when the teachers went through our lockers. That was a terrible invasion of our privacy, and it would be an even worse invasion to read our letters and diaries. Mrs. Lilydale thinks that our letters, etc., are just frivolous, and that it does not matter if she reads them.

But, I must say that I think our diaries, notebooks, and letters are the most important things in our lives. Just about.

Ladies and gentlemen, you might be thinking to yourself: Why do I think that? So! I will tell you.

When you are our age, you are thinking about many important things, such as who you are going to become. Maybe you have to choose subjects for Years 11 and 12, and those subjects will decide what you do at university, and that will change your life!

When you are our age, you do not have much space to do this figuring out.

So where do you do all this thinking?

Not when you talk to your parents: They have known you all your life and can't really imagine you as a grown-up.

No, it is only when you talk to yourself or when you talk to your friends.

And the way that you <u>really</u> talk to yourself and your friends is through things like diaries and notebooks and letters.

When you're an adult, you have so many private places to put things, e.g., homes and attics, filing cabinets and desk drawers.

When you're our age, you spend most of your life at school. And where can you put your diaries and notebooks and letters when you come to school? Nowhere. Except in your locker. That's it.

If you teachers go through our lockers, and read our notebooks, etc., well, you know what you will be doing? You'll be taking the fragile pieces of paper which decide who we are going to be — and you'll be tearing them to shreds.

In a metabolic sense, anyway.

Excuse me. In a metaphoric sense, which means symbolic.

And which is a lot more important than you think.

In conclusion, it is wrong to get in trouble for something you didn't do. But it is even more wrong for you to be able to read our private things.

That concludes my Declaration. However, I have attachments which I will now hand up to the judges, and which I have taken from a folder of material belonging to Cass Aganovic's mother.

Attached and marked with the letter A are copies of Articles 16 and 40 of the United Nations Convention on the Rights of the Child, which say that children have the right to privacy.

Attached and marked with the letter B are copies of cases from around the world in which teenagers are given privacy protection, even in their lockers.

Attached and marked with the letter C is a copy of the notice which Mr. Botherit, our English teacher, put up on the notice board at the beginning of the autumn term and which specifically said that our letters to Brookfield would be "completely confidential."

Emily takes a deep breath, hands over a pile of papers to the judges, and sits back down next to me. She reads over my shoulder, so she can see how her speech looked.

There is general silence — a sort of rippling of disbelief from the stage and across the hall — "Was that really Emily Thompson?" is the impression I get from the rippling.

Emily: Bindy's doing the adjectives again.

Bindy: They're not adjectives.

Emily: YOU CAN'T SPEAK AND TYPE AT THE SAME TIME, BINDY.

Bindy: Watch me.

Note that the above exchange between Emily and Bindy was drowned out by the sound of the entire assembly hall beginning to clap and stamp their feet.

Emily: (returning to the microphone) And anyway, our private papers don't have any evidence at all of our attacking Brookfield. They might have evidence of <u>other</u> wrongful conduct by us, but —

Mr. Thompson: Objection!

Judge Koutchavalis: On what basis?

Mr. Thompson: She's shooting herself in the foot.

Emily sits back down again.

Judge Koutchavalis: Is everybody finished?

Emily: Yes.

Mrs. Lilydale: Well, I rather think that I should be entitled to —

Mr. Thompson: You've had your turn.

Judge Koutchavalis: *(to Judge Anderson)* Then we should make a decision, I suppose — shall we have a little chat?

Whispering between the two judges, which presumably should not be typed, although if I just lean over slightly, I can ALMOST hear —

Judge Koutchavalis: Ladies and gentlemen, we have reached a decision. Although we believe these girls were involved in attacks on Brookfield, there is a right way to go about dealing with that. The right way does not include reading their private things.

Mr. Thompson: As adviser, I must say you have given the correct decision.

Mr. Pappo: You know, it occurs to me that Mr. Thompson might be a biased adviser. Can that be allowed?

Emily: Why is he speaking? Why is Mr. Pappo speaking?

Judge Koutchavalis: As I said, we agree with Emily. The girls should have their things returned to them at once.

Exuberant cheering and stamping in the audience.

Judge Koutchavalis: *(tapping on microphone)* Ladies and gentlemen. I am sure that the girls are pleased that their private things will not be read. But this is not a matter for frivolity. This is serious.

The audience begins to quiet down.

Judge Koutchavalis: (continuing) The real meeting is going to begin in a moment, and we will be discussing a very grave matter. Students at both our schools have been carrying out dangerous attacks. The three girls you are applauding now were seen at Brookfield yesterday, putting oil on the floors of science laboratories. I cannot think of a more dangerous stunt. And despite Emily's clever remarks, we have no doubts about the reliability of the witness who saw them.

Judge Anderson: *(looking solemn)* Yes. I can vouch for the witness myself. He is one of the best students at our school.

Judge Koutchavalis: These girls are in serious trouble, and I am afraid they will be suspended immediately and quite possibly could be expelled.

Audience looks chastened; eyes cast down; some nod heavily; I see that Emily and Lydia are both ashen-faced.

Judge Koutchavalis: Therefore —

She is interrupted — there is the noise of a speeding car just outside the assembly room! — people look up and gasp a bit, as it seems to be very close — squealing tires, slamming car doors, rushing footsteps — the door bursts open — everyone looks up expectantly — it's Cassie Aganovic! And she's with two Brookfield boys; one of the Brookfield boys, dark-haired and rather sexy-looking, runs up the steps onto the stage, two steps at a time, and raises his eyebrows at the judges, indicating where Emily and Lydia are sitting.

Judge Anderson: *(grimly)* Seb Mantegna.

Seb Mantegna: *(taking that as permission)* Thanks. I won't be a moment. *(Goes over to Emily and Lydia and talks to them in whispers which I cannot hear.)*

Emily: *(leaping to her feet and returning to the microphone)* Ladies and gentlemen! Just finally, I have a few <u>very interesting</u> things to show you!

Beckons the other Brookfield boy, who runs up onto the stage, looking serious, carrying a large backpack.

Emily: First, I must show you some half-empty cans of RED SPRAY PAINT!

The other Brookfield boy takes three spray-paint cans out of the backpack and holds them up, one at a time, like a sort of cooking show.

Emily: And now, I must show you some empty plastic bottles of grapeseed oil!

The audience look bewildered; the teachers are beginning to reach toward Em, as if to gently lead her away from the microphone.

Emily: (being a bit humorous) Wait just one minute! Red paint! Wasn't Brookfield attacked with red paint? Grapeseed oil? Wasn't that on the floor of the Brookfield science labs? I guess my friends here must have found these things in the home of an Ashbury student?! I guess it must have been in the home of one of the three girls who have been accused today?! Charlie, can you tell us — is that where you found these things?

Everyone waits — the boy with the backpack (Charlie, I assume) leans hesitantly toward the microphone.

Charlie: *(politely)* No, actually, Em, we found most of this stuff in the bedroom cupboard of a guy from Brookfield.

Confusion from the audience.

Emily: *(being theatrical again)* So that sounds like a Brookfield student might have attacked Brookfield?! Now, why would he want to attack his own school? Charlie, can you tell me the name of the Brookfield student who had these things in his bedroom?

Charlie: Yes, Em, I can. It's Paul Wilson. Our Form Captain there.

There are sharp intakes of breath all around from teachers, judges, etc.

Judge Koutchavalis: Hey! Isn't that the name of the witness against our girls?!

Judge Anderson: *(chuckling a little; unfazed)* Yes, but I don't imagine Paul would —

The tall, handsome Form Captain from Brookfield is standing up — he has sauntered onto the stage and is standing right beside me as I type, smiling slightly, as if this is all a bit of a joke; he talks to Judge Anderson in a low voice.

Paul Wilson: Mr. Anderson, look, you can't believe Seb Mantegna and Charlie Taylor, can you? They hate my guts. I don't know who this girl is they've got with them, but she looks like one of the girls I saw committing the crime. How can anyone believe her? She could be some kind of a freak. She could be a pathological liar or something.

Bindy: *(whispering to him)* No, that's Cassie. Be careful what you say about her, okay? Her father died last year and she was really close to him, so you've got to be nice to her. Otherwise, you'll get everyone mad at you.

Paul Wilson looks at me and blinks. He is quiet for a moment, breathing and blinking.

Judge Anderson: *(looking bemused)* Well, just explain to the people why you've got those things in your room, would you? Explain to me.

Paul: *(stares at him, wide-eyed and confused)* Look. *(uncertainly)* Look, this is ridiculous. *(moves to the microphone)* Everyone, of course there's an explanation. As you know, I do food technology — there was so much grapeseed oil that I took some home and —

A Brookfield teacher stands up from the row of chairs at the back; a small, plump woman.

Plump Brookfield Teacher: I didn't know you were in the food technology class, Paul.

Student in Audience: *(calling out — crudely?)* Whatcha do with the oil in your bedroom, eh Paul?

Paul: *(blustering; confused)* And I got the spray paint from the art supplies, so I could —

Plump Brookfield Teacher: We never use grapeseed oil, actually. I prefer olive oil.

Judge Anderson: *(The color is rushing from his face; he speaks softly.)* Paul. You were at school last weekend, weren't you? For drama rehearsal? And you stayed back to tidy up after we left? Please don't tell me you went into the classrooms and painted "Brooker bites" onto the walls.

I think that Paul Wilson is starting to cry! Yes! Yes!

Paul: Of course not! — I didn't — I just — Mr. And — <u>you</u> know — the, oil —

Judge Anderson is a big man; I see traces of sweat around the collar of his shirt; he pulls at the collar of his shirt.

Across the stage there is a strange little noise from Cassie Aganovic; Paul glances over; I see their eyes meet briefly; Paul Wilson looks back to Judge Anderson.

Paul: Uh — *(His shoulders crumple; he swivels; he runs across the stage, down the steps, and toward the fire exit. He pushes at the door — "Not that one!" exclaims Mr. Botherit — he runs on to the next door, pushes through it, and slams the door behind him.)*

A deathly, stunned silence follows fast upon the echo of the slamming door. There are gasps, etc., which I will not bother transcribing; they can be imagined.

Now: uproar! Everyone talks at the same time — parents, students, and teachers alike — much amazed excitement and confusion.

Judge Koutchavalis: *(beaming)* Well, imagine that! <u>All</u> the attacks on Brookfield were carried out by a <u>Brookfielder</u>!

Judge Anderson: *(shakes his head; grim; a broken man?; at last, distractedly)* Hmm.

Judge Koutchavalis: Let me just consult my handout here. Well! Yes, anyway, two of the three Ashbury attacks were inside jobs! We'll have to change the handout!

Charlie: Yeah, the only thing we didn't find at Paul's was evidence of that Ashbury school song episode. Remember when it was played over our P.A. at regular intervals? But we didn't have much time. There'll be evidence in his place somewhere.

Judge Koutchavalis: I don't doubt it. *(into the microphone; jolly-sounding)* Well, everyone, it looks like Ashbury's in the clear, and we all owe those three girls an apology! They were not at Brookfield yesterday at all! They were probably studying in the library!

Emily: Probably.

Judge Koutchavalis: Yes, that is the nature of Ashbury students. Diligent. Now, just looking into Brookfield's role in the dispute — let's see *(consults the handout)* — yes, well, Brookfield smashed windows, painted rude words, sent a computer virus, dyed our pool purple — the list goes on! Golly. Presumably, this was all carried out by the criminal element at Brookfield in response to attacks which were actually carried out by Brookfielders themselves! How — extraordinary.

Judge Anderson: *(wearying of her good humor)* Extraordinary.

Judge Koutchavalis: At any rate. *(leans to the microphone again)* Well! Ladies and gentlemen, I am sure you are all as surprised as we are by this turn of events, and as relieved to discover the true culprit. But there is still work to do! It is imperative that we discuss the best —

She looks to the audience; they seem to have lost interest in her — parents are now gathering their handbags, continu-

ing to chat animatedly; I hear many references to the refreshments in the staff room.

Judge Koutchavalis: *(pretending this is all as she planned)* So now might be a good time to partake of refreshments! We will reconvene in half an hour and nut out some ideas for forging ties between our schools again. *(The teachers all begin to stand up too; there is an array of chatting and scraping, footsteps, "Oh, I forgot my glasses!" "Is this them on the floor?", etc., etc.)*

Bindy: When can I stop typing?

Emily: *(with a trace of sarcasm?)* Now would be a good time, Bindy.

31. Ashbury High Year 10 Notice Board

THOUGHT FOR THE DAY:
Isn't it great that Ashbury was not to blame?
Turns out it was Brookfield who lit the flame
of the dispute.

Students: On Friday night, a three-hour meeting was held with the objective of restoring unity and peace between our schools. As you will no doubt have heard, it emerged that the ENTIRE conflict was set up by a single, somewhat unhinged Brookfield student.

Nevertheless, steps must be taken to ensure that peace reigns true between our schools.

THE SPIRIT OF COOPERATION

In the second part of the meeting, Mr. Botherit argued (passionately) for the reinstatement of his Ashbury-Brookfield Pen Pal Project. He also suggested that his students be asked to meet and cooperate with their Brookfield Pen Pals, in order to demonstrate the success of that project — and so that the first step may be taken toward peace and unity.

Accordingly, each of Mr. Brookfield's Year 10 English students **must join with his or her Brookfield Pen Pal** and prepare a contribution to the Ashbury Spring Concert! (I shall give the Spring Concert an appropriate new name.) The contribution may be a dramatic, musical, or artistic act, to be performed onstage. Or it may be behind-the-scenes — painting backdrops or decorating the hall, etc.

THIS HAS BEEN A MESSAGE FROM YOUR FORM MISTRESS.

32. Emily and Charlie

Dear Charlie,

Well, I am so happy I feel confused!

It was so much fun on the weekend having a party at Lyd's place and laughing and/or chatting with you and Seb, and everyone drinking, talking, etc., and celebrating happily!

Really, I have to say again, though, that you and Seb and Cass were AMAZING the way you came skidding up in your teacher's Audi, bringing the evidence with you! It was the sexiest thing that ever happened in my life.

I'm just glad that nobody mentioned that Cass had broken into Paul Wilson's bedroom window, as that might have put some confusion into my privacy argument.

Speaking of which, I only wish you had seen me be a lawyer, as I think (modestly) that I was a real hit. Everyone has been congratulating me today, shouting praise from various distances, and I have been shouting back thanks in every direction! I have even thanked *people I'd never heard of*! It is a true taste of fame.

And get this, the legal studies teacher was at the meeting, and she tracked me down today so she could have a really intense conversation in the corridor. About how she hopes I'm planning to do legal studies next year? So I told her I dream of being a lawyer but I'm scared my marks won't be good enough. You should have seen her gasping denial! She was like a fish! "There are *so many ways to become a lawyer*!" she proclaimed. "And getting good marks is *just one of those ways*!" She said that anyone determined enough could become a lawyer as long as they went to see her in her office so she could explain the options.

She also said I had the talent for restraint, which means I don't talk too much.

Have you noticed how bad teachers look close up? Very wrinkled, and some unexpected blackheads on the nose.

Well, I have to arrange something with you as our joint contribution for the Spring Concert. So I have put us down as running the refreshment stall during intermission, selling cakes, chocolates, etc., etc. Okay? Great.

Guess what, Cass says she is going to SING as her contribution! I was just *nom-plussed*, as I thought she was too afraid of singing onstage, but she told me she's not.

You should hear her sing, Charlie. She is an angel in disguise, and I CAN'T WAIT FOR EVERYONE TO HEAR HER. I will be so proud I'll cry my eyes out. You'll cry too, Charlie. For sure.

I'm not sure how she got around the joint Ashbury-Brookfield obligation, though! I mean, she's supposed to do something with her pen pal, and we all know who that is.

I just hope she hasn't started some kind of secret liaison with Paul Wilson. Imagine.

Speaking of secret liaisons, do you want to have one? We could have one at the Blue Danish. I don't really think we should have lessons, where I teach you how to Date a Girl and so on. I think we should just be us. If that is fine with you.

Great.

And soon it will be holidays!

Speaking of holidays, the only thing needed to make everything perfect is if I could get to see my horses for a couple of days, as I think they have probably forgotten my name. But for sure my parents will have to work during the holidays. Still, at least my dad got to see me be a lawyer. Not that he has said anything about it. Maybe he could see that I wasn't actually any good? I guess that's why he hasn't said anything. I guess the legal studies teacher doesn't know what she's talking about. What have I been thinking?

Oh well, you should never trust happiness. Don't even get me started.

Love,

Emily

* * *

Dear Emily,

I'm sorry, Em, but the weirdest thing I have heard all year has got to be that teacher saying you're a girl who has restraint.

You can be as unrestrained as you like with me, though, Em.

And even if your dad doesn't realize that you're a good lawyer, I believe you're a genius, and I might have to rely on those genius legal talents in relation to a particular stolen Audi. On the other hand, the Rattler is thinking about letting it go, since I've promised him free tune-ups for the next five years.

If your parents abandon you for the holidays, I'll take charge of entertaining you. I'll take you for a spin on Kevin's motorbike if you like. You just say the word.

Wilson isn't at school today, by the way. My contact in the principal's office says his parents withdrew him first thing this morning, probably to preempt getting expelled. It's funny to think that every Ashbury attack on our school was actually caused by our Form Captain.

Anyhow, looking forward to crying on your shoulder when we hear Cass sing at the concert.

Love,

Charlie

33. Lydia and Sebastian

Dear Seb,

Have you heard that Cass has signed up to sing in the concert next week? She's got an amazing voice, you know. I just saw her at a rehearsal. I was walking past the hall, where a lot of people are testing out microphones, stacking chairs, talking, etc. Except then I heard Cass testing out a microphone. I looked around the doorway into the hall, and she was standing on the stage, with her eyes closed, singing softly, and the entire room had stopped breathing.

I couldn't believe how calm she seemed — she used to be afraid of singing in front of anyone except Em and me. But there were about fifty people in the room, and every single person was staring at her. She only sang one verse of this old Placebo song she likes, and then she stopped, and right away everyone was begging her to keep going. But she just smiled and looked embarrassed, and put the microphone back.

The only thing I don't understand is how she convinced the teachers that this is a joint act with her Brookfield penfriend. She told me to stop stressing when I asked her.

Anyway, Seb, we have to do something for the concert ourselves. Do you want to just sell tickets?

I've been thinking about what you asked me before you went home on Saturday night. And sorry it's taken me a few days to answer, but okay, the answer is yes. We can give it a try. But if I start to forget my identity, that's it. We go back to writing letters.

Love,

Lydia

* * *

Hey Lyd,

If Cass sings like you say she does, she'll have every guy at that concert falling at her feet. She's cute, eh, and a nice girl too, though she doesn't say much. But, as we said at your party on Saturday, she picked the locks at Wilson's place in approx. 0.5 seconds, which was one of the coolest things I ever saw.

In relation to you and me, that's an excellent decision you've made there, Lyd. No way will you regret it. And if I catch you losing any personality, I'll give you a heads up, and you can go back and get it.

Love,

Seb

P.S. I have an idea for something you and I can do for the concert. Maybe I could come by your place tomorrow and run it by you?

34. Lydia's Notebook

Hey!!!!!! YOU DID IT!!! YOU MADE IT!! Welcome to the FINAL PAGE of your Notebook™. It was quite a journey, wasn't it? But a valuable one.

Go on, write your name in the box!

Write it big and write it proud.

And then, for this final page, have a glass of chardonnay and share some of your musings on what it's like to be a Writer. Because, we guarantee it, if you've got this far, then you *are* a Writer[1] — so fill your glass and fill this space with words!

Yeah, I'm just out here in my rose garden, pouring myself a nice glass of chardonnay, thinking back to my sword-fighting days. I should phone up my best buddy, the plumber, really, and ask him what he thinks about being sunburnt. And when he answers, I'll write down the words EXACTLY AS HE SAYS THEM, because I don't actually have a mind of my own and the fact is, I am really pretty stupid.

[1] For the purposes of the money-back guarantee, a "Writer" is defined as a person who has, at any time in his or her life, used a typewriter, computer, or pen. Guarantee applies only to persons over twenty-one years of age. Guarantee applies only to residents of Regina, Saskatchewan. Credit card and valid photo ID required.

You have the strangest idea of who I am, don't you, Notebook™?

It's been great getting to know you, of course. You're a lot of fun.

But I'm not sure how healthy it is to keep writing to you.

For a start, I think I have this idea that I can do anything by writing. Like I can be myself if I write letters, and I can help my friends if I write Secret Assignments. Like I can change things, punish people, fall in love, and find myself, all by writing the right words.

Maybe I'm just hiding behind the words? Just like I'm hiding behind this idea that everything is dark and terrible — like I hate my parents, and I'm always scared that Em and Cass are going to fail at life, and I'm scared I'll never be a writer. In fact I should just be proud of Em and Cass. And I don't even know why I hate my parents — I can give reasons, like the fact that my mum's spaced out, and my dad can't stop flirting with other women, even though he's such a nerd that no one but my spaced-out mother could ever fall for him. But they're okay really, and they've just had a hard year. Maybe I'm just mad at them for being upset about Cass's father — like I wanted them to be normal and strong while we were the crazy ones.

So maybe I should be dramatic and symbolic, and "Come out from behind the words!" and "Come out from behind the darkness!" As you might hear recommended on American daytime talk shows.

Maybe I should even stop writing stories altogether? Just hang out with Seb and get to know him? He's coming over later today with some idea for the concert. I'm not tap-dancing, if that's what he thinks.

And if I ever do decide to write again, I will never ever write in a Notebook™ like this. Instead, what I'll do — when I decide to start again — what I'll do is, I'll take one of those 48-Page Refill Books (Feint Ruled) that Dad has stacked in his study. And I'll write a story in that book.

And whatever I write, the only thing to get in my way will be the pale blue (feint ruled) lines.

35. Emily's Weekend

IN THE SUPREME COURT OF NEW SOUTH WALES
SYDNEY REGISTRY
COMMON LAW DIVISION
SUBPOENA TO ATTEND AND UNDERTAKE CERTAIN TASKS

To: Emily Melissa-Anne Thompson
52 Hunting-down Circle
Cherrybrook NSW 2126

THE PARENTS HEREBY ORDER that you shall ATTEND AND UNDERTAKE THE TASKS described BELOW:

(a) Go horseback riding
(b) at the Country Cottage;
(c) with your Parents and your Little Brother ("William");
(d) on the first weekend of the holidays, and until you are excused by the Parents from further attending;
(e) because the Parents are so proud of you.

Signed,

. . . . . Benjamin A. Thompson . . . .

(The Dad)

Please note that:

(1) if you do not comply with this subpoena, you may be arrested.

36. Cassie's Diary

So, a funny thing happened last night, Diary.

Mum and I decided to stop seeing Claire the Counselor.

How it happened was this: Claire made us decorate little plastic Christmas trees on her office floor. (It's October, by the way.) Mum was too shocked even to think up some tricky reason why this might be illegal, so we spent the whole time quietly twirling tinsel around tree branches, every now and then sneaking looks at Claire to check that she was for real. Whenever Claire wasn't looking, we opened our eyes really wide at each other, like: *What is going on here?*

So then at the end, Claire said, "You guys like decorating therapy as much as I do?"

Mum and I nodded at her, politely and carefully. And then we didn't say a word on the way out to the car, or even as we got into the car while it went *DING DING DING*, waiting for us to put on our seat belts. Mum looked over her shoulder to reverse out of the parking spot, and then, as she put the car into drive and adjusted the rearview mirror, she said, "Cassie?"

And I said, "Absolutely."

Which was our way of saying that that was the last time we were going near that crazy lady.

Mum said that the main thing is that people at work are now used to her leaving early every second Thursday, and she's going to keep doing that, whatever. Only now she and I can hang out together, without Claire getting in our way.

Then we started saying all the things that were stupid about Claire, such as the way she played applause for us, and the way she squints, and the way there are always two buttons missing from her cardigan, and the way she pretends to be smarter than us, and the way she told Mum to write a letter to Dad but she didn't let me do that too.

That last one was something I said, which made Mum brake a bit dangerously, and say, *"Cassie!"*

And I said, "What?"

And she said, "You don't need *Claire's* permission if you want to write a letter to Dad."

And I just shrugged and said I'd been kind of jealous that she got to do that, whereas I had to talk to a stranger for my homework, which didn't seem fair, and next thing Mum was crying.

Only for a second, though. She cries unexpectedly like for a second sometimes, like a sneeze. Then she turned the cry into a laugh and said, "Did you get *candy canes* for your Christmas tree?"

So then we drove along for a few minutes, listening to music and kind of giggling to ourselves, thinking about Claire's Christmas decorations.

"Listen," Mum said, getting serious again. "If you do want to keep seeing Claire, I mean, if you want to ask her any questions or anything, then you just say so, don't let me steamroller you here."

I thought about it, and I said, "The only question I want to ask Claire is why she told me I had to find a stranger to be a new friend."

"I can tell you why," said Mum, right away. "She knew she was such a crappy therapist that even a perfect stranger would be better than her."

"Well," I said, getting cross, "I don't see why I couldn't just talk to Lydia and Emily. *They're* my best friends."

So then Mum said, "Who knows what's going on in that woman's mind, but I can tell you why *I* might have suggested the same thing."

Then she said she thought maybe I'd changed a bit after what happened, but I didn't know how to be the new self with Lyd and Em. Because they knew me as the old me.

Whereas I could try out the new personality on a stranger, and prove to myself that it worked.

"Do *you* think I've got a new personality?" I said.

"Do you?" She likes to throw questions back like a schoolteacher.

"Yes," I said, "I'm deranged in the head." I said it right away, like a joke.

Mum just laughed, as if it *was* a joke, and she said, "Well, *I* think the amazing thing is this: that you are just as lovely as you ever were, except stronger and braver than before."

Then we slowed down because lights up ahead had turned orange, and she slapped both hands on the steering wheel and said, "The witness may step down," at which exact moment a woman waiting on the curb stepped down onto the road.

So, anyhow, I don't know about that theory of Mum's, that I'm a new person now.

And if I am, when do I get to try out my new personality on a stranger?

Seb and Charlie seem pretty cool. Maybe they can be the

strangers. Or I could just ask Lyd and Em to cut their hair and wear sunglasses.

Whatever, on Monday there was a notice on the board at school saying we had to do something for the spring concert. Because they've expanded it now, to bring in the people with Brookfield penfriends. I could have just put myself down as a ticket seller or something, but it seemed like a second chance to put my hand in the air (although, to be honest, you didn't have to put your hand in the air, you just went to Mrs. Lilydale's office and wrote your name in a book).

So this is what I wrote:

"'In the Stars,' a song performed by Cass Aganovic (Ashbury); words by Matthew Dunlop (Brookfield)."

Then I walked out of the office and thought, *Oh my god, what did you just do?*

Anyway, but today at the rehearsal, I decided I may as well pretend to myself that Mum was right. That I have some kind of a new brave identity now. And I think it worked.

I'm dedicating the song to my dad. Not that I'll say that aloud, okay, because people will think I'm looking for the sympathy vote. But you'll know that I mean it for you. And I'll write out the words for you here:

I saw your name in lights last night.
It's the middle of the night,
and I can't sleep,
thinking all my trumpeting thoughts,
and I get out of bed,

open the curtains,
and look into the night full of stars,
and you know what I saw?
Your name.
Like the stars joined up and spelled the word for me.
Like a sign.

It's not exactly Shakespeare, eh. And like a sign of what? But it works with the music I wrote, and it's straight from one of Matthew Dunlop's letters.

All this time we were trying to figure out who he was, who would have thought he was a songwriter?

37. Ashbury High Year 10 Notice Board

THOUGHT FOR THE DAY:

I thought I would go round the bend!
But it all worked out in the end.
Well done, Year 10.

THE SPRING FOR UNITY! CONCERT

The Spring for Unity! Concert will take place at seven P.M. tonight. The Spring for Unity! Concert looks set to be a marvelous evening. As Mr. Botherit says, the Spirit of Friendship is alive and well again!

THIS HAS BEEN A MESSAGE FROM YOUR FORM MISTRESS.

LATE ENTRY IN THE SPRING FOR UNITY!

We have received a late contribution to the Spring for Unity! Concert. *Barney and Maribelle Learn to Fly*, a children's book* written by Lydia Jaackson-Oberman (Ashbury), illustrated by Seb Mantegna (Brookfield), will be on display in the entryway to the hall this evening.

* Please note that the book is not suitable for children — all the characters suffer startling and gruesome fates on the final page.

FOR SALE — ACID® PRO 4.0 (audio looping software) comes with a content CD which has multi-genre music loops (dance, hip-hop, techno, industrial, rock, jazz, etc.). Recently purchased and used only once. Price negotiable.

Any interest, please contact Lydia Jaackson-Oberman, Emily Thompson, or Cassie Aganovic.

About the Author

A former media and entertainment lawyer, Jaclyn Moriarty now writes full time so she can sleep in each day. She divides her time between Sydney, Australia, and Montreal, Canada, depending on where the summer is.